The Horsemen

By

Bill Shuey

*Randall,
Best Wishes
Bill
9/2019*

Other books by Bill Shuey

A Search for Israel

A Search for Bible Truth

Unholy Dilemma – A Search for Logic in the Old Testament

Unholy Dilemma 2 – A Search for Logic in the New Testament

Unholy Dilemma 3 – A Search for Logic in the Qur'an

Have a good week – Ten years of ObverseView musings

East of Edin

Retribution

A Killing in Dogwood

The Cattlemen

The Texican

This is a work of fiction based solely on the imagination of the author. Actual characters found in the story-line were inserted for authenticity. Other characters, businesses, places, locales, and incidents are either the product of the author's imagination or used in a fictitious manner.

The opinions expressed in this manuscript are solely the opinions of the author and do not represent the opinions or thoughts of the publisher. The author has represented and warranted full ownership and/or legal right to publish all the materials in this book.

The Horsemen

All Rights Reserved Worldwide
Copyright 2019 Bill Shuey

This book may not be reproduced, transmitted, or stored in whole or in part by any means, including graphic, electronic, or mechanical without the expressed written consent of the publisher except in the case of brief quotations embodied in critical articles or reviews.

ISPN 13: 978-1726693370
ISPN 10:

Printed in the United States of America

Dedication

To all those men and women who gave their lives, and still do on the Texas/Mexican border, served in the Philippine-American and Spanish-American Wars, and World War I. And to those hardy souls who transitioned from the cavalry to mechanized warfare.

Horseman

Noun: a rider on horseback, especially a skilled one.

Acknowledgements

As with my earlier literary efforts, the team is what makes the endeavor come together – not just the author.

My sister-in-law, Bern, proofread the book twice and was instrumental in correcting the prose for grammar and punctuation.

April Wade, the English czar, put the final touches on the finished book.

Betty Henderson proofread the book and caught a few snafus.

Marisa Mott – www.cowboykimono.com for designing the final cover art and wrap.

And last, but not least, my wife, Gloria, who is always supportive of my literary efforts, and this was no exception.

Chapter 1

If hell was worse than this, they sure didn't want to go there. Canon shells were screaming overhead, on their way to find American soldiers further downrange. Mortar shells were quietly dropping from the sky, hitting trees and sending shards of arm sized wood flying through the air to impale or tear off body parts. Trees that were struck by canon fire or mortars were falling. Men were screaming, bleeding, dazed, and missing body parts. This was hell on earth! If this continued, the Argonne Forest would become the Argonne cemetery. As far as the eye could see, there was nothing but charred tree stumps and equally burned and broken bodies, which, like many of the trees, were missing limbs.

****

The Meuse-Argonne Offensive was a major part of the final Allied offensive of World War I and stretched along the entire Western Front. The battles raged from September 26, 1918, until the armistice was signed on November 11, 1918, a total of forty-seven days. The Meuse-Argonne Offensive was the largest in United States military history and involved one and one-half million American soldiers. The Offensive was actually a series of Allied attacks known as the Hundred Days

Offensive. The engagement brought about the conclusion of the horrible war. It was the bloodiest operation of World War I for the American Expeditionary Force.

****

There were three brothers: a cavalry officer, a cavalry officer who was assigned as an engineer, and an Army chaplain, who were still alive. With all the carnage around them, they wondered how long they would survive. Before the attack, Nathan Baxter's engineers cut access holes in the barbed wire and hung pieces of cloth on either side of the openings to mark the access points where the doughboys were to cross. Dozens of boys, who were away from home for the first time, were draped over or hung up in the wire, riddled with bullets.

The Germans were dug in behind sand bags with their machine guns cutting down the advancing men like sickles cutting tall grass. Wave after wave of young men advanced and were sacrificed to the kraut's machine guns like blood sacrifices of biblical times. BJ Baxter advanced with his men and watched his young officers being killed as they led their individual units.

Bill Baxter was in the thick of the battle, even though he wasn't supposed to be on the battle line. Chaplains were expected to stay behind the line and not be exposed to actual fighting. Their job was to pray with and for the wounded and provide comfort as best they could.

It was mid-October 1918, and not one of the three brothers expected to see 1919. They really didn't expect to see tomorrow!

Five thousand miles away, the fourth brother, actually not a brother by blood but their constant childhood companion, was having his own problems with killers and bandits during the Mexican Revolution. And then after the Porvenir massacre, an event he wasn't even involved in, he was trying to salvage his reputation and good name. And if that wasn't enough to contend with, he was trying to stay alive.

The year 1918 wasn't a good one for the Baxter brothers or Fred Brubaker!

Chapter 2

James Budwell (BJ) Baxter, Jr., was born on July 1, 1870, while the Slant BB ranch was still located in Hopkins County, Texas. BJ was the oldest son of James Budwell Baxter, Sr., and Sara Bright Baxter. BJ was always a quiet boy. He was the polar opposite of his father in that respect. He wasn't introverted but was lacking in the affable social skills that came so naturally to his dad. What BJ lacked in affability, he made up for in thoughtfulness and an introspective mind. He tended to think a situation through before making a decision. He wasn't overly cautious or hesitant. He just tried to consider all the implications of a decision before he acted.

BJ grew tall like his father, standing about 6' 3" in his stocking feet. He had a medium complexion, dark brown and often unruly hair, steel gray eyes, and arms and legs that were thin but deceptively strong. His mother often remarked that his physique wasn't unlike that of the rail-splitter from Illinois who became the sixteenth President of the United States.

BJ decided early on that he wanted to serve in the Army like his father had, albeit in the Union Army rather than the old Confederacy. BJ's grades in school were good but not eye catching impressive, which made acceptance into West Point Military Academy problematic. BJ announced to his dad that he desired to attend West Point. He then shared the same desire with his god-father, Captain Brubaker. The Captain told him to work on his grades, and he would see if he could get him a sponsor.

Captain Bill Brubaker contacted the offices of John Henninger Reagan and Richard Coke, both of whom were United States Senators from Texas at the time. Captain Brubaker personally asked for their assistance in getting his godson into the United States Military Academy at West Point, New York.

****

John Henninger Reagan had resigned from the U.S. House of Representatives when Texas seceded from the Union and joined the Confederate States of America. He served in the cabinet of Jefferson Davis as Postmaster General. After the surrender of the Army of Northern Virginia at Appomattox Courthouse on April 9, 1865, for all practical purposes, the Confederacy and the war were over. After the war, Reagan called for cooperation with the federal government. That was an unpopular position at the time. He was elected to Congress in 1874, after his predictions of harsh treatment for resistance against the federal government were proven to be correct. He served in the United States Senate from 1887 – 1891. He later served as chairman of the Texas Railroad

Commission and was among the founders of the Texas State Historical Association.

Bill and John Reagan had met a few times during the Civil War when Captain Brubaker had been tasked by General Nathan Bedford Forrest with the job of securing the mail intended for his troops. When John Reagan announced his candidacy for the United States Senate, Captain Brubaker contributed to his senate campaign and spoke on his behalf during the campaign of 1887. Senator Reagan said he would be happy to sponsor William Budwell Baxter, Jr., for entry as a plebe at West Point. With the aid of Senator Reagan, BJ entered the U.S. Military Academy in 1888, the class of 1892 which would graduate in June 1892, and would be commissioned as a Second Lieutenant.

BJ met Robert E. Wood, who was two years his senior, while at the Academy. In fact, he met him more times than he wanted. Wood was a stickler for detail and hung a couple demerits on BJ during his freshman year. Wood went on to become a Brigadier General and then later the Chairman and CEO of Sears, Roebuck and turned the company from a mail-order enterprise into a department store retailer. Wood and BJ became good friends after Baxter's freshman year and, even though they rarely saw each other after graduation, continued that friendship.

After graduation, BJ was assigned to the 10th Cavalry Regiment at Fort Assiniboine in north central Montana. The 10th was one of the original Buffalo Soldier regiments composed of black soldiers serving under white officers. BJ fit in well with the regiment and quickly gained the trust of the black soldiers. Since he had grown up with Wil Byrd on the Slant BB ranches, he had no problem with black folks and thought them otherwise qualified based on merit, not skin color. Shortly after arriving at his first duty assignment at Fort Assiniboine, BJ was assigned to accompany First Lieutenant John Pershing on an expedition in the southern and southwest portions of Montana to round up a large number of Cree Indians, bring them to the fort, and confine them until they could be deported to Canada.

In early August 1892, Colonel Marvin P. Morgan called Lieutenant Baxter to his office and said, "Lieutenant, I am reluctant to send you out with a patrol when you only just graduated from the Point and have only been here a couple months, but Lieutenant Pershing has a bad case of the squirts and is in no condition to make this foray. Lieutenant Jackson is out north of here rounding up other Cree and, therefore, unavailable, so you're elected. We have reports that a small contingent of Cree, who are camped a few miles from here, are refusing to come in to be transported to Canada. I need you to take six troopers, find the Indians, and bring them to the fort. Sergeant Jones is an experienced Indian fighter. He will be with you and provide advice. You will do well to listen to him."

Lieutenant Baxter said, "Yes, Sir. I will do my best." With that, he saluted, did an about face, and walked out of the colonel's office. Colonel Morgan thought to himself, "*I hope that shave tail doesn't get himself and his troopers killed.*"

BJ had met Sergeant Jones and thought him experienced and capable. Sergeant George Washington Jones had fought in several Indian engagements on the frontier. He knew the Indians and would be an asset to the patrol. They left the fort with six soldiers, including Sergeant Jones, and one pack horse. About thirty miles south of present day Lewiston, Montana, BJ's patrol came upon the small group of Cree braves who were camped in a canyon. As they rode towards the Indians, the hostiles grabbed their weapons and took shelter behind rocks. BJ told his patrol to dismount, take out their carbines, and get behind cover.

After getting behind a large boulder, BJ called out in broken Cree, "We are here to escort you to Fort Assiniboine. When we get you there, you are to be transported to Canada with the rest of your tribe." The response was a rifle shot with the bullet ricocheting off the face of the boulder BJ was behind.

BJ looked at Sergeant Jones, smiled, and said, "Sergeant, I don't think they want to go with us or to Canada."

Jones laughed and replied, "Ya think not, Sir? Where did you learn to speak Cree?"

BJ didn't answer, took aim in the direction of the rocks the Indians were hiding behind, zeroed in on a hip that was partially exposed, squeezed the trigger on his Model 1892 Springfield rifle, and was rewarded with a scream.

****

The Springfield Model 1892-99 Krag-Jorgensen rifle was a Norwegian designed bolt-action rifle that was adopted in 1892 as the standard United States Army military rifle. It was chambered in the U.S. caliber .30-40 Krag. All models and variants were manufactured under license by the Springfield Armory between 1892 and 1903. Although Krags were popular, unique, and efficient for the time period, the side loading gate mechanism was slow and cumbersome to reload in combat. Infantrymen carried the standard size Krag, and cavalry units used the shorter model. The Model 1892 was replaced by the M1903 Springfield rifle which was essentially a copy of a Mauser.

****

BJ hollered out to the Indians again, "My job is to bring you back to the fort. I would prefer it was riding on your horses rather than tied over them. That is your choice." With that, one of the Indians ran towards his horse, and BJ shot him through the side. The Indian fell and tried to crawl away without success.

BJ hollered again, "You are cornered and have no place to go. Throw down your weapons, or you all will die here today."

Everything was quiet for a few minutes, and then an Indian hollered, "Don't shoot, white eyes. We come out now." With that, an Indian appeared, dropped his rifle on the ground, and started walking towards the troopers. Seven more Cree followed suit.

BJ looked at Sergeant Jones and said, "Put them in irons, if you please, Sergeant." With that, BJ walked towards the Indians who were on the ground. The one he had shot in the hip was bleeding but lucky that the bullet had missed the hip bone. The other Indian wasn't so lucky and was taking his last breaths when BJ got to him.

BJ had one of the troopers bandage the wounded Indian and help him on a horse. The dead Indian was draped over his horse and his hands were tied to his feet under the belly of the animal. Once everyone was mounted, they started the journey back to the fort. The return trip was uneventful. BJ left the Indians in the care of Sergeant Jones and went to the headquarters building to give his report on the foray to Colonel Morgan.

Lieutenant Baxter reported to Colonel Morgan, saluted, and said, "Sir, we brought ten Cree Indians back. Eight are in good shape. One is wounded, and one is dead. We suffered no casualties."

Colonel Morgan looked at Lieutenant Baxter for a few moments and said, "Well done. I would like for you to dine with Mrs. Morgan and me this evening if it would be convenient." BJ knew full-well from his father, Captain Brubaker, and his West Point training that a request from a superior officer was actually an order. He merely asked, "What time shall I arrive, Sir?"

BJ walked to the stockade, checked with Sergeant Jones, and made sure the Indians were taken care of and that the wounded man had been taken to the infirmary. He then got a bath, changed into his dress uniform, and presented himself promptly at 6 PM at Colonel Morgan's quarters. After introductions, BJ waited for Colonel and Mrs. Morgan to sit, and then he sat down. One of the mess soldiers began serving the meal. Mrs. Morgan started the conversation with BJ. "Lieutenant, I understand you shot a Cree Indian while you were in the field. Is that correct?"

BJ glanced at Colonel Morgan, who nodded his head, and BJ replied, "Yes, Ma'am. I actually shot two, but one survived."

Colonel Morgan entered the conversation by saying, "Lieutenant Baxter, word came to me that you spoke passable Cree. I have the distinct feeling that there is a lot in your past history that you haven't shared with me."

BJ looked at the Colonel and replied, "With respect, Sir, I have been taught all my life to reply to my superiors when asked. I figured the time would come that you would want to know my bona fides and would ask."

Colonel Morgan laughed and said, "Alright, Lieutenant, I'm asking. Tell me about yourself."

BJ went on to tell the Colonel that he had been born on a cattle ranch in Texas. Then his father and Captain Brubaker had sold their holdings in Texas, drove their longhorns to the cattle market in Kansas, and then drove their breeder stock on to Montana Territory. Though he had been young, he could remember much of the journey and his father's and Captain Brubaker's dealings with the Indians.

Colonel Morgan interrupted and asked, "Excuse me. This Captain Brubaker you spoke of, by any chance was he chief of scouts for General Nathan Bedford Forrest during the Civil War?" BJ replied that he didn't know exactly what his father and Captain Brubaker did during the war, but yes, they had mentioned serving under General Forrest. Colonel Morgan went on to say, "Us ole timers are well aware of the story of Captain Brubaker threatening to shoot a Confederate Army Surgeon who refused to treat your father. I just never associated you with that Baxter and Brubaker. You have to admire an officer who would threaten to shoot a sawbones. Did your father and Captain Brubaker meet during the war?"

19

BJ explained that his father and Captain Brubaker were born on adjacent farms in the Huzzah Valley of Missouri, one hour apart, and had been together all their lives.

Colonel Morgan continued, "Interesting, and you were tutored by your father and Captain Brubaker?" BJ explained that he grew up around Indians and was taught to respect them and treat them with dignity. His father had taught him how to track, read trail sign, and other needful things that kept one alive on the frontier.

Colonel Morgan was thoughtful for a few moments and asked, "Were the two Cree you shot the first humans you have had occasion to shoot?"

BJ said, "No, Sir. I shot my first man when I was nine years old, but I didn't kill him. Dorothea, our chuck wagon cook, killed him when he tried to run me over with his horse. The Cree was the first man that I have killed, and I didn't enjoy the experience." Colonel Morgan opined that BJ's past explained a lot. He had asked Sergeant Jones his impression of the Lieutenant after they had returned from the foray and had been told that he was "sterling," a fine young man who knew what he was about. The colonel didn't share that with BJ however.

The conversation ebbed, and BJ excused himself, thanked the Colonel and Mrs. Morgan for a fine meal and entertaining evening, and went to his quarters. When he arrived and got out of his dress uniform, he took out his Colt M-1873 .45 caliber handgun with JBB engraved on the butt plate. His father had given him the pistol as a present when he graduated from the academy. He wiped the weapon off, added a touch of oil, wiped it off again, checked the barrel, and placed it back in its holster. The pistol was a tool, and he had been taught to keep his tools in good working order. His life could depend on it. Leading men on the frontier wasn't a game, and a misfire or jammed weapon could lead to an early grave.

Having concluded an interesting day, he turned in for the night.

Chapter 3

Nathan Forrest Baxter was born on August 30, 1871, at the Slant BB ranch in Hopkins County, Texas. Nat was named after Nathan Buford Forrest, who was the general his father and godfather served under during the Civil War. Nat had two older siblings: Mattie Lea and James Budwell (BJ), Jr. Nat and BJ were fourteen months apart in age and as close as brothers could possibly be. Whatever BJ did, Nat wanted to do. Nat and BJ looked enough alike to be mistaken as twins when they were young children. As they got older, they developed their individual distinguishing features. Nat was tall like his older brother, almost 6' 4", with brown wavy hair and the same complexion. The distinction was in the differences in the physique of the two men. Where BJ was willowy, Nat was thick of chest, arms, and legs. Nat's nickname at West Point Military Academy was "The Mule."

Nathan followed his older brother in applying for acceptance at West Point Military Academy and was accepted without a problem. The fact that his older brother was a sophomore helped, as did Nat's excellent grades, and Senator Reagan's sponsorship sealed his appointment. Nathan Forrest Baxter was admitted to the academy in 1890, the class of 1894.

Shortly after his second year at West Point started in mid-summer 1891, Nat was approached by Cadet Captain Dennis Michie who was the academy football coach. Michie had been the Captain of the football team in 1890 and 1891. Michie told, not asked, Nat, to present himself for fall football practice. Nat tried to explain that he had never played football and knew nothing about the game. Undeterred, Cadet Captain Michie merely said, "Be there, cadet." When the dog days of August arrived, Nat found himself on The Plain practicing football. The Mule was taught how to be a pulling guard who, hopefully, would lead the runner carrying the football through or around the other team's defensive line. Army had a good year in 1891, winning four games, tying one, and losing one. Fortunately, on November 28, 1891, they went to Annapolis and won the only game that really mattered by beating Navy 32 to 16.

****

In 1890, Cadet Michie felt that the West Point cadets could beat the Navy cadets in a football game, so he got some of his classmates together and challenged Navy to a game. The inaugural game was played on a frozen field at West Point where Navy trounced Army 24 – 0, starting an annual tradition between the academies which continues to endure.

Cadet Captain and football coach Michie graduated from the Point in the class of 1893 and was commissioned a second lieutenant.

During the battle of Santiago, Captain Dennis Michie commanded the 6th and 16th Infantry Regiments. On July 1, 1898, Michie led a patrol along the San Juan River. As he was deploying his men for an assault on a hill, he was killed by a Spanish sniper's bullet. When Army's football stadium was opened in 1924, it was named Michie Stadium in honor of the man who introduced football to West Point.

****

In 1892, Nat played on the West Point team again, this time, with Laurie Bliss as the head coach. Now nicknamed "The Black Knights," Army posted a 3-1-1 record, and on November 26, 1892, lost to Navy 4 to 12. Laurence Thornton "Laurie" Bliss only coached the one season at West Point. He later served as the head football coach at Lehigh University in 1895 and, after leaving the academy, played with the Chicago Athletic Association team. Nat graduated from the academy in June 1894 and missed the opportunity to avenge the two losses to Navy. Actually, the Army v. Navy game was discontinued from 1894 to 1898. The games were cancelled because an Army general and a Navy admiral became embroiled in an argument after the 1893 game which almost resulted in a duel. Fearing emotions over the game were getting out of hand the War Department ordered the cancelation of the annual game.

****

Nathan Forrest Baxter was commissioned as a 2nd Lieutenant in the U.S. Army in June 1894 and followed his brother as an officer in the Long Gray Line of West Point graduates who served their country. The Long Gray Line is the continuum of all graduates and cadets of the United States Military Academy at West Point, New York. The term is uttered affectionately by West Point graduates and refers to the unique ties which bind every West Point graduate to all the others who have come before and all those who will come after. It reflects the process that all cadets at West Point have experienced. The program is a demanding four year period of instruction which remains largely unchanged to the present day.

****

After receiving his commission, Lieutenant Nathan Baxter was assigned to the 6th Cavalry Regiment at Fort McKinney near the Powder River in northeastern Wyoming. Lieutenant Baxter reported to Fort McKinney as the fort was being closed and was sent with the 6th to various frontier forts. On June 1, 1898, Lieutenant Baxter was told to report to Florida where he was assigned to the 9th

Cavalry (Buffalo Soldiers) for transportation to Cuba. Lieutenant Nathan Baxter, like the other officers, was forced to leave his horse in Florida because of the cramped quarters aboard the ship. The 9th finally arrived in Cuba on June 24, 1898, and was posted alongside Teddy Roosevelt's Rough Riders. The Rough Riders called the men of the 9th "the Weary Walkers" because they had been forced to leave their horses in Florida. Ironically, so had the Rough Riders!

The Battle of San Juan Hill began on July 1, 1898, with some 8,000 American soldiers and volunteers involved in the taking of Kettle and San Juan Hills. Nat and his troopers were assigned to the right flank, along with the Rough Riders, to take Kettle Hill. Nathan and his men had to cross a thicket consisting of a heavy entanglement of vines and bushes that made visibility beyond a few yards impossible. As they began clawing their way through the briars and brambles, the Spanish began firing into their midst. Around 9 AM, Nathan and his Buffalo Soldiers passed U.S. troops who were pinned down by enemy fire. When the Spanish became fully aware of the 9th's advance, they began firing grapeshot, a cluster of small iron balls fired from cannon, at the advancing men. Nat was hit in the left shoulder by one of the balls, and two of his troopers were killed during the onslaught of cannon fire.

Whoever said that getting shot didn't cause much pain was full of crap. Nat was in agony. He was taking deep breaths and trying to stay calm to avoid going into hypovolemic shock. Nat lay on his back next to the two dead troopers and waited for the field medic to arrive when two more troopers who were behind him on the advance fell from grape shot. The two soldiers were alive but badly wounded and crying out in pain. When Nat heard voices speaking in Spanish, he was scared to death for both himself and the wounded soldiers. As the voices grew louder, Nat saw two enemy soldiers advancing, carrying rifles with bayonets attached, to dispatch the wounded men. Nat drew the Colt .45 single action revolver with NFB engraved on the butt plate. His father had given him the weapon the day he was commissioned from the Point. Nat cocked the hammer, took aim, fired, cocked the hammer, and fired again. The nearest Spanish soldier was struck in the chest area and went down like a fallen tree. The second man was hit in the mid-section, lay on the ground fifteen yards away with his intestines leaking fluid on the ground and screamed constantly.

    The field medic arrived, bandaged Nat's wound, moved to the two wounded soldiers, treated their wounds, and said he would get a field ambulance to move the two troopers to a field infirmary. The medic said he would take Nat back with him and come back for the two wounded troopers. Nathan responded, "No, I won't leave my troopers until they are in the ambulance."

The troopers of the 9th and 10th continued to advance along with the Rough Riders, now under covering fire provided by Gatling Guns, and were the first to arrive at the top of Kettle Hill immediately before noon. Shortly thereafter, San Juan Hill was taken by the combined forces. The 9th held San Juan Hill until July 4. A truce was initiated in order to allow both sides to exchange prisoners and allow the wounded to be taken to field hospitals. The Spanish and American dead were removed from the field during the truce.

The Army surgeon removed the shrapnel from Nat's shoulder and had him placed in a bed. The wound became infected, and he was forced to stay in the field hospital for two days while the 9th was involved in minor skirmishes with the Spanish. They were also used to guard enemy prisoners. On July 6, Nathan was released for limited duty and returned to his unit. While recuperating, Nat met Theodore Roosevelt, the man who had led the Rough Riders up San Juan Hill. They formed an association which only men-in-arms during combat can share. That association with the future president would benefit the Baxter brothers during the ensuing years.

****

"The Rough Riders" was a nickname given to the 1st United States Volunteer Cavalry. The Rough Riders was one of three regiments formed in

1898 for the Spanish-American War. It was the only one of the three to see action. After the Civil War, the majority of Union soldiers left the military, returned to their homes, and went back to their old occupations or found new employment. The mass exodus of soldiers left the Army, other than general officers, small and understaffed of qualified regulars. To rectify the problem, President McKinley called for 125,000 volunteers to help with the Spanish-American War effort.

Colonel Leonard Wood was in charge of the military forces sent to Cuba and personally took charge of the 2nd Cavalry Brigade. Theodore Roosevelt resigned his position as Assistant Secretary of the Navy to lead a volunteer group made up of college athletes, cowboys, ranchers, miners, and other outdoorsmen. The Rough Riders then became known as "Roosevelt's Rough Riders." The Rough Riders received the Lion's share of publicity for the taking of San Juan Hill. The reality was that the taking of the hill was a cooperative effort. The 1st Brigade commanded by Brigadier General Samuel S. Sumner, consisting of the 3rd, 9th, and 10th Cavalries dismounted, actually did much of the heavy lifting during the engagement.

The press, Buffalo Bill's Congress of Rough Riders of the World, and Frederic Remington's painting "Charge of the Rough Riders at San Juan Hill" made Roosevelt's name a household word. The publicity ultimately led him to the vice-presidency and then to the White House.

****

When all the hostilities in Cuba had ended, Nat was sent back to the United States, remained with the 9th Cavalry Buffalo Soldiers and was assigned to Fort Bliss near El Paso, Texas. Lieutenant Baxter reported in on November 14, 1898, and discovered his function was to take part in preventing hostilities growing out of disputes as to ownership and control of immense salt lakes at the base of the Guadalupe Mountains of West Texas. By the time Nat arrived on the scene, the issue had been settled, but there was still deep seated resentment, friction, and occasional violence on both sides. Beyond that, since the Army was between wars, Nat's biggest challenge was trying to keep the troopers busy so as to avoid boredom, drinking, and the resulting fights.

There was training, training, and more training. The training was intermingled with work details. And then there was weapons cleaning and repair, care and maintenance of the mounts, repair of tack, and more training. Nat was as bored as his troopers and ready for another war!

Chapter 4

William Huzzah Baxter, the youngest son of James Budwell Baxter, Sr., was also born in Hopkins County, Texas, on December 30, 1872. He was given the name William after his god-father, William Travis Brubaker, and Huzzah after the valley in Missouri where his father was born. Bill was never like his brothers in their love of guns, cattle, and frontier life. He was always quiet, serious, and studious. Bill looked much like his brothers: tall, ruddy complexion, brown hair given to unruliness, and the same steel gray eyes.

Bill always pitched in and did his part on the ranch without complaint. His family realized early on that that he was different and destined for some vocation which didn't involve cattle or firearms. He did, however, share in his brothers' love of horses.

Bill had displayed a curiosity regarding the Bible at an early age and would sit and read the book for hours when he didn't have chores on the ranch. For Bill's birthday in 1885, his parents gave him the 1853 Oxford University Press King James Version of the Bible. A Bible would be an unusual gift for most thirteen year old boys on the frontier, but Bill thought it a great gift. On Bill's sixteenth birthday, his parents got him the Matthew Henry commentaries. Bill read the Henry commentaries from cover to cover, made notes on elements he found intriguing or confusing, and gave them considerable thought.

On September 23, 1893, Bill entered the Iliff School of Theology in Denver, Colorado.

****

Iliff was founded in 1889 as a seminary and school of religious studies of the University of Denver. In 1892, it was named Iliff School of Theology after John Wesley Iliff, who had wanted to establish a school to train men to serve as ministers in the Territory of Colorado. The cornerstone of Iliff Hall was laid on June 8, 1892, and construction of the buildings was completed in 1893.

In the summer of 1900, Iliff closed due to financial and organizational problems. On August 27, 1903, Iliff School of Theology was incorporated as an independent institution separate from the University of Denver. It reopened on September 10, 1910, as an antonymous school of theology and was a Methodist seminary.

****

Bill was an exceptional student at seminary. The only problem the instructors had was his unquenchable curiosity and probing inquiries regarding Bible exegesis for which they had no reasonable explanation. Belief was easy enough until one got into the weeds of looking at various scriptures that didn't agree one with the other. When a large number of contradictions became evident, Bill's confidence in the entire Bible as a source document became problematic. Be that as it may, Bill's focus was on helping his fellow men. He didn't let his misgivings regarding biblical texts overcome his goals. Bill graduated from seminary in May 1898 with an excellent grade average, was ordained as a minister, and was assigned to a Methodist Episcopal Church South, in Billings, Montana. Bill didn't pastor a church but rode on horseback, visiting houses of worship on a circuit. The circuit found him preaching at various small churches around the Billings area and spending a couple days at each location ministering to the individual spiritual needs of the small congregations. Reverend Baxter served in the capacity of traveling preacher for a year and then decided that riding around on horseback and preaching wasn't his calling. The preaching he enjoyed, riding a horse was part of his heritage, visiting and comforting the sick and infirm was an honor, and performing baptisms was uplifting. Old people who craved attention complaining about their various ailments wore on him. Bill had been offered a pastorate position and realized that being responsible for a congregation with full time complainers wasn't his calling. He decided to join the Army chaplain Corps.

****

The U.S. Army Chaplain Corps is one of the oldest and smallest branches of the Army. The Chaplain Corps dates back to July 29, 1775, when the Continental Congress authorized one chaplain for each regiment of the Continental Army, with pay equal to that of a captain. In addition to chaplains serving in Continental regiments, many militia regiments had ministers serving as chaplains who joined them as volunteers.

Since the War for Independence, chaplains have served in every American war. Over that period, the U.S. Army Chaplain Corps has evolved. Roman Catholic chaplains were added in the Mexican War and Jewish and Negro chaplains during the Civil War.

The military chaplain's responsibilities include performing religious rites and ceremonies, conducting worship services, providing confidential counseling, advising commanders on religious, spiritual and moral matters, and visiting and comforting the wounded and infirm. Ten Army chaplains have been killed in the line of duty. Army Major Charles Watters was awarded the Medal of Honor for his bravery in ministering to fallen comrades during the battle of Dak To, Vietnam, in 1967.

****

Bill was sworn into the Army Chaplain Corps in June 1899 and assigned to the 9th Cavalry Regiment. The 9th Cavalry was one of six original regiments of the Army set aside for black enlisted men. The units were authorized by congress on July 28, 1866. Colonel Edward Hatch, who had no military experience prior to the Civil War but proved to be an excellent leader of the Iowa cavalry regiment, was the 9th's first commander. Initial recruits came from the New Orleans area, and twelve companies were organized and on their way to Texas by February 1867.

Following a succession of black chaplains, Lieutenant William Baxter became the first white chaplain assigned to the regiment. He was received with no small degree of resentment.

Shortly after being assigned to the 9th, the regiment was assigned to the Philippines as part of the American forces fighting against Philippine nationalists.

****

The Philippine-American War was an armed conflict between the First Philippine Republic and the United States that lasted from February 4, 1899, until July 2, 1902. The Filipino nationalists viewed the conflict as a continuation of the struggle for independence that began in 1896 with the Philippine Revolution. The U.S. regarded it as an insurrection. The conflict arose when the First

Philippine Republic objected to the terms of the Treaty of Paris, under which the United States took possession of the Philippines from Spain, which ended the Spanish-American War.

The war resulted in the death of at least 200,000 Filipino civilians, mostly due to famine and disease. The conflict, and especially the ensuing occupation by the United States, changed the culture of the Philippine Islands and lead to the ending of the Catholic Church's hold on the Philippines as a state religion. Following the end of hostilities, English was introduced into the islands as the primary language of government, education, business, and industry.

****

Lieutenant William Huzzah Baxter arrived in the Philippines in September 1899. He was just in time for the Cavite campaign which was conducted between October 7 and 13 of that year. The campaign was under the command of General Lawton. Bill reported to Colonel William Bisbee. Colonel Bisbee asked Lieutenant Baxter to visit with the sick and wounded in the field hospital and help them with spiritual comfort and encouragement as best he could. This was a task he would find daunting and humbling. Bill felt he was swimming upstream with the Negro soldiers because they resented him for having replaced a black chaplain they all liked. Even though Bill had nothing to do with the decision, he had to deal with the fallout. Bill could feel the resentment but just went to work, and, little by little earned the respect of the soldiers.

In late 1899, the U.S. Army attacked Banos in Laguna and Imus and Bacoor in Cavite. General Lawton headed south with three columns. One column swept the lines between Imus and Bacoor and along Laguna de Bay. A second column moved along the west shore of Manila Bay, with warships providing fire support. The third column advanced down a narrow peninsula from the Cavite Naval Station to Novaleta. Lieutenant Baxter accompanied the first column and came under heavy Filipino fire. Several soldiers were wounded, and the capability of the medics to treat the wounded was overwhelmed. Chaplain Baxter was scared to death but tried to ignore the whistling of bullets. Bill helped bandage the wounded, placed them on litters, and helped carry them to field ambulances.

On the second day of the engagements, October 10, 1899, Bill was retrieving a wounded black soldier when he was shot through the right upper leg which made him unable to move the soldier quickly to the safety of the U.S. Army line. Slowly but surely, Bill inched along using only the one uninjured leg to crawl, dragging the wounded soldier while trying to keep as low to the ground as possible. Finally, he got to within a few feet of the column line, and another bullet hit his right lower leg. Soldiers grabbed him, pulling him and the wounded soldier behind the cover of a wagon only to discover that the soldier Bill had been dragging was dead. For his act of courage and compassion in trying to save the wounded soldier while under enemy fire, Lieutenant William Baxter was awarded the Certificate of Merit Medal. He was one of the very few military chaplains to ever win the award. Much more important than the medal, by risking his life for a Negro trooper, Lieutenant Baxter had earned the respect of the Buffalo Soldiers.

    Bill was treated in the military field hospital, and against the advice of doctors, was up the day following his injury, on crutches, visiting the other wounded patients, trying to cheer and console them. Bill had recovered sufficiently that he could join the soldiers on the second San Isidro campaign in early November 1899. On November 10, while talking with soldiers along the Pampanga River, Bill was hit in the arm by a stray bullet. The bullet only plowed a furrow along the side of his forearm but caused a great deal of bleeding. A second bullet hit a trooper in the shoulder. Bill threw himself on the soldier, shielding him from the bullets that were whizzing through the air. In a few minutes, corpsmen came and carried the wounded soldier away, and Bill walked to the infirmary to have the arm bandaged. When Colonel Bisbee heard of Lieutenant Baxter being wounded again, he went to the field hospital and spoke with Bill while a corpsman was bandaging his arm.

    After they visited for a couple minutes, Colonel Bisbee said, "Lieutenant Baxter, I want you to stay off the line. Spend your time doing religious services for the men, counseling them, and visiting them in the field hospital, but stay away from the shooting."

Bill replied, "With respect, Sir, my place is with the men. If they need spiritual help, I want to be there to do what I can."

Colonel Bisbee responded, "Lieutenant, the Army has never lost a chaplain, and you aren't going to be the first. This is not a suggestion. I don't want to have to send the first dead chaplain home in a box, and you don't want to be court martialed for disobeying my order. Am I making myself clear?" Bill uttered the perfunctory, "Yes, sir," without a hint of guile, and thanked the colonel for his concern.

After his arm was bandaged, Bill went and checked on the wounded soldier and found him with his shoulder heavily bandaged and resting in a bed in the field hospital. After chatting for a couple minutes, Bill asked if the soldier would like for him to write a note to his parents and tell them he was wounded but would be fine. The young man said that his father was dead, but he would appreciate the chaplain writing his mother who lived on a small farm near New Orleans. After getting the complete address information, Bill visited with other wounded soldiers.

Bill noticed a young white soldier lying on a cot, walked over, engaged him in conversation, and discovered the man was from a farm just off the

Yellowstone River near present day Corwin Springs, Montana. The trooper told Chaplain Baxter that his name was Michael Cheyhill, Jr., and thanked him for taking the time to visit with him. As they both had roots in Montana, Bill felt a sort of kinship to Cheyhill. The meeting seemed innocuous enough, just a chance meeting between two men who shared the same general location as their home. Neither man knew it at the time, but they were linked by a common incident that had happened many years prior.

Bill didn't disobey Colonel Bisbee's orders, but he did push the definition of "the line" to the limit. He continued ministering to the soldiers near the battlefield until the end of hostilities on April 1, 1901. Emilio Aguinaldo swore an oath accepting the authority of the United States over the Philippines and pledged his allegiance to the American government. The war was declared over on April 16, 1902. Lieutenant Baxter was transferred back to the United States as the post chaplain at the United States Cavalry School at Fort Riley, Kansas.

Lieutenant William Huzzah Baxter was wounded three times in combat even though he was a non-combatant. He received the Certificate of Merit Medal and the Philippine Campaign Medal, not bad for an officer who never fired a weapon during the conflict.

Chapter 5

Frederick William Brubaker, the son of William Travis and Betty Jean Brubaker was born on November 8, 1873, on the Slant BB ranch in Hopkins County, Texas. Freddie was a fun loving child who was given to playing tricks on the Baxter brothers. He went to Dallas public school and then worked as a teamster while trying to figure out what he wanted to do with his life. After driving freight wagons for a couple of years, Fred landed a job with the Dallas County Sheriff Department as a deputy sheriff. From the time Fred was a little boy, he had been mesmerized by Honks Pickens. Pickens had been the ramrod on the Baxter/Brubaker ranches in Texas and Montana. Pickens had served a couple stints with the Rangers, one in Laredo and the other in Dallas. The Texas Rangers had a spotty reputation as a law enforcement agency. Sometimes they did remarkable work, and sometimes they seemed to be unconcerned about crime. But there was an allure about the Texas Rangers that appealed to Fred.

On his twenty-ninth birthday, Frederick William Brubaker applied for a job as a Texas Ranger. Bill Brubaker had met Governor James Stephen "Big Jim" Hogg and knew him well enough to ask for his help in getting his son an appointment with the Rangers. In fact, Captain Brubaker had met Governor Hogg's father,

Brigadier General Joseph L. Hogg, during the siege of Corinth, Mississippi, in 1862. Unfortunately, the elder Hogg had come down with dysentery and died during the siege. The fact that Bill knew the governor's father held him in good stead with the younger Hogg. Bill liked Big Jim. You couldn't help but like a man named Hogg who would name his daughter Ima.

With Governor Hogg's influence and his experience as a deputy sheriff, Fred Brubaker was accepted as a Texas Ranger, sworn in, and stationed in Company "A" based in Houston, Texas. Fred's first few months were less than exciting with most of his time spent serving warrants and studying Texas criminal law. In late April 1904, Fred and Ranger Blythe Evans were assigned the job of trying to track down Claude "Sweet Tooth" Barbee who was wanted for cattle rustling in Texas and had killed Deputy Kinney Hamilton on a cattle ranch in the remote San Andres Mountains, sixty-five miles west of Tularosa, New Mexico Territory, in 1900. The rangers were cautioned to take no chances as Barbee had shot the deputy and then walked over to the wounded lawman and shot him three more times, execution style, while he lay on the ground.

Eugene Rhodes, the ranch owner, had wired Sheriff Pat Garrett in Las Cruces, New Mexico, advised him of the murder, and asked him to come and arrest Barbee while he was in the area. For whatever reason, Garrett never responded and made no attempt to catch Barbee. Barbee was reported to have taken up with two known outlaws. One was named Frank "Blockey" Jackson and the other Tom Nixon. They had a history of robbing freight stations and mercantile stores. Their latest robberies had been a freight station in West Columbia and a store in Pearland, Texas. The Rangers couldn't enforce the New Mexico murder warrant but could hold Barbee for the New Mexico authorities, if they were able to capture him.

Fred and Ranger Evans left Houston for Pearland, Texas, on January 7, 1904, armed with a handbill which supposedly displayed a fair likeness of Claude Barbee. Blythe Evans had been with the Rangers for seven years and had yet to fire his sidearm. Fred had never shot another human being, and he wasn't sure how he would react if confronted with the necessity of taking a human life. He was more than a little proficient with his .45 Colt single action Army that his father had given him when he was accepted as a deputy sheriff. He had shot the revolver and worked on it with a tiny file to relieve some of the stiffness and smooth out some of the resistance in the trigger pull. After tinkering with the pistol for about a month, he had it to his liking. Fred wore a custom made cross-draw holster that his father had crafted by a Dallas saddle maker and gave to his son with the pistol. Neither the revolver nor the holster was ostentatious. Captain Brubaker told him it was better to keep a low profile. Other than the initials FWB engraved on the butt plate the pistol, it was just a finely tooled and extremely accurate Plain Jane Model M1873P Colt with the standard five and one-half inch barrel.

Fred and Blythe got to Pearland around lunch time on the 7th, stabled their horses, grabbed their rifles and Fred's shotgun, and headed for the Pearl Hotel. Bud Baxter, Fred's father, had given him a Model 1892 Winchester .44-40 when he was accepted to serve with the Rangers. The Model 1892 was essentially the same weapon as the Model 1876 Winchester with only slight improvements. Fred's mother, Betty Jean, always a practical woman, figured the Winchester Model 97 12 gauge riot gun could prove mighty useful if her son needed to defend himself or defuse something at close range. She gave him the weapon and urged him to be careful. After getting their rifles, shotgun, and saddle bags stored in their rooms, they headed for the Doolittle Café for supper, ate a nice meal, topped it off with a slice of apple pie and hot coffee, went to their rooms at the hotel, and turned in for the night.

The next morning, Fred and Blythe went to the marshal's office and talked to the acting marshal, William Zychlinski, who was also the founder of the town. The regular town marshal had left after the terrible hurricane of 1900 destroyed the majority of the town, including his home. A full-time replacement had yet to be hired. Mr. Zychlinski wasn't much help other than confirming that three men had indeed robbed the general store. The acting marshal apologized because he couldn't be of more help. With that, Fred and Blythe walked to the general store and showed the handbills to the clerk. The store clerk was able to identify two of the three men on the wanted posters as being the ones who robbed him.

Since they had come up with nothing of value in their visit to Pearland, other than confirming the identity of two of the robbers, they got their horses and rode to the Brazoria County sheriff's office in Angleton, Texas, dismounted, hitched their horses, and walked into the office, introduced themselves and asked to see the sheriff.

****

Brazoria County took its name from the Brazos River which flowed about six miles southwest of Angleton, Texas. Brazoria was the county seat when the county was organized on December 20, 1836. It remained the county seat until 1896 when Angleton replaced it as the seat of government. Brazoria County is on the bottom land on the Gulf Coast at the mouth of the Brazos Rivers. The Brazoria County sheriff's department was formed in March of 1836 which gives it the distinction of being the oldest sheriff's department in the State of Texas.

****

After waiting a few minutes, Fred and Blythe were ushered into Sheriff F. M. Harvin's small office. Sheriff Harvin wasn't exactly friendly but made up for it by being less than helpful. After introductions, Sheriff Harvin said, "Well, well, the Texas Rangers are here to save the day. Doesn't the governor think we can catch these thieves without the help of the Rangers?"

Blythe spoke up and replied, "Sheriff, we just go where we are told to go and do what we are told to do. If you have a problem with the Rangers being in what you think is your territory, I suggest you take it up with the governor. Now, can we ask you a couple questions?"

Before the sheriff could respond, Fred piped up, "Sheriff Harvin, if you already have them locked up in the jail, it will save us a lot of looking."

Fred's prodding obviously made Sheriff Harvin mad, and he responded, "Son, I was catching thieves and murderers when you were shiteing yellow. You boys ask your questions so that I can get back to work."

Other than the sheriff looking at the likenesses on the handbills and saying they fit the description his deputies had got from the people who were robbed, he had little to add. When the sheriff started writing on a pad on his desk and completely ignoring the two rangers, Fred and Blythe thanked the sheriff for all his help and left. They figured their horses would be fairly safe in front of the sheriff's office, so they loosened their saddle cinches and left them standing there.

After leaving the sheriff's office, the Rangers poked around Angleton for a couple hours, stopped at the saloon, and chatted with people on the street in the attempt to coax some information that might be helpful. While in the River Saloon, they overheard a man telling of seeing three men camped on the Bravos River southwest of town when he was coming in from his ranch. Blythe interrupted and asked the rancher if he would look at some handbills. The man was glad to oblige and said that they looked enough like the men he had seen that it might be them but he had seen them at a distance and couldn't be sure.

Fred and Blythe went to the Brazos Café, had supper, walked back to the sheriff's office, retrieved their horses, tightened the cinches, mounted, and walked them south out of Angleton in the direction where the man said he had seen the men camped on the river. Neither Fred nor Blythe had their badge exposed and rode along at a leisurely pace as if they didn't have a care in the world. They smelled the smoke from the campfire before they saw the camp. As the rancher had said, there were three men sitting by the campfire drinking coffee. Blythe felt they should approach the camp cautiously but head on. They walked their horses up to within twenty feet of the camp fire, stopped, and asked if they had a cup of coffee to spare.

A short man, who was about as wide as he was tall, looked them over and finally said, "Sure. Step down from your horses."

Both Fred and Blythe dismounted with their horses between themselves and the men at the campfire. Fred came around his horse with the Winchester 97 shotgun pointed in the general direction of the men and said, "Each of you need to be real careful what you do next and how you do it. I want all three of you, starting with you on my left, to take your pointing finger and thumb, pull your pistol out of its holster, drop it on the ground, and slide it away with your foot." The short heavy man started to get up, and Fred said, "Don't do anything stupid, fatty." The portly man glared at Fred but sat back down, and all three did as they were told.

Blythe said, "We are Texas Rangers and have warrants for Claude Bisbee, Tom Nixon, and Frank Jackson for armed robbery. I am going to throw a pair of manacles to each of you, and I want you to secure them to your wrists. Then we will get on with taking you fellas back to Houston."

After the handcuffs were on the three men, Fred saddled their horses, took their rifles out of their scabbards, unloaded them, searched their saddlebags, tied all three rifles to the back of his saddle, and put their pistols and knives in his saddlebags.

Since it was to be a full moon, Fred and Blythe decided to ride back to Houston that night, keeping the three men between them in single file.

Fred reminded the three men that he had no intention of chasing around in the brush if they tried to get away. He would merely put a load of buckshot in their hide if they tried to run. With that bit of encouragement, they set out for Harris County. They got to the Harris County jail about mid-night, got the three prisoners locked in cells, and then Fred picked up the phone and asked an operator to connect him with the Brazoria County sheriff's office. In a couple minutes, the phone rang and Fred told the night deputy to tell Sheriff Harvin that he could stop wearing himself out looking for the three robbers because they were locked up in the Harris County jail.

Sometimes a young pup can show up an ole dog. It was a fun phone call to make!

Chapter 6

On a chilly morning on April 15, 1879, four men said goodbye to their wives and children, crossed the Yellowstone River, and set out across Montana Territory to try and find work as drovers. Or, at least, that was what they told their families. Three of the men were the Cheyhill brothers: Peter, Michael, and Joseph. The fourth man was named Edwin Marsey. The Cheyhill brothers were thieves: cattle, hogs, and chickens. They would basically steal anything that wasn't tied down. They had no history of violence, but they were poorly motivated to work and thought thievery a more profitable profession than physical labor. Edwin Marsey was another story. He had killed at least two men and was just plain mean through and through. They set out, headed northeast in the hopes of finding game or perhaps a trail drive headed north. On the 18th of April, the four men picked up the tracks of a large herd of cattle headed towards the southeastern corner of Montana Territory. The men trailed the herd from a distance, far enough away that they wouldn't be detected.

Late on the night of April 20th, the three brothers eased their horses into the herd of cattle and began quietly cutting cows out. The fourth man circled around the herd to try to steal whatever of value was in the camp or on the chuck wagon. Nothing went the way it was planned. Peter was shot by one of the drovers. He was badly wounded and was losing a lot of blood. Edwin Marsey was shot and wounded by a young boy and then killed by a mulatto woman.

The three brothers made it as far as Brayton's Trading Post near Belle Creek, Montana Territory, stopped to rest, gather themselves, and see if they could get Peter's wound to stop bleeding. In mid-afternoon, two men entered the trading post, one from the front door and one from the back. They ordered the men to stand up. When Peter Cheyhill, the brother who had been shot, attempted to get to his feet, he collapsed. The men marched Michael and Joseph Cheyhill out of the trading post and to a large boxelder tree and hanged them. Peter had bled to death. The two men cut down Michael and Joseph and took them to the trading post with instructions for the owner, Rufus Brayton, to give them a proper burial. They then rode off.

When Brayton had gone through the men's pockets in search of greenbacks or coins, he found a letter addressed to Michael Cheyhill. The men had little to nothing to take. So Brayton copied the address and wrote a note informing Mrs. Michael Cheyhill that her husband and two other men were dead. Brayton went on to tell her where the bodies could be found. Brayton gave the letter to a man traveling through to post when he arrived at civilization. It was still cool in Montana Territory and cold at night but not cold enough to keep the bodies from decomposing. Brayton dug a shallow grave close to the trading post, laid the three men side by side in the hole, covered them with their blankets, and mounded the dirt. He had no way of knowing if the letter would find Cheyhill's widow and had no way of knowing if someone would come for the bodies if the message was received.

A month later, two men, riding on a farm wagon, drove up to the trading post and asked Brayton where the Cheyhill bodies were located. The men dug up the remains, wrapped each in their individual blankets, and placed each body on the wagon. One of the men looked at Brayton and asked, "What were the men's names who killed my nephews?" Brayton told them he had no idea who they were. They had just ridden in, took two of the men out, hanged them, and told him to bury the three men. All Brayton knew for sure was the two men were cattlemen because they had told him they had hung the men because they had tried to rustle their cattle. Whether the men were moving cattle north or south, or where they had ridden when they left the trading post, he didn't know.

The same man looked hard at Brayton and asked, "Did you find any money on them? And where are their weapons, horses, and saddles?"

Brayton responded, "They had a couple dollars between them, and I applied it to their grub and whiskey bill and my labor for burying them. I will get you their side arms and rifles. Their mounts are in the corral, and saddles and tack are in the shed. With that, the two men saddled the three horses, hitched them to the wagon, and rode off with the three bodies, horses, and gear. Brayton never saw or heard from them again.

The men transporting the remains arrived in what is now Park County, near Corwin Springs, Montana, in the southwestern part of the territory, now state. The Cheyhill brothers had small homesteads near the Yellowstone River, were dirt poor, and without prospects. The two men who retrieved the brothers were Martin and Enoch Cheyhill. They were the paternal uncles of the deceased men. The nephews' father, whose name was Matthew, had been killed by a grizzly bear while elk hunting a couple years prior to the hanging.

Once the funerals were over and Michael, Joseph, and Peter Cheyhill were laid to rest, Martin took all the great-nephews aside. There were a total of five boys: Michael Jr., Cabel, Seth, Jacob, and Joshua. The Cheyhill's were big on biblical names. Once everyone was assembled, Martin, being the oldest living Cheyhill, promised the boys that the killers of their fathers would be found and treated in like fashion as were their fathers. Cabel spoke up and said, "Well, Uncle Martin, since we don't have any idea who the men were or where they might have been going, how do you intend to find them?"

Martin responded, "Enoch and I will get on the trail tomorrow morning and try to find evidence of a large herd of cattle that is either moving south to market or north to find grazing land. We'll trail them, capture one of the drovers, question him, and then do what needs to be done if they are the guilty party."

Caleb looked at his brothers and cousins, then turned to his uncles and said, "Our fathers have been dead for more than a month. That means the cattle herd went north or south more than a month ago. All the evidence of the cattle's passing is gone. I fear you are wasting your time."

Enoch and Martin left the following morning and headed for southeastern Montana. They traveled for days and saw nothing providing evidence of a herd of cattle having passed through. Five days out of the Yellowstone River area, Enoch and Martin were camped beside a small copse of trees when they noticed that it was suddenly quiet, very quiet. Not a bird was chirping or a squirrel chattering or moving. Both men grabbed their rifles and got behind the nearest trees.

They didn't have long to wait before the first arrow came whizzing in and struck Enoch in the thigh, embedding in the muscle. Since the arrow didn't pass all the way through, there was no way to remove it. Enoch and Martin knew they were in trouble, terrible trouble, and there was little chance of escaping their situation alive. Martin cut the shaft near the skin on the fletching end. That's all that could be done at the time. In a couple moments, two more arrows whizzed through the air, and each hit a horse. Neither mount was killed, but they were in a frenzy, broke loose from their tethers, and ran off. They were now trapped in the small stand of trees and could only wait for the inevitable.

They didn't have to wait long. An Arapaho brave stood and fired a rifle, hitting Martin in the chest above the left lung. Both men were now seriously wounded and had no way of escape. The Indians merely waited and let the two brothers bleed. After a couple hours, the Arapaho started cautiously approaching the two men who put down their rifles and started pleading for their lives. The Arapaho just laughed and got out their knives and started having fun with the two wounded men. First, the Indians scalped both of the Cheyhill brothers while they were still alive. The Indians then sat by the fire and watched the blood run from the men's heads down their faces. Finally, both men passed out, and the Indians hacked them to death with their knives, retrieved their ponies, gathered the dead men's pistols and rifles, and left the corpses to the buzzards and animals to dispose of.

After three months, it became apparent to the Cheyhill clan that Uncles Martin and Enoch weren't coming back to the Yellowstone area. They had no way of knowing if their uncles had found the men who killed their husbands and fathers. If they had, they could have also been killed by them. And it was possible they had suffered some other mishap. They were to never know the disposition of their great uncles. The boys would have to wait years and a couple wars before they were able to identify the men who had killed their fathers. Unfortunately, by the time they finally discovered who had killed them, both the men were dead, but their sons weren't!

Chapter 7

On the 17th of May 1905, Fred Brubaker was called into the Ranger office in Houston and handed a warrant for the arrest of Ben Kilpatrick, aka The Tall Texan or Benjamin Arnold. Kilpatrick was an outlaw most of his adult life. He had been a member of the Wild Bunch and robbed trains and banks in Nevada, Montana, and Texas.

****

Ben Kilpatrick was one of the most prolific train robbers of the Old West. He was born in Concho County, Texas, on January 5, 1874, and grew up working as a cowboy there. While working as a cowboy, he met and fell in with a hard bunch including Thomas and Sam Ketchum and William Carver. Kilpatrick was 6' 2" tall which earned him the nickname of The Tall Texan. He had very peculiar eyes, pale yellow with a violet spot in them. He was an excellent shot with pistol or rifle and feared nothing.

Kilpatrick and his cowboy friends came to the conclusion there was an easier way to make money than working cattle and formed the Ketchum Gang which robbed trains in New Mexico. In 1898, he branched out and joined the Wild Bunch and holed up in the Robbers' Roost in Utah for a time. After a few years with Butch Cassidy, Sundance

Kid, Harvey Logan, and William Carver, he decided to go it alone for a while and went back to Texas with Laura Bullion in tow. Laura had been Carver's girlfriend, and when she and Kilpatrick started their affair, Ben thought it best they put some distance between themselves and Carver.

****

The warrant that was handed to Fred was for a train robbery that Kilpatrick and Bullion had committed near Galveston, Texas, on November 6, 1904. News of the robbery and escape of the robbers spread far and wide. It seemed that a man and woman who fit the description of Ben Kilpatrick and Laura Bullion were seen by some drovers at a small cabin alongside the Guadalupe River, west of Victoria, Texas. The men who had noticed the couple traveled the trail from the ranch on which they worked to Victoria frequently. The cabin had been abandoned for several months, and now, it was suddenly occupied by a man and woman.

The drovers had stopped to be sociable and were met with a reproof and a cock and bull story about the woman having inherited the cabin from her dead uncle. The drovers knew John Tabor owned the cabin and was in Arizona in a sanatorium trying to recover from consumption. Since the drovers doubted the story, they notified the sheriff of Victoria County, who contacted the Rangers.

Fred wondered why the sheriff didn't just take a deputy or two and check out the man and woman. Since he was the junior member of the Houston Ranger Troop, he didn't ask many questions. Fred was paired up with Blythe Evans again. They got their gear together and set out for Victoria which was about 125 miles southwest of Houston. They camped overnight twice and arrived at the sheriff's office in Victoria around noon on May 20th. IIc and Blythe hitched their horses to the rail in front of the sheriff's office, went inside, and asked to see the sheriff. The man who was in the office said that the sheriff, George Henry Heck, was away on a trip to see his daughter in New Orleans and wouldn't be back for a week or so. Blythe asked the man who the sheriff had left in charge. He was told that the acting sheriff was named Rufus Ledbetter and that he was out talking to a rancher about some missing cattle.

It became obvious to Fred and Blythe that they were getting nowhere fast, but Blythe plowed on and asked, "Well, is there a deputy who can come with us and point out the cabin in which Ben Kilpatrick and Laura Bullion may have been sighted?"

The dispatcher seemed to be nervous and said, "I can't send anyone on my own. Deputy Ledbetter can go with you or send someone else when he gets back."

Fred was getting irritated and said, "Any idea when Ledbetter might return?" The dispatcher said that if he didn't get invited to stay to supper, he should be back before dark. Fred and Blythe looked at each other and tried not to laugh.

Blythe looked at the dispatcher and said, "We'll be at the Victoria Café for the next hour or so. If Ledbetter gets back, have him walk over. If not, we'll be back after we eat." They walked out of the sheriff's office, crossed the street, walked about seventy-five yards to the café, and had a large bowl of chili, a glass of beer, and then coffee. They didn't see hide or hair of Deputy Ledbetter. After their second cup of coffee, they paid their bill and walked back to the sheriff's office. Deputy Ledbetter hadn't showed up.

Fred and Blythe waited around the office until it was fully dark and then decided that Ledbetter was obviously gonna be late coming back. They were discussing whether to get a hotel room when, out of the blue, the dispatcher spoke up and said, "Deputy Ledbetter is sweet on Lizzy Cantrell."

Fred and Blythe looked at each other in bewilderment, and finally, Blythe said, "So?" The man said that Ledbetter was at the Circle C checking on the missing stock. Lizzy's father owned the Circle C ranch. Ledbetter might just spend the night and come back the next morning.

Blythe looked at Fred and said, "I've had enough of this horse crap. Let's go see about this our own selves." With that, they walked out of the office, mounted their horses, and headed down the trail towards the Guadalupe River and the cabin.

They had just gotten to the outskirts of town when Fred looked over at Blythe and said, "Has it occurred to you that we don't know where we're going? It's dark. How are we gonna find this cabin unless we stumble upon the place in the blackness? And then how would we know we have the right place?"

Blythe pulled up, turned his horse around, and said, "Let's go back to town, stable the horses, get a hotel room for the night, and try this again tomorrow. I have allowed myself to get irritated with this sheriff's office, and it's tainting my judgment." Blythe and Fred were up at daybreak, ate breakfast at the Victoria Café, and went to the sheriff's office again. Lo and behold, Deputy Ledbetter was in the office drinking coffee.

Blythe said, "Deputy Ledbetter, we are going to the cabin on the Guadalupe River where the drovers saw the man and woman. We could use a deputy to go along with us, point out the cabin, and provide backup in case things go badly, and they put up a fight."

Ledbetter said, "I'll go with you. It probably ain't them anyway." Blythe and Fred got their horses. Ledbetter met them at the livery, and around 9 AM, they headed down the trail towards the river. In about an hour, they arrived at a rise which gave them a good view of the cabin.

Blythe said, "Let's fan out a mite and get maybe thirty feet between us just in case things go wrong."

They rode forward, and when they got to within fifty feet of the cabin, the door partially opened, a rifle barrel appeared, and a man's voice said, "What do you men want?"

Deputy Ledbetter spoke up and said, "I'm Deputy Ledbetter, Victoria County sheriff's office. I need for you to put the rifle down and step out on the porch where we can talk." The door slammed shut, and in a couple seconds, the glass from the front window was knocked out. Ledbetter wheeled his horse around and hollered, "Oh shite. Let's get back out of rifle range." With that, all three men raced their horses to a small copse of trees along the river, dismounted, and took out their rifles. Fred also pulled out his Winchester shotgun and slung it over his shoulder.

Fred had noticed as they approached from the rise there were no windows on the downriver side of the cabin. He had no way of knowing if there was a door or window in the back or on the other side of the building. They were at a standoff with the people in the cabin. Whoever was in the cabin probably couldn't get out, but on the other hand, they couldn't approach the cabin without losing their cover and exposing themselves to rifle fire.

Fred looked at Blythe and Ledbetter and said, "I'm going to circle back around, get behind the rise, and see if I can get a better field of vision on the front and far side of the cabin." With that, he mounted his horse and took off. Within fifteen minutes, Fred had gotten to a point where he could leave his horse, crawl forward, and take cover behind a couple large stumps. He ground picketed his horse, crawled forward, and got behind a stump where he could cover the front door and a small window. He had just got settled when a bullet hit the top of the stump. It was a good 100 yards to the cabin. Whoever was shooting at him knew which end of the rifle the bullet came out of.

Fred had a box of shells and a fully loaded Winchester 92 .44-40, so he figured he might as well let the occupants know he also knew a little something about shooting a rifle. He lay completely prone behind the stump, wriggled to the right side, took aim at the window, and fired. What little glass that was left in the window exploded into small glass fragments and flew all over the inside of the little cabin. Fred had no way of knowing, but his bullet had caused some cuts and minor bleeding on both the occupants.

While Fred had the front of the cabin covered, Blythe and Ledbetter started towards the cabin. When they were within fifty yards, a bullet hit Blythe in the lower leg, missing the bone, but tearing out a hunk of hide and soft tissue. Both men started shooting at the window of the cabin, and Ledbetter helped Blythe limp back to the trees. The bullet wound was nasty looking and bleeding freely.

Ledbetter got a piece of cloth from his saddlebags, made a compress, and bound the leg with a couple pieces of the cloth.

Blythe was in no condition to walk and was slightly dizzy from the shock and loss of blood. It was now mid-afternoon, and they were still at a stand-off. Deputy Ledbetter decided that he needed to get Ranger Evans back to Victoria and have the sawbones take a look at his leg, but he hated to leave the other ranger alone. He helped Blythe on his horse, and they made the same circular route Fred had taken. Ledbetter stopped his horse alongside Fred's picketed horse and dismounted, crawled up the rise, and hollered loud enough for Fred to hear. He said he was going to take Ranger Evans to town to have his leg looked at by the doctor. Fred knew that Blythe had been hit by a bullet but had no idea how bad it was. Fred told Ledbetter to go ahead and come back with a couple deputies.

At dusk, Fred saw two forms heading for the river. He brought his rifle up and snap-shot. The larger of the two spun around, fell, and disappeared over the river bank. Fred wanted to go down the incline and try to get a better shot at the man but realized he would be giving up his cover. There was no doubt the man could shoot. After about an hour, Deputy Ledbetter and two other deputies rode up at a gallop. Fred told them what had happened. He told them he didn't know how badly hurt the man was or where he might be.

It was now fully dark, and with only a half-moon, the four men had little visibility. They tried to keep the cabin and the place where Fred had last seen the two individuals between them. When they got to the place where Fred thought the man was located when he had shot him, they found a good bit of blood on the ground but no body. The two people had about a two hour head start floating down the river and heavy cloud cover was developing. The deputies and Fred had little choice but to head back to Victoria.

Fred checked on Blythe and told him what had happened. Evans would be fine but would have a nasty scar to show off. Evans spent the night at the doctor's office, and Fred went back to the hotel. Fred got up early, ate breakfast at the café, and took a plate to Blythe. He then went to the sheriff's office to call back to Houston and advise the Ranger office of the circumstances.

Around 9 AM a farmer who lived a couple miles downriver of the cabin rode up to the sheriff's office. He came into the office and said that a man and woman had stolen two of his horses and lit out going northwest. He said that the man had a bad limp and sure rode funny. When Fred was told what the farmer had said, he laughed because he had apparently shot the man in the arse.

Fred waited two days until the doctor released Blythe to travel and then they slowly rode back to Houston, taking several breaks, and spending two nights on the road. There was little doubt that it had been Kilpatrick and Bullion, even though their identification hadn't been confirmed. Innocent people don't shoot at lawmen.

****

Kilpatrick escaped, made it back to New Mexico, and for some reason, decided to go to Missouri where he was apprehended, tried, and taken to the federal prison in Atlanta, Georgia. After spending a few years in the penitentiary, Kilpatrick was paroled. After his release, Kilpatrick and an accomplice did a couple train robberies near Memphis, Tennessee, and then a couple small robberies in West Texas.

On March 12, 1912, Kilpatrick and Ole Hobek, a friend from prison, decided to rob the Galveston, Harrisburg, & San Antonio Railroad Train No. 9 as it pulled out of Del Rio, Texas. The bandits stopped the train half way between Dryden and Sanderson where they had an accomplice with horses waiting. Hobek stayed with the engineer while Kilpatrick went to the baggage car with David Trousdale, the Western Union express agent on the train. Kilpatrick filled a sack with money, and as he turned to leave, Trousdale hit him on the head with an ice mallet killing him instantly. Trousdale then picked up Kilpatrick's pistol. When Hobek got tired of waiting and came to the baggage car, Trousdale shot and killed him. The botched robbery, known as the Baxter's Curve Train Robbery or the Sanderson

Train Robbery, was one of the last train robberies in Texas.

When the train carrying David Trousdale got to Sanderson, he received a hero's welcome. It wasn't just every day that a middle-aged man could overcome a gunman with an ice mallet and then kill another gunman in a gunfight.

Chapter 8

In 1877, General Phil Sheridan suggested that a fort be built on or near the Milk River in Montana. His logic was to man the fort in order to ward off possible attacks from the north by the Sioux who had migrated to the Cyprus Hills in Canada. The Nez Perce were also a threat, and some of the tribe had migrated to Canada. Lieutenant Colonel, later Major General, J. R. Brooke recommended the site where Fort Assiniboine was to be established. The fort was constructed in Hill County six miles southwest of the present day Havre, Montana. The fort was named for the Assiniboine people.

The fort was located on a massive military reservation which stretched south to the Missouri River, north to the Milk River, and encompassed the Bear's Paw Mountains. At its maximum usage, the fort encompassed 704,000 acres and had a staff of 750 officers and enlisted men. The fort had 104 buildings in 1880 and was one of the largest military facilities ever built in the United States.

****

Lieutenant James Budwell (BJ) Baxter remained at Fort Assiniboine until the outbreak of the Spanish-American War in 1898.

In June of 1895, Sergeant George Washington Jones was leading a four man reconnaissance patrol when they came upon a group of men driving a herd of around 100 head of cattle. Cattle wasn't the business of the military, and the patrol just stopped and watched with fascination as the men drove the cattle, steered wayward cows back to the herd, and maneuvered their horses. Jones had been in the cavalry for more than twenty years and had seen excellent horsemen, but these cowboys were as good with horses as his troopers.

When the men who were driving the cattle noticed the four black soldiers, they pulled their rifles out of their scabbards and began shooting at the troopers. Sergeant Jones and his men were well outnumbered and weren't expecting a bunch of cowboys to shoot at them. Before they could get their mounts turned around and get out of rifle range, Private Elemis Jones (no relation to GW) and Corporal Moses Simpson were hit by bullets. Jones caught a bullet in his upper arm just below the shoulder, and Simpson was hit in the upper right leg just below the hip joint. Both men were able to stay in their saddles and get out of rifle range.

The cattle drovers' decision to fire on the soldiers was senseless and stupid. The Negro soldiers had no idea that the men weren't the owners of the cattle. Beyond watching the drovers work the cattle, they had no interest in the men anyway. When the rustlers panicked, they made a horrible mistake. The rustlers should have known they were sealing their fate once they engaged the army troopers without provocation. On the other hand, stealing cattle doesn't require a great deal of intelligence.

It was about twenty-five miles back to the fort, and Sergeant Jones sent the uninjured trooper at a gallop to the fort to get help and send the surgeon's ambulance to transport the two wounded men. The ambulance and a six man patrol led by Lieutenant Baxter met Sergeant Jones and the two wounded troopers ten miles from the fort, loaded the two injured men into the ambulance, and started back to let the Army surgeon treat the men.

When Lieutenant Baxter arrived at the fort, Colonel Broadwater was waiting on the parade ground for the patrol to arrive. After the colonel checked on the status of the wounded men, he told BJ to follow him to his office. When they got to Colonel Broadwater's office, he told BJ to close the door and said, "I don't give two hoots in hell about cattle rustlers per se, but when they shoot my soldiers, I have a great interest. There are officers on the post who outrank you but since you have the cattle expertise and know the area, you are elected. Take Sergeant Jones and a detachment of ten troopers, find that cattle herd, and arrest or kill the rustlers. I expect the men to be punished for shooting my troopers before you come back to the post. That's all, Lieutenant Baxter." BJ gave the perfunctory, "Yes, Sir," saluted, did an about face, and walked out of the colonel's office. The Colonel obviously had a briar under his saddle over the shooting of his men!

BJ walked up to Sergeant Jones and said, "GW (out of earshot of the men, BJ would call Sergeant Jones 'GW'), we're gonna need pack horses, food stores for twelve men for ten days, ammunition, and cooking equipment. I want to leave at daybreak tomorrow. You select ten men that you can depend on. That will be all."

Sergeant Jones saluted and said, "Yes, Sir." Jones and quickly went off to make the arrangements for the detail. At 5 AM the next morning, Sergeant Jones was standing by his mount, and ten troopers were lined up and standing at parade rest. BJ walked up leading his dun color gelding named Sunny. He returned Sergeant Jones' salute, told him to have the troopers mount up, and the detail got under way.

The cattle herd that Sergeant Jones had come upon was headed north, no doubt to cattle markets in Saskatchewan or Alberta. Unless the rustlers (honest cowboys don't shoot at soldiers) had ridden off and abandoned the cattle, they wouldn't be difficult to find.

What exactly to do when they found them was the dilemma. BJ didn't have a problem with shooting the drovers if fired upon. On the other hand, he had no interest in hanging rustlers. The Army had no authority to deal with civilians in that manner. At 11 AM, the forward scout came galloping back to the detail, saluted, and told BJ that the herd was about three miles ahead. The presumed rustlers were still with the herd. BJ pulled up and told Sergeant Jones that he wanted the detail to continue on in a column of twos until they sighted the herd. Then he wanted the troopers to fan out with ten feet between each horse. They would approach at a trot with their rifles at the ready. No one was to shoot until BJ fired. Then they were to fire at will until told to cease firing.

Nothing happened until the detail got to within seventy-five yards of the herd. Then, one of the rustlers fired on the cavalry detail. BJ signaled the troopers to stop their horses. The patrol dismounted. Each trooper used their saddle for a rifle support and took aim at a rustler. BJ said, "Fire at will," and squeezed the trigger of his carbine. The Buffalo Soldiers were armed with the new Springfield Model 1892 Krag-Jorgensen rifles, in the .30-40 Krag caliber which had a five shot magazine. The rifle had an effective range of 3,000 feet, which was just over one-half of a mile. The rustlers might be excellent horsemen, but the Buffalo Soldiers spent a lot of hours firing their rifles and were without equal regarding marksmanship.

Twelve men sighted their weapons, and after BJ fired, eleven rifles fired in unison. The troopers worked the bolt of their rifles, chambered another shell, sighted, and fired again. After two volleys, eight rustlers and four horses were on the ground and the cattle were stampeding. The remaining three rustlers whipped their horses into a full gallop, headed west, and never looked back. BJ remounted and walked Sunny towards the downed men followed by Sergeant Jones and the troopers. Of the eight men on the ground, five were, without a doubt, grave yard dead. The other three weren't up to a barn dance.

Sergeant Jones placed manacles on the wounded men and seated them side by side. BJ walked up to the three men and said, "Well, fellas, this didn't go well did it? I need to know who came up with this great idea." None of the three men said anything, and BJ looked at them and said, "You don't seem to understand. I'm not going to hang you. On the other hand, I have been given no orders to take you to the fort. As far as I am concerned, we can leave you bleeding right where you are and let the buzzards, wolves, and other scavengers take care of you. We are out this way often and can get the manacles in a week or two."

The man sitting on the right end of the three said, "Please, Lieutenant, don't leave us out here. I'll tell you who was in charge of this gang. His name is Jack Sully, and he was one of the three men who lit out from here and left us." BJ looked at Sergeant Jones who just shrugged his shoulders. Neither of them had ever heard of Jack Sully.

****

At the height of his cattle rustling career, Jack Sully had a gang of twelve men and was reputed to have stolen more than 50,000 head of cattle and 3,000 horses. United States Deputy Marshal Johnny Petrie attempted to arrest Jack Sully on May 16, 1904. When the outlaw refused to surrender, he was killed by Marshal Petrie in the ensuing gunfight.

****

BJ took the three wounded and five dead rustlers back to the fort. The five dead men were buried in a mass grave on a knoll about seventy-five yards outside the main gate of the fort. The three wounded men recovered, were tried by a military tribunal, found guilty of attempted murder, and assigned to ten years at hard labor in the fort stockade at Fort Assiniboine. The prisoners were assigned to duties that were the most undesirable: cleaning latrines, mucking out horse stalls, and cleaning up horse droppings on the parade ground. The soldiers loved having the rustlers around to take care of the duties they hated to perform.

The cattle herd was allowed to just graze after they stopped running. They would either become feral over time, or the rancher who owned them might find them, round them up, and take them back to his ranch. Either way, the Army wasn't in the cattle business and had no idea of how to notify the rightful owner of the livestock.

BJ wanted to take a detail and go after Sully and the other two men, but Colonel Broadwater nixed the request. The Colonel felt that Sully and the other men would head for the safety of Canada. With their head start, BJ would never catch up with them before they got to the border. Five dead rustlers and three in confinement was a good day's work. The Colonel was happy with the results and commended Lieutenant Baxter for his leadership in the foray. When the Colonel was happy, happiness abounded at Fort Assiniboine.

Chapter 9

On a chilly morning on February 26, 1906, Texas Ranger Fred Brubaker was summoned to the office of Ranger Captain Smith. Fred immediately wondered what he had done to cause the captain to want to personally see him. As far as he knew, he had done nothing wrong, but Captain Smith was notorious for chewing on his ranger's posteriors when he thought they needed his attention. A good rule of thumb around the ranger headquarters was to find something to do that would keep you away from the office and Captain Smith. After waiting about ten minutes, Captain Smith told Fred to come into his office and have a seat.

Captain Smith lit a cigar, took a long draw, expelled a cloud of smoke, and said, "Brubaker, I have a special assignment for you. We have a visitor coming from Scotland Yard in London, England, who will be here with us for a month. Your assignment and most importantly is, don't let him get hurt while he tags along with you observing our methods and operating procedures. Thanks for volunteering and have a nice day or month as it were." Fred got up, smiled, and thanked Captain Smith for his confidence in him and for entrusting him with this wonderful opportunity to represent the Texas Rangers on this special assignment.

Captain Smith said, "Put a lid on the horse crap, Brubaker, and just make sure the Limey doesn't get hurt."

****

The London, England, police force was created in 1829 by an act of Parliament introduced by Sir Robert Peel, the home secretary. In honor of Peel, the metropolitan policemen are called "bobbies" and sometimes "peelers."

The name of Scotland Yard was derived from the location of the original Metropolitan Police headquarters at 4 Whitehall Place. The rear entrance of the building was on a street called Great Scotland Yard. The Scotland Yard entrance became the public entrance to the police station. Over time, the name of the street and the Metropolitan Police station became synonymous.

The population of London, England, in 1905 was in the neighborhood of six million souls, with 13,000 metropolitan policemen to combat crime in the sprawling city.

****

The Scotland Yard investigator who was to accompany Fred was named Colin Mannford Picknard-Lee. Colin was a pleasant enough fellow, but he sure talked funny. It took half a minute to pronounce his entire name. After Colin and Fred were introduced and chatted for a few minutes, Brubaker asked the Englishman if he was hungry. Colin replied that he would fancy some fish and chips. Fred had absolutely no idea whether the English fellow wanted to eat fish or change into better clothes. Fred decided to take Colin to the San Jacinto Café which was situated on the river bank overlooking the San Jacinto River. Picknard commented that the San Jacinto looked somewhat like the Thames River, only a bit smaller.

During their meal, Fred asked Colin why he wasn't visiting with the Houston police department. It just seemed to make sense that a big city policeman would want to train with a big city police department. Picknard explained that, in the English countryside, there were watchmen and constables who attended to minor crime. When a major crime was committed, that required thorough investigation Scotland Yard would be called. Chief Superintendent Marcum Davies thought that by spending some time with the Texas Rangers, Picknard might learn some helpful things regarding rural policing.

When they returned from their lunch, Captain Smith called Fred into his office and gave him a warrant for the arrest of Annie Rogers, aka Della Moore or Maud Williams. Rogers had been involved with Butch Cassidy's Wild Bunch. She had been charged with being an accomplice during a train robbery and imprisoned in Tennessee. Rogers was released from prison on June 19, 1902, and took up residence in Baytown, Texas, where she worked in a saloon as a "hostess," some would say prostitute. There had been a series of robberies in and around Baytown. Fred was to arrest Annie Rogers and bring her to Houston for questioning and possible charges for her part in the crimes. Captain Smith thought arresting Rogers would be a safe enough mission with little possibility of violence. The main thing was it would give Picknard something to talk about when he got back to England. Boy, did it ever!

Fred got Colin a horse and saddle from the livery, saddled his own horse and the Limey's, and set out on the twenty-five mile ride to Baytown. Picknard had been on a horse while in training in England but had never ridden to any extent. After thirty minutes in the saddle, the Englishman was ready to walk. They finally got to Baytown after frequent stops to allow Picknard to rest his hind quarters. Fred got directions to the Bay Saloon, rode to the building, hitched both horses, and entered the drinking establishment. Picknard walked into the saloon spraddle-legged. Once inside, Colin commented that he was less than impressed with the saloon and said that the pubs in England were much cleaner and more civilized.

Fred walked to the bar and asked the barkeep where he would find Annie Rogers. The man responded that he didn't know anyone by that name. Fred responded, "How about Della Moore or Maud Williams?"

The bartender said that Maud Williams worked at the saloon but wouldn't be in before late evening. After getting directions to the small house outside Baytown on Cedar Bayou that she was renting, Fred and Picknard mounted their horses and headed to the woman's house. Fred never took anything for granted and had brought his shotgun and rifle as well as the Colt .45 he always had on his side. He had learned that the simplest things could go awry. Many lawmen had been shot, and some killed, because of their assumptions and carelessness. As they neared the house, Fred cautioned Colin to stay with his horse. Better yet, stay behind his horse just in case things went wrong. They did, very wrong.

Fred dismounted, cautioned Colin again to stay behind his horse, walked to the porch, and knocked on the door. In a couple minutes, a woman's voice was heard saying, "What do you want?" Fred identified himself as a Texas Ranger and said he had a warrant for Annie Rogers. Just as he finished, the right front window burst outward sending shards of glass onto the porch. A pistol appeared. Fred flattened himself against the house just as the pistol fired. Luckily, the bullet missed Fred by a couple inches. Fred fired through the wall in the direction of the shooter and was rewarded by a scream. He had no idea where he had hit the man, but a hunk of .45 lead does considerable damage wherever it hits the human body. The front of the house had two windows, one on either side of the door. Immediately after Fred fired his revolver, the window glass on the left window burst outward sending more glass onto the porch, and a rifle barrel appeared. Fred, who was between the door and the left hand window, grabbed the rifle barrel and jerked outward as hard as he could, and the rifle discharged. A man's upper body appeared when he was jerked off balance while trying to hold onto the rifle. Fred put a dent in his head with the butt of his Colt .45 and pulled him on out the window. Once on the porch, Fred rolled the man on his stomach against the porch wall and put manacles on his wrists. The man was bleeding like a stuck hog. The shards of glass Fred had pulled him through had cut the man in several places.

When Fred turned around to check on Picknard, the investigator's horse was down and thrashing around. The rifle discharge had hit the animal in the neck and caused an enormous amount of bleeding. No doubt, a major artery had been hit. Fred hollered to Picknard to stay behind the horses and, when the horse stopped thrashing, to lie down behind the animal and stay there.

Fred turned his attention to the house, and a man hollered, "I'm hit, and bone is sticking out of my arm. I need a doctor."

Fred, always the glib one, said, "I'm afraid I didn't bring a sawbones with me. Come out the door, and I will take you to Baytown and get you to a doctor."

Nothing happened for a couple minutes. Then the door opened and a male voice said, "Don't shoot, I'm coming out." Fred told the man to keep both hands where he could see them and walk out the door.

When the man cleared the door, Fred told him to turn around slowly. When Fred was convinced that the man wasn't armed, he told him to walk slowly to the horse that was standing. Fred hollered to Colin, "There are manacles in my saddlebags. Stay behind the horse and put a pair on this fellow when he gets to you." To the wounded man, Fred instructed, "Walk straight and slow. Do anything out of the way, and I'll put another piece of lead in you."

When the man got to the horse, Colin called out, "Ranger Fred, there is a bone sticking out of his left arm."

Fred replied, "Put the manacles on his wrists, not the bone."

Fred had two men in custody but had no idea how many others might be in the house. If this was the gang that had been doing the robberies, there could be more inside. Fred hollered, "Annie Rogers, I have never shot a woman, but that doesn't mean I won't. Come out with your hands held high and empty. If I have to come in, you will probably get to ride to Baytown tied over a horse's back."

In a couple minutes, a female voice said, "Alright, alright. I'll come out. Don't shoot me. I'm unarmed." Fred told the woman to come ahead with her hands on top her head. When the woman walked through the door, Fred was taken aback. The woman who appeared was a slightly built attractive woman with black hair and dark eyes. Fred took the woman by the arm, stood between the door and window, and asked her if there was anyone else in the house. She said no. Fred then hollered to Colin and asked him if he knew how to shoot a rifle. The Englishman answered in the affirmative. Fred told him to keep the rifle pointed at the woman and shoot the men who were cuffed if they tried to get away.

Fred then cautiously entered the house and began searching the four rooms. The house was empty. He came out of the house, walked the woman to the horse, took out a pair of manacles, and put them on her wrists. He then went to the barn behind the house and saddled the three horses that were in the stalls. Fred and Colin helped the two men on their horses. The Englishman got onto the saddle of the third horse. Annie Rogers put her foot in the stirrup, and Colin pulled her up behind him. About thirty minutes later, Fred, Colin, and the three suspects arrived at the Baytown jail.

The man with the broken arm was identified as Franklin "Bay" Williams, a no-count who hung around the saloons and brothels along the wharf. When Doc French examined Williams' arm, he announced that it had to be removed at the elbow to prevent gangrene from setting in. The second man was Bob Nevils, a career criminal. Nevils and

Williams were charged with attempted murder. After Williams recovered from the amputation, he and Nevils stood trial, were convicted, and sent to the Texas State Prison in Huntsville, Texas. Annie Rogers was taken back to Houston, questioned, and released for lack of evidence.

****

Annie Rogers' actual name was Della Moore. She was born in Tarrant County, Texas, in 1869. She left home in 1893 and found employment as a prostitute at the bawdy houses of Fannie Parker in Mena, Arkansas, Fort Worth, and San Antonio, Texas.

After being released in Baytown, no one ever heard of Della Moore again. Some said she changed her name again and went back to work for Fannie Parker. Others said she married a whiskey drummer and moved to Saint Louis, Missouri. As with many people in the old west, she simply disappeared never to be heard from again.

****

Colin Picknard spent the rest of his time following Fred around like a puppy dog. He was convinced Marshal Brubaker was a famous Texas gunman. He went back to Scotland Yard with a wonderful story. The police at Scotland Yard didn't carry firearms and thought them uncivilized. After his adventure with Ranger Brubaker, Colin could see the logic of carrying a weapon. Captain Smith chewed on Fred for getting the Englishman involved in a shootout, but there was a slight grin on his face while he was chewing.

Smith commented, "Brubaker, if I sent you out to get kids to stop playing marbles in the street, you would find a way to turn it into an altercation."

Fred replied, "Captain, I guess some folks just don't appreciate my charm and wit."

Chapter 10

At 7 AM, May 17, 1897, Corporal Lester Sharp came running into the officer's mess, rushed up to Lieutenant James Baxter, saluted, and blurted out, "Lieutenant Baxter, Colonel Broadwater wants to see you forthwith, Sir." BJ had finished his potatoes and eggs and was on his second cup of coffee when the corporal had come running in. He got up, took his mess tray to the kitchen, drained his coffee cup, placed it on the tray, and walked out of the dining hall.

When he arrived at the headquarters building orderly room, Colonel Broadwater's office door was open, and he was pacing back and forth. BJ thought to himself, "*Whatever is going on, it ain't good.*" BJ knocked on the door, entered when the colonel waved him in, and saluted. Colonel Broadwater told him to sit down and then walked to the door and closed it. When he got to his desk and sat down, he looked at BJ and asked, "Who in the hell do you know in Washington, D.C.?"

BJ looked at the colonel in bewilderment, shook his head and finally said, "Colonel, as far as I know, I don't have any friends in Washington, D.C. Why do you ask, Sir?"

The colonel looked at BJ with cold eyes and said, "I have a communique for your eyes only from Russell A. Alger. Do you know who he is?"

BJ looked at the colonel and said, "Someone named Russel A. Alger is the Secretary of War. Is that who you are asking about? I have never met and don't know the gentleman." The colonel said nothing and handed an envelope to BJ. Lieutenant Baxter asked, "Am I to open it, Sir?"

The colonel, obviously irritated, said, "The communique is addressed to you. Unless you can divine what is in it without opening it, I would suggest you see what this is all about." Colonel Broadwater went on to say, "I got an envelope myself, and about all it said was that I was to give you all the support and supplies that you requested. If I seem a little testy, it is because I'm not accustomed to taking instructions from lieutenants."

BJ was trying to read and listen to Colonel Broadwater's ranting at the same time. He merely said, "Yes, Sir, I fully understand. But this isn't of my doing, and I'm as much in the dark as you. I have absolutely no idea why I would be singled out to perform this mission. True enough, I grew up in the area where all the military payrolls are being stolen, but that hardly qualifies me for this type mission."

Colonel Broadwater responded, "Be that as it may, the Secretary of War seems to think you have some special talent. He has requested that Lieutenant James Budwell Baxter, Jr., do some undercover work for the Army. So you will saddle up and do the job, lieutenant. Unfortunately, I have absolutely no control over this mission, but if you screw it up, I will share some of the blame. That is the way it works in this man's Army, so get the job done."

BJ responded, "Yes, sir. Going into the area in uniform would be a waste of time. The Army represents the government, and rightly or not, we're blamed for giving the soiled lilies who work in the saloons venereal diseases. Or at least that was the situation when I was living in that area."

It seemed that three Army payrolls, at least two gold shipments, and Army supplies had been stolen as they passed through Montana for delivery to the different frontier posts. Mr. Alger didn't think that uniform soldiers would have any luck investigating the thefts. Since BJ knew Montana and had lived there and was recommended by someone, (Alger didn't know BJ Baxter from Adam's house cat), he had been selected for the undercover job. BJ had absolutely no idea how his name got picked. Surely there were other officers with ties to Montana. Obviously, Secretary Alger had been given reason to believe that Lieutenant Baxter could sniff out the culprits. What exactly BJ was supposed to do then remained somewhat of a mystery.

BJ's mind was going at a gallop as he was trying to figure out what he was to do and exactly how to accomplish it. He looked at Colonel Broadwater and said, "Sir, this hit me kinda cold. Would you allow me to go to my quarters, think on this, come back, and discuss the particulars with you later this morning?" The colonel had simmered down somewhat and merely waved BJ off with his hand without a response.

When he got to his quarters, BJ read the instructions again. There really weren't any specifics beyond outlining the thefts and the general location where he should look. After reflecting on the situation, BJ put together a list of what he would need: a horse with no government markings, a used western saddle, a Winchester Model 1873 and scabbard with no government markings, civilian canteen, civilian gun belt and holster, a full set of civilian clothes with a change of shirts, and a pair of well-worn civilian boots. Some of the items he had in his quarters; others, he would have to borrow. He was also going to need someone to accompany him. The problem was there was nothing but white officers and enlisted Buffalo Soldiers at the fort. He could be gone for weeks or possibly months, and taking a fellow officer was out of the question. Taking a Negro soldier would bring too much attention. He had no solution but sure didn't want to be alone when and if he confronted the outlaws.

After eating lunch at the officer's mess, BJ went to the headquarters building and asked to see Colonel Broadwater. When he went into the colonel's office, BJ handed him the list of items he felt he would need. Colonel Broadwater looked the list over, sat silently for a couple minutes, and said, "I don't see anything that doesn't make sense. I apologize for barking at you. It seems you have no more control over this assignment than I do."

BJ said, "No need, Colonel. No offense taken. One more thing, Sir, I've been thinking about this. As an Army officer, I have no arrest authority. I will need to be appointed a U.S. Marshal in order to have any jurisdiction or authority to do anything if I find these outlaws."

Colonel Broadwater thought a minute and said, "I see your point. I will send a telegram and inform Mr. Alger's office of your request. I have been thinking about you being by yourself, and I think I have the solution. But it would be your decision." Colonel Broadwater went on to explain that Sergeant Melvin Spurgeon was an excellent soldier and knew cattle, having grown up on a ranch in Texas. Sergeant Spurgeon had gotten into an argument with a young lieutenant at Fort Custer, Montana, and was accused of striking the officer. A court martial was convened, but before a verdict was reached, General John Schofield, Commanding General of the U.S. Army, interceded and all charges against Sergeant Spurgeon were dropped. As punishment for his offense, Sergeant Spurgeon was assigned to Fort Yates in Sioux County, North Dakota, to twiddle his thumbs and be lost to obscurity. No one seemed to know why General Schofield got involved or why he wanted Spurgeon exiled to a fort whose only mission was to manage Sioux Indians. Obviously, the general knew Spurgeon from some military action and felt he owed him a favor. It was later discovered that Spurgeon had saved the general's, then captain, life during the Indian Wars. Although Spurgeon hadn't asked for General Schofield's help, the general intervened on his behalf. The general was also irritated that Spurgeon had struck an officer and ordered him sent to Fort Yates as punishment.

Colonel Broadwater closed by saying that he felt sure Spurgeon would be more than happy to accompany BJ. On the other hand, if Spurgeon got angry and hit him, Colonel Broadwater didn't want to know about it.

Spurgeon was notified and volunteered. Mr. Alger made the arrangements and had Melvin Spurgeon and BJ Baxter appointed Deputy U.S. Marshals. Arrangements were made for BJ and Spurgeon to meet at Miles City in Custer County, eastern Montana, at the junction of the Yellowstone and Tongue Rivers on or about June 1, 1897. The wire to Fort Yates instructed Spurgeon to dress in civilian clothes, bring nothing with military markings, use his own name, and register at the Olive Hotel. Both Baxter and Spurgeon had each other's name and the meeting location. Whenever they arrived, they were to find the other man.

BJ left the fort on May 29, rode his horse to Fort Benton, loaded his saddle and rifle scabbard on the top, tied his horse to the back, and rode in a stagecoach from Fort Benton to Helena, Montana. He then took a series of trains, riding in the livestock car with his horse, to Miles City,

Montana. He checked in at the Olive Hotel on the evening of May 31, tired, in need of a bath, and hungry. Spurgeon arrived on the morning of June 1, asked for BJ's room number, found him gone, went back to the desk clerk, got a room, and left a message for Baxter. When BJ got back to the hotel and received the message, he went to Spurgeon's room. They made their introductions and had their first face to face meeting.

Melvin Spurgeon was at least ten years older than BJ. Judging by the redness of his face and his twisted nose, Spurgeon was obviously a drinker and brawler. He looked as if he had blocked a fair number of punches with his face. After BJ talked with the man for a few minutes, he took a liking to him. Melvin was plain spoken, affable enough, and unpretentious. He was just a cowboy who got tired of cows, joined the Army, and made the cavalry a career. When he wasn't soldiering, he was drinking and fighting. Spurgeon was like many men on the frontier: honest, loyal, rugged, and a good man to have your back. Lieutenant Baxter reminded Melvin that there was to be no rank used and no deference. He was just BJ, the sergeant was just Mel. And both were just deputy U.S. Marshals of equal status until the mission was over. BJ reminded Melvin that it would be his arse the Army would come after if something went wrong. Since that was the case, Melvin was to let him make the major decisions.

Mel smiled and said he would do his best to forget that BJ was an officer and try real hard to just treat him like another guy. After getting the preliminaries behind them, BJ and Mel discussed their plan of action and the places they would sniff around trying to get some idea of who and where the bandits might be.

Saloons were always the best place to get information. Even if a bartender couldn't help with information, there was always a refreshment to be had. They decided to make the circuit.

Chapter 11

Harvey Alexander Logan, better known as Kid Curry, was orphaned early in life and became a cowboy as a teenager. While still in his twenties, Harvey turned to rustling cattle, robbing banks and trains, and was considered the wildest of Butch Cassidy's gang called "The Wild Bunch."

Harvey Logan was born in Iowa in 1867. When his father died, his mother moved the family to Missouri where she died in 1876. Harvey lived with an aunt and uncle for a time and then left Missouri with his three brothers and moved to Texas. His first real job was breaking mustangs on the Cross L ranch near Big Spring, Texas.

While in Texas, Harvey met a man named "Flat Nose" George Curry and changed his name to Kid Curry. For whatever reason, he liked the name Curry better than Logan. At age sixteen, Curry was involved in a saloon brawl in Pueblo, Colorado, where he carved up a drunk with a broken whiskey bottle. He then headed to southern Wyoming to avoid arrest. In 1884, Harvey and his brothers, Lonnie and Johnnie, homesteaded a plat in Montana in present day Chouteau County, a short ways from the Landusky mining camp.

In 1894, Harvey Logan and Powell "Pike" Landusky got into a fight when Landusky accused Harvey of having a sexual relationship with his young daughter. As the fight ended, Harvey was walking away when Landusky drew a pistol. Johnnie tossed a revolver to Harvey. Landusky's gun jammed and Harvey proceeded to shoot the man in the head. As it turned out, it was Lonnie who was sporting with the miner's daughter. Or, at least, she named him as the father of her child.

The law was now after Harvey. With a bounty on his head, he headed to New Mexico and joined up with the Black Jack Ketchum gang. In January 1896, Harvey returned to Montana with his brothers, Lonnie and Johnnie, and got into a shootout with James Winters, a bounty hunter who was searching for the outlaw. During the exchange of gunfire, Harvey's brother Johnnie was killed. Harvey and Lonnie returned to New Mexico, robbed a train and got into an argument with Kctchum over the divvying up of money from the train robbery. They took the share they were given and headed to Colorado.

Harvey and Lonnie worked on a ranch for a time and then started a gang of their own that included Lonnie, Walt Putnam, Tom O'Day, and George Curry. In April 1896, Harvey was reputed to have killed Deputy Sheriff William Deane of Powder River, Wyoming. Harvey was now wanted for murder and his gang was broken up when most were caught during a failed bank robbery.

Undaunted, Harvey put together another gang which included Lonnie, James Andrew "Dick" Liddell, Bronco Bill Smith, and James "Spooks" Tilder. They found a gold mine that didn't require any picks or shovels in the trains that brought gold out of the Black Hills along with the Army payrolls which were shipped into Montana and sites further west.

****

BJ and Mel had no idea who they were looking for or how many men they would be up against if and when they found the bandits. After arriving in Miles City, Montana, they began their quest to find and apprehend the outlaws. Realizing that a saloon is always the best place to start searching for information, BJ and Mel went to the First Chance Saloon on Main Street of Miles City, ordered a beer, and looked around the room. Every working individual looked pretty much alike in the 19th century west. The men displayed lots of dirt, tobacco juice stained mustaches, spurs, chaps, and well-worn slouch hats. Mel turned out to be a talker and in a couple minutes had the bartender telling him his life history. Mel, in turn, was telling the bartender that he and BJ were representing a cattle buying consortium out of the mid-west and were hoping to find cattle to purchase. They knew that the horrible winter of 1886 – 87 had killed a lot of free-range cattle and had driven the price of the remaining cattle through the roof. Or, at least in the short term, cattle prices were higher than normal. Montana ranching had transitioned into smaller ranches, less free-grazing land, and an influx of farmers who were willing to try and withstand the extreme winters.

BJ saw an opening in the palavering, interrupted, and asked the bartender, "We are going to be riding around the countryside looking at cattle and such. Do you think we will be safe out by ourselves with all the robberies that are going on around here?"

The bartender laughed and said, "Well, unless you are carrying a few sacks of gold or an Army payroll, I think you will be fine."

BJ tried to appear less than convinced and responded, "Does anyone have any idea who these outlaws are? Who should we be careful to try to avoid?"

The bartender started to get a little spooked but said, "Rumor has it that it is Kid Curry and his gang of bandits that are doing the robbing, but I actually have no idea." BJ followed up by asking what this Kid Curry looked like, but the bartender claimed he had never seen the man and had no idea. BJ figured they had pushed their questioning as far as they could without raising suspicion, so they thanked the bartender and left the saloon.

Next BJ and Mel walked to the edge of town to The Bob Saloon which was rustic, to say the least. Actually, there were more customers sitting outside the building than inside. Once inside, they could see the logic of staying outside to drink. The place was filthy and smelled like something had crawled under the floorboards and died. BJ and Mel both ordered a beer and walked outside and tried to start up a conversation with a couple of the men. The men just grunted, looked suspiciously at them, and said little. They finished their beers, set the mugs on the ground by the porch, walked back to the Olive Hotel, went to BJ's room, and discussed what they had found out. That conversation didn't take long at all.

The office of the Secretary of War had devised a code for Western Union telegrams to keep BJ informed of payroll shipments going west and gold shipments headed east. The code was simple enough. If there was a payroll shipment, the wire would say, "Cattle prices are better in the far west. Try to get cattle shipped on the train by June 18." If there was a large gold shipment out of Helena, the wire would say, "Cattle prices are picking up in the east. Try to get cattle on the train by June 18." Since the Northern Pacific Railroad passed through Miles City going both directions, BJ hoped a telegraph message wouldn't raise suspicion.

BJ decided to ride out to the old Slant BB spread where he had grown up. It would give him and Mel a chance to look at the countryside and possibly find something or someone that seemed out of place. They got their horses from the livery, went by the general store, and purchased enough coffee, bacon, beans, and hardtack to last them for a week. Once they were supplied, they headed southeast with a plan to make a large circle and end up back in Miles City. On the second day after leaving Miles City, BJ and Mel saw buzzards circling a mile or so ahead. Mel remarked, "Looks like a group of wolves got a cow or maybe an elk." BJ thought he was probably correct, but they decided to investigate anyway.

When they got closer, they saw a horse standing by a man who was on the ground. BJ and Mel reigned in their horses, dismounted, and picketed them along with the other horse. They got closer to the man and saw no obvious wounds on his back. They gently rolled the man over onto his back and saw a wicked looking gash in his scalp above his left ear. There was a copse of trees 100 yards east, down a slight slope that led to a creek. BJ and Mel laid the man over his saddle and led the horses to the trees. Mel got a campfire started, and BJ took the man's coat off to examine him for more wounds. When the coat was removed, BJ saw a deputy sheriff badge on the man's shirt above the left pocket.

Once the fire was burning, Mel joined BJ in checking the man for more wounds. There was a flesh wound on the man's left upper arm, but it wasn't serious, more of a deep scratch really. Mel got his canteen, took the man's bandana off, soaked it with water, and began cleaning the dried blood off the man's head. When he finished, Mel got some salve out of his saddlebags and smoothed it on the head wound. He then put a relatively clean bandana around the man's head and put a bit of the salve on the wound on the arm. There wasn't really anything more they could do for the wounded man but keep him warm and wait to see if he was going to wake up. It was Friday the 5th of June, and they figured, based on the dried blood, that the man had been shot the day prior to their finding him. That meant he had probably been unconscious for the better part of an entire day. Friday night came and went with BJ and Mel taking turns checking on the man. Nothing had changed on Saturday morning. As the day progressed, the man moved his right hand a mite a couple of times but never said anything. Around dark on Saturday, the man awoke and whispered, "Water." Mel gave the man a small sip from his canteen. The deputy moved his head slightly to look at both men, said nothing more, and closed his eyes.

BJ and Mel didn't really know what to do. They were two days away from Miles City and knew of nothing that was closer. BJ had left this area of Montana in 1886 and had no idea what in the way of stores or trading posts might have sprung up since. Around 9 PM, the man opened his eyes, and with a strained voice, said, "Could I have some vittles?" Mel got busy heating some bacon and beans. BJ tried to talk to the man, but he was disoriented and couldn't remember what had happened. BJ continued to question the man, being careful not to push him too much. The man ate his food, had some more water, and went back to sleep. BJ figured the questions could wait until the next morning.

Sunday morning was clear and cool until the sun began to peek over the copse of trees. The man awoke early and asked for coffee. BJ fished around in the man's saddlebags and found a black cup. He poured his cup half-full of coffee, which was as strong as a blacksmith. The man took a couple sips and said, "Good coffee. Just the way I like it. It's about strong enough to choke a mule. I'm Caleb Daniel Cheyhill, a deputy sheriff from Yellowstone County. Who might you two be?" BJ and Mel introduced themselves as cattle buyers and asked Caleb who had shot him. Cheyhill said he had never seen the men before. They just rode up, asked him if he was the law, and when he replied yes, they shot him. No doubt thinking he was dead, they left him on the ground, bleeding. BJ and Mel asked Caleb if he was able to ride or needed to rest another day. He said he was ready to leave.

The three men rode along together headed north, and in a few hours came upon a small herd of cattle which had been gathered in a small arroyo just south of the small settlement of Cohagen, Montana. As they got close to the herd, they saw two men sitting by a campfire. Caleb pulled out field glasses, took a look at the men, and said, "That's the two who shot me." They spread out, putting a few feet between each horse, and walked their mounts towards the camp. When BJ, Mel, and Caleb got to within twenty yards of the campfire, the two men stood up, reached for their rifles, and stopped in mid-stride when Mel hollered, "Leave the rifles be and put up your hands." Both the men reached for the pistols, and before Deputy Cheyhill could react, BJ and Mel drew and fired in unison. BJ's bullet hit the man on the left in the chest, and Mel's found the same area on the man on the right. Both men went down like a sack of corn and didn't move.

Caleb looked at BJ and Mel and said, "Cattle buyers my arse. Who are you two?"

Chapter 12

All three men dismounted and walked towards the downed men. One was dead, and the other wasn't long for this world. The live one looked at them and said, "You three have bit off more than you can chew. When we don't show up with these cattle, there will be a lot of men looking for the three of you." With that, his eyes rolled back in his head, and his lights went out.

Caleb looked at BJ and Mel and said "I seem to remember asking you men who you were." BJ said he was James Baxter but was called BJ, and his friend was Mel Spurgeon. Caleb waited a couple moments and said, "That's not what I meant, and you know it. I appreciate you saving my life, but cattle buyers from back east don't shoot pistols like the two of you. I need to know the truth of who you two are."

BJ and Mel looked at each other, shrugged, and BJ said, "We are Deputy United States Marshals who are in Montana to try and find the bandits that are robbing gold shipments and Army payrolls. We would prefer you keep that information to yourself."

Caleb thought a few moments and replied, "Why don't we combine our efforts? The outlaws that are rustling cattle might well be tied up somehow with the same bandits who are robbing the trains. Three guns are better than two."

BJ reflected for a few moments and said, "You're welcome to tag along, but cattle rustlers aren't our interest. Cattle rustling is a local problem and isn't the concern of the federal government. Let's get these men in the ground and then we can discuss it some more." Caleb had a small Ames T handle shovel strapped behind his saddle and got busy starting a grave. BJ and Mel took turns relieving the deputy. The three men got a hole big enough for the two men in less than an hour. They rolled the two men into the hole, covered them, placed their saddles next to the grave, took the rifles and scabbards off the saddles, put their pistols in Caleb's saddlebags, and tied the scabbards containing the rifles to BJ and Mel's saddles. BJ slapped the horses on the rump and watched them run off toward the northwest.

Caleb said, "I would wager that those horses would lead us to the rest of the rustlers."

BJ said, "We'll play one more hand with you and see what shakes out, but I feel obliged to remind you that rustlers aren't why we're in Montana. I don't believe in coincidences, and it would be a minor miracle if the people we are looking for and your rustlers were the same folks." When they got to within ten miles of the old Slant BB ranch, BJ saw two Conestoga wagons parked near Cottonwood Creek. Several people were milling around the wagons. The three men rode up to the wagons and greeted the people who were assembled there. They were met with hostile stares.

BJ said, "May we get off our horses and maybe get a cup of coffee?"

The younger of the two men said, "We don't cotton much to cowboys. Aren't you folks satisfied with running us off our homestead?"

BJ looked at the two men and responded, "Someone may have run you off your stake, but it wasn't us. My companion and I have only been in Montana for a week or so. This young man is Caleb Cheyhill, a deputy sheriff from Yellowstone County. I understand someone got your tail feathers ruffled, but it wasn't us."

The man doing the talking introduced himself as Ralph Emery and his father as Micah and said, "We had homesteaded an abandoned ranch about ten miles from here. We filed the proper papers over in Billings at the federal office. We started putting in a garden and were grazing these few head of cattle that you see when a group of rough looking men came and run us out. They gave us the choice of leaving or being buried there. We left!" Emery went on to explain that his father abhorred guns for any purpose other than hunting. They had felt that this close to the 20th century, the west would be suitable for living and raising a family. Apparently, they were mistaken.

BJ knew Emery had to be talking about the Slant BB that his father and Captain Brubaker had built and left in the spring of 1886. There were no other ranches in the local area, but it had been eleven years since the Baxters and Brubakers had left the ranch facilities. Unless people had used the cabins, they would have been awfully run down by 1897. BJ had been cautioned while at the Academy that everything uttered by an officer to others was to be on a need to know basis. In this case, no one needed to know that he had grown up on the abandoned ranch.

Ralph Emery apologized for their lack of manners. He then asked the three men to please get down off their horses. When they sat on their haunches, he gave each man a cup of coffee and a piece of cornbread. BJ, Mel, and Caleb thanked the Emerys and were introduced to their wives and children. The Emerys were understandably worried. They had traveled a long ways to get run off the property they had settled on.

Caleb looked at Mel and asked if he could talk to him alone for a couple minutes. Cheyhill asked Mel if the federal government would have jurisdiction over the men throwing the Emerys off their homestead. Mel looked at Caleb and said, "I don't rightly know what jurisdiction, if any, we might have. You will have to take that up with BJ. He is in charge of this operation." Caleb apologized and said that he had just presumed, since Mel was older, he would be in charge.

Mel merely said, "Nope." Cheyhill didn't want to be too obvious or get the Emerys' hopes up, so he saved the question to take up with BJ later.

BJ walked down to Cottonwood Creek and reminisced about his time on the Montana ranch. He was throwing pebbles into the stream when Marie Emery walked up and stood beside him. BJ looked at Mrs. Emery and said, "Ma'am, with all due respect, you shouldn't be out here with me away from the camp. Your husband may find it improper." BJ had looked the woman over at the camp, hopefully, without being too obvious. She was gorgeous with light brown hair, a healthy complexion, blue eyes, and well-proportioned in all the right places. He felt bad about looking at another man's wife, but the woman was strikingly beautiful.

Marie looked at BJ, smiled, and said, "Well, if I had a husband I would hope he would be jealous of me being alone with a good looking man. I'm Ralph's sister. Micah Emery is my father. Ralph's wife got pneumonia and died while we were traveling out here from Potosi, Missouri. I took on the task of managing his children." Marie went on to say that she missed the rolling hills of southeastern Missouri and the quaint unassuming people she had grown up around.

BJ felt like his face was on fire and apologized for his obtuseness. Marie didn't need to know, but he felt compelled to tell her that his father had grown up in the Huzzah Valley just a few miles from Potosi, Missouri. He went on to say that his youngest brother was even named William Huzzah in honor of the area of his father's youth. BJ opined as much to himself as to Marie, "What a small world it is that we would meet here in

Montana when both of our roots are in the same area of Missouri." They continued talking, and BJ got over his initial embarrassment, shyness, and self-consciousness. He found he really enjoyed the company of the young woman. It was approaching dusk, and BJ suggested it might be a good idea to start back to the camp. Marie placed her hand on his arm, agreed, and they walked back to the camp together.

When they got back to the camp, Ralph invited the three men to spend the night. They accepted and had supper with the Emerys. After they had eaten, Mel asked BJ if he could have a word. They walked over to one of the wagons, out of earshot of the Emerys, and Mel said, "I feel bad for these sodbusters. We may have federal authority by virtue of our Army and marshal status to right this wrong, but do we want to get involved and get distracted from our mission?"

BJ listened to Mel and said, "I don't know that I want to get involved in this issue. On the other hand, it won't take long to ride over and get the lay of the land. I just discovered one coincidence. You never know when there might be another. We will ride over to the ranch in the morning, but let's not tell the Emerys what we have in mind. I don't want to get their hopes up."

The next morning, BJ, Mel, and Caleb were up early and enjoyed the aroma of freshly brewed coffee and the smell of bacon being cooked. Marie walked over to BJ and handed him a steaming cup of coffee and said, "Good morning, Mr. Baxter."

Mel and Caleb just looked at each other as Marie walked away. Caleb said, "What are we, chopped liver." Mel smiled and commented that the poor girl only had two hands, so she couldn't possibly carry three cups of coffee. Obviously, she had to decide who to bring the coffee to.

BJ felt his face flushing and turning scarlet when Caleb said, "Yep, in a pig's eye. No doubt our coffee is on the way. Let's not hold our breath." After waiting a few minutes, Mel got up, walked over to the camp fire, and poured himself and Caleb a cup of coffee.

They ate breakfast with the Emerys, got their horses saddled, and were getting ready to mount their horses when Marie walked over, placed her hand on BJ's arm and said, "Be careful, Mr. Baxter. I hope to see you again."

Caleb smiled at Mel and said under his breath, "Yep, like you said, the girl just has two hands. There's nothing else going on here." BJ just ignored them, and they got underway.

They rode fairly near the old ranch house, arriving about 9 AM. Caleb surveyed the layout with his field glasses. He figured there were at least five men in or around the house, based on the number of horses in the corral. He scanned all the way to the horizon in three directions and saw no evidence of cattle. He turned to BJ and Mel and asked, "If they aren't using the ranch to graze stolen cattle, what do they want it for. Why would they run the Emerys off?"

While they were watching, three men came out of the ranch house, walked to the corral, saddled their horses, and rode out towards the west. The three lawmen waited thirty minutes to allow the three riders to get far enough away so that they couldn't respond if there was gunfire from the ranch. They then rode down the incline towards the ranch house.

They were about to realize that they weren't riding into a church social.

Chapter 13

As the three lawmen neared the ranch house, two men stepped out on the porch. The men didn't look like your normal cowboys. Both men were rough looking, wore two holsters holding revolvers, and weren't smiling. The smaller of the men had a nasty scar on his left cheek and said without preamble, "What do you three want?"

BJ had kinda appointed himself as the spokesman for the three lawmen and responded, "The older man and I are U.S. Marshals, and the other man is a Yellowstone County deputy sheriff. We are following up on an allegation that you folks wrongly evicted the rightful owners of this property."

The man with the scar responded, "I don't give a shite what you heard. Turn your horses around and git or there are going to be some dead lawmen." BJ, Mel, and Caleb didn't move, and the scar faced man went for his pistol. Mel shot him in the chest as he was getting off a shot. BJ rushed his shot a bit, shot low, hit the other man in the knee, and shattered the kneecap. The man collapsed on the porch in a heap and screamed in agony.

All three lawmen dismounted and walked to the porch. The man Mel had shot was gasping for breath and was coughing up frothy blood. The other man was cussing a blue streak and screaming in pain. BJ walked into the old ranch house and saw a couple of bags lying in a corner of the room. When he picked them up, he noticed a Loadstone Mine logo imprinted on the side of the bags. Now, BJ was really beginning to believe in coincidences. As he searched the house, he found money wrappers lying in a pile next to the fireplace. As he continued searching, he found almost $20,000 in greenbacks and around ten pounds of gold nuggets and dust. Obviously, these were the men who were robbing the Army payrolls and gold shipments from the mines.

BJ walked out on the porch, smiled, and told Mel and Caleb what he had found. Neither man could believe their good fortune in stumbling on the robbers more by happenstance than any skill or investigative work. BJ asked Caleb to take their horses to the rear of the ranch house so they would be out of sight. He and Mel dragged the dead man inside the house. They then helped the man with the ruined knee through the door and into a chair which was against the wall. BJ took a look at the man's knee. It was shattered by the bullet. If the man didn't get gangrene, he was always going to have a bad limp. He wrapped the knee and asked the man his name.

The man said, "You ruined my leg. I ain't telling you shite."

BJ drew his Bowie knife out of the sheath, held it by the flat side of the blade and struck the man's injured knee, prompting a string of cursing and sobbing. BJ said, "I rushed my shot, or you would be dead. I would rather you just tell me your name and the names of your accomplices, but we can do it the easy or hard way. That's up to you. I've got no place to go."

The man continued to curse BJ. BJ drew back to hit the knee again and the man said, "Ok, ok. I'll tell you what you want to know. I'm called 'Bronco Bill' Smith and the dead man is James 'Spooks' Tilder. The three men who rode off are Harvey and Lonnie Logan and Dick Liddell. Harvey likes to call himself Kid Curry." Smith went on to tell BJ that the three outlaws had gone to Broadus, Montana, to case a bank and Western Union office with the intent of robbing them when the gold shipments arrived from Helena on the Union Pacific railroad.

Smith laughed and said, "You are fair with a pistol, but you haven't ever been up against the likes of Kid Curry or Dick Liddell. They both are hard men and excellent with a gun. When they realize you took their gold and greenbacks, they are going to come after you. If I was you, I would take off and hope I never meet them. They will kill the three of you easy enough."

BJ smiled and said, "Funny you would say that. We heard the same threat from two of your crew who were herding rustled cattle. That was right before we put them in the ground, and now you make the same boast. But I'll take that under advisement. I think I will wait around here and have a chat with them when they come back." All three lawmen armed themselves with their Winchester rifles and stood by the front windows watching for the men to return. Late the following afternoon, three men appeared on a ridge and approached the ranch house. When they were 100 yards from the house, they stopped, sat on their horses for a few minutes, turned their horses, and rode back the way they had come. BJ looked at Mel and Caleb and said, "They stopped, turned around, and rode off?"

Smith laughed and said, "You didn't ask me if we had a signal for them to ride into the courtyard."

BJ turned to Mel and Caleb and said, "You two take Smith and Tilder to Miles City and turn them in to the sheriff. Mel, you take the greenbacks to the Western Union office and have them wire the money to the Secretary of War's office. Include a note telling Mr. Alger's office that we are still after the bandits and have killed three and captured another, and don't forget to get a receipt for the money. Turn the gold into the bank and get a receipt for it also. I'll go to the Emerys, tell them what happened, and caution them to wait until we finish with the robbers before they return to the ranch. If Logan finds them there and knows they put us on to them, he will kill them all. These are bad men. I will stay with the Emerys until the two of you get back."

Mel turned to Caleb, smiled, and said, "Isn't that nice of him? I guess rank has its privileges."

BJ just smiled and said, "Don't lose the dead man or the cripple."

With that, BJ got on his horse and started towards the Emery's camp. When he arrived, Marie was happy to see him as were Ralph and Micah, but probably not for the same reason. BJ filled them in on what had happened and cautioned that they shouldn't return to the ranch until the Logans and Liddell were arrested or had left the territory. The bandits would be seeking revenge for losing four of their henchmen along with the gold and cash and would no doubt take it out on them. BJ ate supper with the Emerys, visited with Marie until late at night, and turned in.

Mel and Caleb showed up at the Emery's camp around 10 AM the next morning. BJ, Mel, and Caleb talked the situation over and decided to head to Broadus and see if they could smoke out the Logans and Liddell. BJ told Marie he would be back and see her before he left the area, and she asked, "Do you promise?"

BJ told Marie he would come back and let her know the outcome of his attempt to find the three remaining bandits. Marie looked up at his face, wrapped her arms around him and, with tears in her eyes said, "Don't get yourself killed." And with that, she tiptoed, kissed him on the lips, and ran off.

Caleb looked at Mel, winked, and said, "Ain't that just the sweetest thing you ever saw?"

BJ, Mel, and Caleb mounted their horses and started towards Broadus, Montana. As they rode along, Mel opined, "These critters are going to know we are following them and may find a nice place to lay in wait and ambush us." BJ and Caleb both nodded in agreement and said they had thought of that possibility. The three lawmen rode slowly and warily and kept a keen lookout for possible hiding places where the outlaws might waylay them.

An hour before sundown, they approached a passageway between a copse of trees on the right and some large boulders on the left. The passageway was 200 yards wide and contained little, if any, cover. Mel reined in his horse, looked at BJ, and said, "I don't like the looks of this. We could get caught in crossfire with no cover to protect us."

BJ looked the situation over, looked at his companions, and said, "I tend to agree. Let's swing right and pass through the trees, and keep well away from the edge of the forest."

Mel said, "You two go ahead. Try to gauge the middle of the forest and come out there into the passageway. I will ride alongside the tree line and see if I can flush them out. Two hundred yards is a long ways for a .44-40 carbine to hit anything, so I think I will be safe from anyone in the boulders. If you hear shooting, come on the run."

Mel rode his horse at a fast walk and weaved in and out of the tree line. His weaving would make it difficult for a shooter to get a bead on him from the boulders on the other side of the passageway. Mel couldn't see anyone but felt he was riding right into the teeth of an ambush. When he had ridden one-quarter of a mile, a man appeared from the tree line fifty yards away, took aim, and fired as Mel came out of the trees. The bullet hit Mel low in the stomach area, and he fell out of the saddle still holding on to his rifle.

In the forest, BJ and Caleb heard the rifle shot, turned their horses, and rode as fast as possible through the trees toward the sound of the shot. Mel rolled behind a tree to get out of the line of fire and waited for help to arrive. BJ and Caleb came busting out of the trees, and both men fired at the outlaw who was standing in the tree line. One of them hit the man. He spun, fell, and crawled behind some trees. A shot came from the boulders and hit BJ's saddle pommel. It took a man who was an excellent shot to get that close at two hundred yards. Whatever else the shooter was, he sure knew his way around a rifle. BJ and Caleb turned their horses back into the trees, dismounted, and started working their way towards Mel.

BJ got to his wounded friend first and immediately saw that the wound was bad, real bad. About that time, the wounded outlaw came busting out of the woods on his horse and headed across the passageway towards the boulders. BJ leaned against a tree, took careful aim, squeezed the trigger, and saw the man tumble out of the saddle and start half crawling and half limping to the boulders. The man was carrying two bullets but was still moving. He was one tough guy.

****

The outlaws could be seen weaving through the boulders, the wounded man riding double behind one of the bandits. As it turned out, Dick Liddell was the wounded man and holed up in a house near Hardin, Montana, until his wounds healed enough that he could travel. After convalescing, Liddell made his way to Missouri and bought a couple race horses. He died of a heart attack while watching the Queen City races in Covington, Kentucky, on July 13, 1901. He still had one piece of lead in him compliments of BJ Baxter.

****

Harvey and Lonnie Logan returned to New Mexico and went on to South Dakota where they robbed a bank in Belle Fourche. During a shootout, Harvey was wounded, captured, and jailed in Deadwood, South Dakota. He escaped on October 31, 1897. Lonnie Logan returned home to Dodson, Missouri, and was killed in a gun battle with Pinkerton detectives and local lawmen in the winter of 1900. Harvey traveled around resorting to petty thefts and then joined Butch Cassidy's Wild Bunch. Later, he went out on his own.

On June 7, 1904, Harvey Logan and two associates were involved in a holdup of the San Francisco Express Number 5 train near Parachute, Colorado. Two days later, a posse caught up with

Logan and his accomplices. During the shootout, Harvey was severely wounded. Rather than return to prison, he took his own life on June 9, 1904.

Sometime prior to Harvey Logan aka Kid Curry's death, William Pinkerton, head of the Pinkerton Detective Agency, opined concerning Logan, "He has not one redeeming feature. He was the only criminal I know of that does not have one single good point."

Chapter 14

BJ and Caleb got Mel on his horse, supported him between them, and slowly rode to Broadus, Montana, where they found the office of Doctor Bray Follup. They got Mel off his horse, half carried and half dragged him, and got him on a bed in a room behind the doctor's office. Doc Follup was a cantankerous ole coot and told BJ and Caleb to go get a beer and come back in a half-hour. He would let them know the prognosis on their friend after he examined him. They did as they were told!

When they came back, Doc Follup told them that the wound was serious. He wasn't sure what the bullet had hit or how much internal damage it had done. The bleeding had seemed to stop once Mel was immobilized in bed. It would be a day or two before the doctor would know if the wound would become septic. If the bullet perforated an intestine, their friend would probably die. If not, he would probably recover. Doc Follup cautioned that it was rare that a man recovered from a bullet wound to the abdomen. He smiled slightly and commented that he didn't want to get their hopes up.

Caleb looked at BJ and said, "I think I had better get back to work on the cattle rustling problem. I appreciate you taking care of me more than you will ever know. I would have died had you and Mel not come along when you did." Caleb and

BJ shook hands. Caleb went to Mel's bedside and wished him well, thanked him as he had BJ, turned, and walked out the doctor's office with a tear in his eye. Melvin Spurgeon was a decent and brave man.

Before walking into the street, Caleb turned, looked at BJ, and asked, "What year was it that your father and his partner took their herd to Montana?"

BJ thought for a few moments and said, "I can't be exactly sure. Kids don't take much stock in the year. I remember riding a horse on part of the drive, and I shot a man who tried to steal our supplies off the chuck wagon. I had to be between eight and ten years old, probably. That would mean the drive would have occurred sometime between 1878 and 1880. Why do you ask?"

Caleb looked at BJ and said, "During the spring of 1879, my father, two of my uncles, and a family friend were either shot or hung by men running a cattle drive through southern Montana. My two great-uncles went in search of the men who hung them and never came back. We don't know if the same men killed them or if something else happened to them."

BJ looked at Caleb and said, "My memory of the drive is somewhat murky, as I was a young boy, but I don't remember any hanging. My father and his partner had problems with rustlers and Indians more than once. I remember my father and Captain Brubaker shot men who were trying to steal our cattle. I don't remember the events you are describing. I'm sorry for your loss."

Caleb said, "My brother and three cousins have vowed to find the men who killed our fathers and settle that score."

BJ said, "Caleb, that would have been about twenty years ago. It might be time to let it go. Don't misunderstand me. I'm only saying what I'm saying. It is doubtful that whoever killed your father and uncles did so just to pass the time of day. You might want to try and learn the whole story before going off half-cocked." With that, the two men shook hands, and BJ went back in the doctor's office.

BJ asked the doctor if there was anything he could do and was told, "No, nothing." BJ went to the Western Union office and sent a telegram to the War Department and gave them an update on their progress. BJ interjected that he thought the bandits who had been robbing the gold shipments and Army payrolls were either dead, jailed, or headed out of Montana. He also informed them of Mel's injury. He added that he was going to stay in Broadus and monitor Sergeant Spurgeon's progress until he either recovered or died. BJ spent the night in Broadus at the Sagebrush Hotel. The next morning, he walked back to Doc Follup's office and checked on Mel. There was no change in Mel's condition. He told the sawbones and Mel that he was going to go to the sodbusters camp to tell them that it was now safe for them to go back to their homestead. BJ said he would be back in a couple days.

Mel smiled weakly and said, "Yes, I'm sure at least one of them will be relieved to see you." BJ took Mel's hand, squeezed it, and said he would see him in a couple days.

When BJ rode into the Emery camp, Marie came running and leaped on him like a hurricane, crying, laughing, and kissing him on the cheek. Ralph, Micah, and the rest of the family were standing there wide-eyed, wondering at what they were watching. BJ was as red as a beet and wasn't really sure what to do. After a bit, Marie calmed down, said that she was glad to see that he was alright, and asked about Caleb and Mel. He sadly told her that Mel had been shot, and it didn't look good.

When the initial greetings were over, BJ told the Emerys that they could return to their homestead. One bandit was dead, another in jail, another wounded, and the last two headed west. One of the two that was headed west was carrying two bullets in his hide. BJ thought everything would be fine. The Emerys were exuberant at the knowledge that they could return to their homestead, all except Marie.

Marie turned to her father and said, "Mr. Spurgeon is going to need someone to nurse him back to health if he lives. I'm going to Broadus with BJ. Mama can look after the children until I get back." There was no discussion, just the pronouncement by Marie.

BJ escorted the Emerys to the old Slant BB ranch house and spent the night in the old tack shed. He went to the house the next morning to find breakfast nearly ready. Marie had heard BJ on the porch and was standing with a cup of hot coffee in her hand. BJ took the cup and said, "I could get used to this." When he realized the implications of what he had just said, he blushed. Marie just smiled.

In about an hour, Marie came walking up with a valise, wearing riding breeches, and said, "I'm ready to go to Broadus and look after Mr. Spurgeon." BJ didn't quite know how to react, so he merely took the valise and walked her to the horse Ralph had saddled for her. He attached the valise to the saddle pommel, turned, and shook hands with Ralph and Micah.

Ralph looked at BJ, laughed, and said, "She's got you roped, tied, and almost branded. I guess I'd better start thinking of you as part of the family." After shaking hands with BJ, Ralph walked off towards the barn laughing to himself as if he was the cat who had swallowed the canary. Mr. Emery shook BJ's hand and thanked him again for helping them.

Mrs. Emery came up with a twinkle in her eye and said, "You take care of my little girl, BJ Baxter. I'll hold you to that!" BJ had no idea of what to say. He wanted to remind Mrs. Emery that he was just taking Marie to Broadus so she could nurse Melvin Spurgeon. He had the feeling that he was the only one of the group that didn't know what was really going on.

BJ and Marie got to Broadus and went to the doctor's office. Doc Follup looked at BJ and told him that it didn't look good. Mr. Spurgeon wasn't getting any better, and his strength was ebbing. Marie looked at the doctor and said, "I'm here to take care of Mr. Spurgeon, so you can attend to your other patients. If you don't mind, just put me a cot in his room, and I will do what I can to make him comfortable."

Doc Follup looked at BJ and said, "That's quite a woman you have there. Not strong willed at all!" BJ wanted to say that she wasn't his but, again, felt he was the only one that didn't understand the situation.

Sergeant Melvin Spurgeon died of septicemia during the early morning hours on Independence Day 1897. The bullet had burst an intestine, caused spillage of its contents, and caused a bad infection which worsened, spread through his bowels, and eventually killed him. BJ went to the Western Union office and rousted out the telegraph operator. He had him send a wire to the War Department informing them that Sergeant Melvin Spurgeon had died from a gunshot wound while trying to apprehend the railroad bandits and asked for burial instructions.

During the mid-afternoon on the 5th, the telegraph operator found BJ at the Olive Hotel and delivered the response from the War Department.

Secretary Alger personally sent his regrets. A second wire instructed BJ to bury Sergeant Spurgeon at the city cemetery in Broadus, Montana, affix a suitable grave marker, and have the undertaker send a bill to the War Department.

At 2 PM on July 7, 1897, the remains of Sergeant Melvin Spurgeon were interred at the Broadus Cemetery. Most of the residents didn't know Sergeant Spurgeon from Adam's house cat. They knew he had been shot by the outlaws that were stealing the gold shipments and military payrolls. Everyone in town knew he had been fighting for his life in the doctor's office. Virtually the entire town went to the funeral. Even the town drunk was in attendance. No doubt, he came because the saloon was closed during the burial. After the graveside rites, BJ and Marie went back to the Olive Hotel and ate an early supper. As they were eating, BJ looked at Marie and said, "Would you consider becoming the wife of an Army officer?"

Marie's eyes twinkled, and she responded, "Any particular officer?"

BJ responded, "Miss Emery, would you marry me?" After receiving a resounding "Yes," BJ excused himself. He told Marie he was going to find the preacher that did the funeral and see if he would come to the old Slant BB ranch and perform the wedding ceremony. The preacher agreed, and they set the date for July 10 at 2 PM at the ranch. BJ sent a telegram to his parents and informed them of the upcoming wedding.

BJ and Marie left the next morning and rode to the old Slant BB ranch where they announced they were getting married on Saturday. Ralph just laughed, Mrs. Emery cried, and Mr. Emory just smiled. The wedding went off without a hitch, and James Budwell Baxter, Jr., and Marie Elizabeth Emery were married. They got Marie's meager possessions together and put them in panniers on the packhorse BJ had rented at the livery in Broadus. They said their goodbyes to the Emery family and rode to Broadus. This time, they shared his room at the Olive Hotel. To say that BJ and Marie's courtship and marriage was a whirlwind affair diminishes the term whirlwind.

BJ went to the telegraph office again. This time, he sent a wire to Colonel Broadwater at Fort Assiniboine informing him that he was returning to the fort in about a week with a wife. He asked the colonel if he would be kind enough to have married officer's quarters prepared for them.

BJ returned the pack horse to the hostler at the livery. He then put their horses on the train, placed the panniers in the livestock car, and they took their seats in the Pullman car. They rode the train to Billings, Bozeman, Butte, Helena, Great Falls, and then took a stagecoach, with their horses tied behind, to the fort. When they got out of the coach, they were met by Colonel and Mrs. Broadwater. Mrs. Broadwater embraced Marie, took her arm, and scurried her away to the colonel's quarters to let her freshen up. Colonel Broadwater looked at BJ, grinned, and said, "I was under the impression you were to go to Montana to catch outlaws, not get caught." Colonel Broadwater laughed at his joke, pumped BJ's hand like it was a well pump, and thanked him so much for bringing someone to be a companion to his wife. Life at Fort Assiniboine was dreary at best for officers' wives with only a couple females to talk to. The theory that all women had things in common to discuss wasn't necessarily true.

In February 1898, Lieutenant James Baxter was deployed, along with the 10th Cavalry Regiment (Buffalo Soldiers), to Florida by train and then transported to Cuba on a troop carrier in anticipation of the looming war in Cuba. BJ and Marie talked about whether she wanted to go back to the ranch in southeastern Montana or wait in their quarters at the fort. As near as she could tell, Marie was six months pregnant with their first child and liked the idea of being at the fort where there was a doctor and Mrs. Broadwater. She elected to wait at Fort Assiniboine for BJ to return.

With that settled, BJ readied himself for his deployment to Florida.

Chapter 15

On February 20, 1898, BJ, now First Lieutenant Baxter, and the 10th Cavalry Regiment left for Cuba. After training in the oppressive heat of Chickamauga, Georgia, BJ and his troopers hurried up only to wait. Then they hurried up only to wait some more, then moved to the port at Tampa, Florida, only to wait some more for transport to Cuba. The sense of adventure had lost its luster. To say that the situation at the port was ruled by confusion would be an understatement. There were thousands of Army and volunteer soldiers awaiting transport. The latrines were inadequate, mess facilities were scarce and viable information nonexistent. BJ, the 10th, and other elements of the dismounted cavalry were assigned space on the Leona, a coastal merchant ship. The Leona set sail with thirty-one other transports for the island of Cuba on June 14, 1898.

The short trip to Cuba was a horrible experience. The Leona became separated from the convoy for the better part of a day. An east wind began blowing, and the soldiers below decks became seasick. The stench from the considerable vomit was overwhelming. The soldiers were hungry but, in the prevailing conditions, unwilling to eat the field rations which were less than palatable during normal conditions. The troopers' woolen uniforms were ill suited for a tropical climate and certainly not for the ship's wretchedly hot and cramped hold. The soldiers were miserable in the sweltering heat. The troopers stripped off their wool blouses, and the officers pretended not to notice.

After the torturous crossing, the 10th disembarked at Daiquiri, thirteen miles east of Santiago, on June 22, 1898. There were no port facilities, and small boats were used as tenders to move the men as close to shore as they could. The men were then put out and had to wade to shore in waist deep water with their equipment. Two men drowned during the transfer.

The first engagement with the enemy was with Spanish soldiers at Las Guasimas. BJ led a patrol and came under heavy fire, with two of his men being wounded. Even though bullets were flying all around him, BJ came through the firefight unscathed. The Spanish were routed, but the 10th suffered one dead and ten wounded.

Food supplies and shelter were big obstacles. They could fight the Spanish soldiers, but they had to eat to fight. Many of the troopers had thrown away most of their gear. First Lieutenant John Pershing, six years senior to BJ even though they shared the same rank, was in charge of getting supplies to the 10th. Pershing did a remarkably good job considering the conditions. The island was filled with narrow jungle trails. There was confusion on the beaches and lack of military precision and organization.

In 1897, Pershing had been appointed as a tactical instructor at West Point. While at the Academy, Pershing became known for his strictness. The cadets (behind his back, of course) referred to him as "Nigger Jack" because of his prior service with the 10th Cavalry. Before he left the academy, the epithet was softened to "Black Jack," a nickname that stuck with him throughout his career.

By June 30, enough American troops had landed to begin the advance on Santiago. The 10th moved to within five miles of the city and set up camp on a hill near the El Pozo hacienda.

At 8 AM on July 1, the artillery barrage began from both the American and Spanish cannons. Most of the Cuban insurgents fled the field. Lieutenant Colonel Theodore A. Baldwin, commander of the 10th, ordered Lieutenant Pershing, since he knew the jungle trails, to guide the regiment and ensure an orderly advance to their objective. BJ and the troopers were subjected to continuous artillery and rifle fire during the march. In the confusion, the 10th got mixed in with elements of the 71st New York Infantry, making advancement on the clogged jungle trails nearly impossible. As if things couldn't get any worse, some genius sent an observation balloon above the advancing troops, which revealed the Americans' location and route of approach. The Spanish concentrated their fire on the area below the balloon. The observers in the balloon hollered to the troops below that the Spanish were firing at them. While the observation was certainly true, it was hardly necessary or helpful.

Lieutenant Baxter and his men crossed the Aguadores River in waist-deep water with Lieutenant Pershing directing traffic. BJ saw Major General Joseph Wheeler, the division commander, and his staff on their horses while crossing the river. A Spanish shell exploded between Pershing and Wheeler, both men got soaked but were otherwise unscathed.

BJ's troopers joined other elements gathered at the edge of a wooded area below San Juan and Kettle Hills and began taking fire. Spanish snipers, hidden in elevated positions, were decimating the American cavalrymen. Everyone was awaiting orders. First Lieutenant Jules Ord of the 6th Infantry finally had enough and hollered, "Follow me. We can't stay here." Following Ord's lead, the Rough Riders, and parts of the 10th, joined the attack. They all crossed the San Juan River, screaming and rushing forward. In the smoke and confusion of battle, the troopers of the 10th became separated from the main force. Some joined the 6th in charging San Juan Hill and some intermingled with the Rough Riders running up the slopes of Kettle Hill.

BJ and Pershing were in the contingent going up San Juan Hill with the Rough Riders. Gatling guns were brought forward and brought to bear on the Spaniards. Under cover of artillery fire and the Gatling guns, the 6th, led by Lieutenant Ord, was the first to reach the summit. Shortly after reaching the top of the hill, Lieutenant Ord was killed by enemy fire.

The victory came at a high price. Dead and wounded American soldiers lay all over the hillside. The 10th Cavalry lost half its officers and about twenty percent of its men. BJ was bloodied by minor shrapnel wounds and a minor gunshot wound to his shoulder but wasn't badly hurt. He was one of the lucky officers. Sadly, five of BJ's men lost their lives during the attack.

Around 3 AM, Spanish artillery began firing at the American positions. After the cannon barrage slackened, some entrenchment equipment and ammunition arrived but not food or water. The conditions were miserable. Some soldiers left their trenches to get water from a water hole a mile to the rear. Tearing off the heavy woolen blouses was the order of the day.

On July 3, BJ heard the heavy explosions of shells fired by the U.S. fleet. The Spanish were trapped in Santiago, and General Shafter sent a message offering a truce. A deadline of July 4 was given but later extended. One of BJ's wounds had festered, and he opened the pus-filled gash with his knife and drained the yellow fluid as best he could. With all the severely injured, medical attention was lacking for the walking wounded. The wound eventually closed, and the infection was fought off by his body.

As the truce talks dragged on, the rainy season began, soaking the men and filling the trenches with water. All around BJ, men were coming down with malaria and yellow fever. BJ became nauseated, vomited several times, and lost his taste for food. Lieutenant Pershing was sick but kept working and secured food, bed rolls, tenting, medical supplies, and cooking utensils for the beleaguered men.

Finally, on July 17, 1898, the Spanish surrendered Santiago, and the campaign ended. Lieutenant John Pershing was recognized for his outstanding work in keeping supplies coming to the soldiers in the field. Colonel Baldwin opined in a letter to Pershing, "You did some tall rustling, and if you had not, we would have starved."

While engaged in the taking of San Juan and Kettle Hills, BJ met and impressed Theodore Roosevelt, the leader of the Rough Riders. Although BJ never asked Roosevelt for any help or special consideration, the future president did influence his postings and career advancement through the ensuing years.

BJ and what were left of his men loaded on a ship and endured a seven-day cruise back to the United States. He had lost twenty pounds during the month-long stay in Cuba. Several hard lessons were learned during the short Spanish – American War. Weapons needed to be upgraded and converted to smokeless powder. Younger commanders who could actually physically lead men were needed in the field. The most important lesson learned was that the logistical challenge of keeping fighting men supplied while in the field was a daunting task. If the Army couldn't keep a steady stream of food, water, and ammunition coming to the line, the prospects for success in battle were poor.

The observations made and lessons learned by BJ while in Cuba would be of great benefit to him when the war to end all wars required his participation.

****

BJ and the remnants of the 10th began the long journey back to Fort Assiniboine and arrived on August 4, 1898. BJ was haggard, tired, and still battling bouts of nausea and vomiting, but the good news was he was on the mend. When he arrived at the fort, he was greeted by Colonel and Mrs. Broadwater and Marie. Marie was holding a bundle in her arms which contained three month old James Budwell Baxter III. He was a fine looking and loud baby boy who had been born on May 13, 1898.

In late November 1898, Colonel Broadwater called BJ to his office and informed him that the War Department was transferring him to the 8th Cavalry for deployment back to Cuba. Based on his experience in Cuba during the war, it was felt he would be beneficial to the peacekeeping operations on the island. The colonel went on to say that he hated to lose him. He also said that Marie and the baby would be welcome to stay at Fort Assiniboine until BJ could find suitable quarters in Cuba and arrange transportation. The colonel added that BJ should be prepared to be on the island for a period of up to four years. After talking it over, Marie decided that she wanted to go home to Montana to be with her family since she wouldn't in all likelihood see them for a few years.

BJ escorted Marie and BJ III back to the old Slant BB ranch, now Emery homestead, to be with her family until he could make arrangements for her transportation to Cuba. After spending Christmas with the Emerys, he made his way to Savannah, Georgia, for transportation to the island. Marie spent the winter at the ranch, for the most part, huddled by the fire, and joined BJ in April 1899.

The mission in Cuba was basically to protect American citizens on the island and keep interlopers from destroying their property. Most of the time, the job was boring and monotonous. BJ tried to keep his company of troopers sharp with drills and inspections, not enough to make the men resent him but adequate to keep them occupied and battle ready.

While on the island, the Baxters increased their family. Madison Kay was born on February 3, 1900, and William Nathan, named in honor of BJ's two brothers, on May 17, 1901. Marie had a very difficult pregnancy with William, and the Army physician recommended that she not attempt to have more children. BJ and Marie agreed that three young children were about all they could handle even with the help of the Cuban nanny.

When BJ's tour in Cuba was over, he was transferred to the Army Cavalry Training Facility at Fort Oglethorpe, Georgia, and reported in on January 15, 1903. The facility was later named Fort Jackson in 1905. The billet at the Cavalry Training unit was considered a "plum" assignment and an avenue for advancement. Even though BJ hadn't requested the posting, there were whispers of favoritism. Marie and the kids joined BJ, and he spent his days helping mold young riders into competent cavalry members. In BJ's opinion, being with his beloved cavalry horses was the "plum."

Once settled in, BJ wrote his father a letter and described his conversation with Caleb Cheyhill and asked if there was a chance that he and Captain Brubaker could have been the men that killed or hung his family members.

Chapter 16

Following the Civil War, promotions for Army line officers virtually ceased because of the drawdown of the military. The overwhelming number of Union officers who had been promoted during the war between the North and South held the higher ranks for years. There were limited opportunities for honest men during Reconstruction, so many older officers just stayed in the Army, thereby clogging up advancement for those younger officers entering the military. For example, John C. Schofield, who Schofield Barracks, Hawaii, was named after, served in the rank of Major General for almost twenty-six years. He was not an exception.

In order to unclog the promotion flow, in 1882 Congress mandated that officers must retire at age sixty-four and could retire earlier if they had forty years' service. Like any bureaucracy, officers in the Army figured out a way to take advantage of the retirement restrictions. An officer could select his retirement date, which was always one day after he filled the grade of a retiring officer of the next higher rank. He would serve one day in the higher rank, retire, and receive retirement pay at the new rank. In January 1904, a single vacant officer position was filled by five men in five days, each retiring one day after attaining the new rank. In 1906, congress noticed the abuse of the retirement and promotion systems and changed the law to require officers to serve for at least one year after promotion. Lieutenants James and Nathan Baxter were caught in the promotion quagmire but felt they were contributing by serving their country, and there was always to be a next war and opportunity for advancement, if you survived.

****

Both Nathan and BJ wrote their father and Captain Brubaker expressing their disappointment and frustration with promotion potential in the Army. Both men received replies urging them to stay the course. Everything was cyclic, even the military. There would come a time when the Army needed leadership and would be looking for career officers who had displayed leadership skills and perseverance. Both Mr. Baxter and Captain Brubaker agreed that the unrest in Europe would cause the United States to get involved at some point. President Roosevelt had no authority to promote below the grade of general, but he had been impressed with both BJ and Nathan Baxter. Then vice-presidential candidate Roosevelt had visited with Bud Baxter and Bill Brubaker while in Dallas in 1900. Having the President of the United States in your corner wasn't a bad thing.

On November 1, 1899, Lieutenant Nathan Baxter volunteered to go with the 9th Cavalry (Buffalo soldiers) to the Philippines as part of the expeditionary force to put down the guerrilla-style warfare against American forces. On November 15,

1899, Nathan and his platoon of troopers left by rail from El Paso, Texas, headed for San Francisco, California, for transportation to the Philippines.

Nathan was eating breakfast in the dining car of the train. Sergeant Samson Lightfoot came into the car, approached his table, saluted, and started to say something. A large man wearing a slouch hat, sidearm, and moustache said, "Lieutenant, get that nigger out of the dining car. White folks are trying to eat."

Nat ignored the man and said, "What is it, Sergeant Lightfoot?"

Before Sergeant Lightfoot could answer the man prodded Nat on the shoulder and said, "I guess you didn't hear me. I said…" And that is all the man got out of his mouth before Nat pivoted, came up out of the chair, and used his left knee to strike the man in his cod sacks with enough force to lift him off his feet. The man's eyes crossed, he went down to his knees, wriggling in pain, and fell to his side.

While the man was rolling on the floor, screaming in pain, Nat looked back at Sergeant Lightfoot and said, "You were saying, sergeant?" Sergeant Lightfoot did his best not to grin. He went on to say that the men were eating their packaged field rations and would love some coffee, but they weren't allowed in the dining car. Nat told the sergeant to return to his men and that he would see what he could do.

After Sergeant Lightfoot left, Nat sat back down, finished the last of his coffee, got up, stepped over the man who was still moaning in pain, and relieved him of his sidearm. He walked up to the head steward and said, "I would like a large pot of coffee, cups, and some donuts would be nice for my troopers. They are black men who are on the way to the Philippines into combat and maybe die fighting a white man's war. I will have the troopers that would like coffee assemble in the first livestock car. Thanks for your help. By the way, put that jackass's pistol away for safekeeping."

The steward, who was a giant black man and also struggling not to grin, looked at a kitchen helper and said, "Get a large portable pot full of coffee, twenty cups, and three dozen donuts, and take everything to the livestock car. If they want more coffee, make them another pot, and if there are more than twenty men, get more cups."

Nat went to the Pullman car and told Sergeant Lightfoot to move the troopers to the first livestock car, and coffee and refreshments would be forthcoming. Lightfoot looked at Nathan and said, "You is something, Lieutenant. I thank you and so do the men." After hearing about the incident on the train, the men of the 9th thought Nathan Baxter was the greatest officer in the Army.

When they arrived at The Presidio in San Francisco, California, Nathan assembled the men for processing and transportation to Manila, Philippines. The Presidio was ill-equipped to handle the influx of soldiers, and mess facilities were too small for the large number of men. The temporary tent camps were crowded and latrine facilities inadequate for the vast number of users. Nathan's troopers began getting sick due to the poor hygiene and cramped quarters. Nathan went to the company commander and requested that his men be placed on the next transport. The colonel told him that every officer wanted his troops on the next transport, but he would see what he could do. Three days later, Lieutenant Baxter and his platoon were on the S.S. City of Peking and headed for the Philippines.

The crossing was less than pleasant. The platoon was billeted in third class at the very bottom of the ship with other black units. The hold compartment was cramped, the food less than palatable, latrines horrible, and bunks stacked one upon the other. Nathan and the other officers were placed in rooms in first class. They reached Manila on January 3, 1900.

****

General Elwell Stephen Otis was placed in charge of all American forces in the Philippines. The War Department had directed Otis to avoid military conflict. Arguably, he did more to encourage conflict than prevent engagement. General Otis refused to accept anything less than unconditional surrender from the Philippine Army and often acted without consulting his superiors in

Washington, D.C. Otis acted punitively against the Filipinos under the presumption that their resistance to United States forces would collapse within weeks, if not days. Even after the Filipino resistance persisted, General Otis claimed they had been defeated and that continued American casualties were the result of "isolated bands of outlaws."

The America media on the Philippine islands began reporting atrocities committed by American soldiers. The War Department ordered General Otis to investigate the credibility of the stories. In an effort of covering up the atrocities, General Otis had his aides send a copy of each newspaper clipping to the commander of the unit involved. Each commander was issued instructions to convince those individuals who had made the claims to write retractions of their original statements. General Otis' efforts were met with mixed results. Some men recanted their original claims, and some were made unavailable for further comment.

General Otis claimed Filipino guerillas tortured American prisoners in "fiendish fashion." Late in 1899, Filipino resistance leader Emilo Aguinaldo responded by suggesting that foreign journalists or representatives of the International Committee of the Red Cross be allowed to inspect his treatment of prisoners. Otis refused, but Aguinaldo managed to smuggle four reporters: two English, one Canadian, and one Japanese, into the

Philippines. The Filipino resistance leader gave them unfettered access to the American captives.

The correspondents returned to Manila and reported that American captives were "treated more like guests than prisoners" and were "fed the best that the countryside had to offer." Otis had the four reporters expelled from the Philippines as soon as their stories hit the news wires. U.S. Navy Lieutenant J. C. Gilmore was released by his Filipino capturers when they were pursued by American cavalry. The lieutenant insisted he had received "considerable treatment" and that he was no more starved than his captors.

F. A. Blake, representing the International Committee of the Red Cross, arrived to investigate alleged atrocities. General Otis ordered him confined to Manila. Blake managed to slip away from his escort and toured the field. While he never made it past the American lines, he saw burned-out villages and "horribly mutilated bodies with stomachs slit open, and occasionally, decapitated." Wisely, Blake waited until he returned to San Francisco to post his findings.

****

Lieutenant Nathan Baxter and his platoon of cavalrymen arrived amidst the political turmoil swirling around the war.

On November 13, 1899, Emilo Aguinaldo decided that a guerrilla war would be the new strategy. This new operational plan on the part of the Filipinos made the American occupation all the more difficult during the next few years. During the first four months of the guerrilla war, the Americans suffered nearly 500 casualties. Instead of attacking in force, the Filipinos would engage the Americans with a small group, shoot some soldiers, blow up a troop or supply wagon, and then blend back into the jungle.

Colonel Pablo Tecson's band of Bulacan guerrillas, which included his brothers Alipio and Simon, constructed several fortresses in the mountains near Makahambus. On May 25, they managed to ambush Captain Charles D. Roberts' six man scout patrol, killing three and taking Roberts and the other two captive. Tecson released the two wounded prisoners after treating their wounds but held Roberts. The Americans organized a campaign to attempt to gain Robert's release.

On June 4, 1900, Company E of the 35th Infantry was ambushed as they approached Makahambus Hill. Lieutenant Baxter and his platoon were involved in a flanking maneuver to the left side of the hill to prevent the guerrillas from taking that route as an avenue of escape. Lieutenant Grover Flint of the 35th attempted to flank on the other side of the hill, was ambushed, and was wounded along with two of his soldiers. Meanwhile, Nathan and his troopers set up a defensive position in a gorge. Volleys of cannon and rifle fire drove the approaching American forces of the 35th back down the hill. More of the retreating soldiers were killed or wounded by booby-trapped pits with sharpened bamboo spears hidden under foliage than by rifle fire. The American infantry attempted three attacks, only to be driven back by rifle fire from the entrenched Filipinos each time.

Finally, the Filipinos, short on ammunition and fearing a larger scale attack, started withdrawing. Twenty-five to thirty Filipinos came down the hill towards the gorge Nathan and his men had taken cover in, and a firefight ensued. During the engagement, four or five guerrillas were killed or wounded. Since the Filipino bodies were dragged away, it was impossible to tell. Nathan's platoon suffered one man wounded but not seriously. After the Filipinos disappeared into the mist, Nathan waited more than an hour. When no further withdrawing Filipinos were encountered, he withdrew his troopers to his staging area.

Having only one man wounded, and he not seriously, was a good result of the foray. Nathan and his men wouldn't always be so fortunate.

Chapter 17

On May 5, 1900, General Otis was relieved of his command and was replaced by General Arthur MacArthur, Jr., father of future Five Star General Douglas MacArthur. On December 20, 1900, the elder MacArthur placed the Philippines under martial law by invoking U.S. Army General Order 100. He announced that guerrilla abuses would not be tolerated. He further stated that guerrillas who wore no uniform and shifted from civilian to military status would not be treated as a uniformed opponent. Filipino leaders who continued to work for Philippine independence were rounded up and deported to Guam.

On July 4, 1901, General MacArthur was relieved of his command and replaced by General Adna Chaffee as Military Governor. William Howard Taft was appointed as Civil Governor. Chaffee and Taft spent a good deal of time in heated debates concerning methods and plans for prosecuting the effort against the guerrilla forces. Taft won the struggle for control and became the sole executive authority on July 4, 1902. Chaffee remained as commander of the Philippine Division until September 30, 1902. Even though he was the military commander, Chaffee was neutered by Taft's overlording.

General Arthur MacArthur, Jr., returned to the United States and served in several high level commands but never achieved his goal of becoming General of the Army. MacArthur received the Medal of Honor for his actions at Missionary Ridge as an eighteen year old during the Civil War. He held the distinction of being one of the last living Civil War officers. On September 12, 1912, MacArthur went to Milwaukee, Wisconsin, to address members of his Civil War unit. While on the dais, delivering his prepared comments, he suffered a heart attack and died.

William Howard Taft went on to become president and a Supreme Court Justice. He is the only person to ever hold both positions. The Philippine-American war was as consumed with political infighting as effective concentration of forces against the enemy.

****

On September 11, 1900, Captain Devereux Shields led a detachment of fifty-four 29th U.S. Volunteer Infantrymen into the mountains of Torrijos to find and engage the forces of Filipino Colonel Maximo Abad. Lieutenant Nathan Baxter and his twenty man platoon were behind Shields' troops to help defend against a surprise Filipino attack from the rear.

Colonel Abad was informed ahead of time of Shields' movements by local guerrilla scouts. Abad assembled a force of some 180 to 250 regular Filipino soldiers and a large number of bolomen,

Philippine natives who wielded a long single-edge knife called a bolo. The bolomen were later estimated to have numbered anywhere between 300 and 2,000. Since you didn't see them until they attacked, it was hard to estimate their numbers.

On September 13, 1900, Abad positioned his men along a steep ridge overlooking Shields' access avenue. Neither Shields nor his men had any actual combat experience and were easy prey. Abad's troops opened fire on the column, which resulted in a fire-fight that lasted several hours. Nathan and his platoon of cavalry dismounted were on the extreme edge of the skirmish line. They fired on the enemy when they could see a target of opportunity. While Shields and his men were concentrated on the exchange of gunfire, the bolomen began encircling their position.

As the battle escalated, Nathan's platoon received increased rifle fire. Private Micah Jackson caught a rifle slug through his left lung. Jackson was just a kid, really, a poor boy from rural Mississippi who wanted a better life than that of a sharecropper. He had persuaded his parents to sign for him to join the Army. Nathan put a compression bandage on the wound, bound him with a field dressing, and told him he would be alright. He knew he wouldn't.

Shields quickly realized the obvious fact that he was almost completely surrounded. He ordered a withdrawal, which quickly turned into a disorganized full-blown, fiasco. Nathan and his

Buffalo Soldiers saw what was happening and Nathan said, more to himself than anyone who might be listening, the famous words of military commanders from the beginning of time who are confronted with an overwhelming force, "*Oh, shite, what do I do now?*" Nathan wasn't so worried about the Filipino soldiers because they would take him and his platoon prisoners, and no doubt, treat them well. His great concern was the bolomen who outnumbered them at least twenty to one and might well hack them to pieces with their large knives.

The Filipinos were so focused on Shields and his column that they didn't even notice Nathan and his platoon lying in the tall grass and ran by them, while chasing Shields and his men into a rice paddy. After the Filipinos had swept by them, Nathan led his platoon, with two men carrying Jackson, to another rice paddy and took cover behind a dike. Shields, completely surrounded, wounded, and with no recourse, raised a white flag and surrendered.

Nathan and his platoon stayed at the dike until the early morning hours. He then quietly led his men back to the staging area. Sometime around midnight, Private Jackson had taken his last breath. The men were all saddened by the death of Jackson. Everyone liked the kid. They were eaten up by mosquitoes and covered with leaches, but they made it back to the staging area alive and weren't captured. Nathan was debriefed by the regimental commander who wanted to know why he hadn't engaged the enemy when they were overrunning Captain Shields' position. Nathan tried to keep his responses civil and courteous and replied, "With respect, Sir, had I engaged the Filipinos, more of my men would have died. We would have been captured by the Filipinos or murdered by the bolomen. Shields and his column were severely outnumbered and had no chance of escaping whether I sacrificed my men or not. If I had engaged the enemy, my troopers would have been killed for naught, and it would have been a more embarrassing loss than we suffered. I have no problem with engaging the enemy, but sometimes being foolhardy only gets men killed for no good purpose."

The colonel listened in silence and when Nathan finished responded, "Given the situation on the ground, I would have made the same decision. Well done, Lieutenant. Your display of sound military judgment saved the lives of your men. I will include that in my report. The Army will be looking for someone to blame, my report will ensure it isn't you."

****

The resounding defeat and capture of Shields and his men sent shock waves through the American command structure. All at once, they were confronted with the stark reality that they were engaged with a wily and resolved enemy who should be taken seriously as a worthy adversary.

MacArthur responded to the embarrassing defeat by issuing an order to Brigadier General Luther Hare to arrest every male over fifteen years old as a potential enemy and hold them hostage until Abad surrendered. General Hare used the hostages as bargaining chips and secured the release of Shields and his men. The Army destroyed all the food and shelters they could find in the interior of the island. All the villagers who were found were moved into towns. Abad and most of his Filipino soldiers continued to elude the Army. The Filipino civilian population was suffering. Many of the landowners joined the Federal Party and turned against Abad. The American Army's harsh tactics and the defection of Filipinos led to the surrender of Colonel Maximo Abad in April 1901.

****

Between 6:20 and 6:45 AM on the morning of September 28, 1901, villagers in Balangiga attacked the unsuspecting soldiers of Company C, 9th U.S. Infantry Regiment, while they were in the mess facilities unarmed eating breakfast. Valeriano Abanador, the town police chief, grabbed the rifle of Private Adolph Gamlin, one of the American sentries, hit him in the head with the rifle butt, knocking him unconscious. The overpowering of the sentry served as the signal for the rest of the communal laborers in the plaza to rush the other sentries and soldiers who were in the mess facility.

Abanador gave a shout, church bells were pealed, and conch shells blown to signal the attack. Some of the soldiers were hacked to death before they could reach their rifles. Others fought almost barehanded with steak knives, kitchen trays, and chairs.

Of the seventy-four men in Company C, thirty-six were killed during the attack, including Captain Thomas W. Connell, First Lieutenant Edward A. Bumpus, and Major Richard S. Griswold. All told, twenty-two more men were wounded and four were missing in action as a result of the attack. Eight men later died of their wounds. Of the seventy-four men in Company C, only four escaped the slaughter completely unscathed.

The villagers captured around 100 rifles and 25,000 rounds of ammunition. The Filipinos suffered twenty-eight dead and twenty-two wounded. The townspeople buried their dead, headed for the safety of the hills, and joined the guerrilla forces.

The Balangiga massacre was described as the Army's worst defeat since the Battle of the Little Big Horn in 1876. The events of September 28, 1901, happened for a number of reasons: lack of alertness on the part of the sentries, underestimating the strength and resolve of the villagers, failure to have rifles at hand while the soldiers were eating, and lack of understanding of the enemy. An aggravating factor was the fraternization between the soldiers and the townspeople. The *tuba* drinking between troopers and male villagers lead to an overly relaxed atmosphere which resulted in disaster.

****

The day following the massacre at Balangiga, Captain Edwin Victor Bookmiller, the commander in Basey, province of Samar, Philippines, sailed with Company G, 9th Infantry Regiment, for the town aboard a commandeered coastal steamer, the SS Pittsburgh. When he arrived, he found the town abandoned. After burying the American dead, the American forces set fire to the bell tower.

The attack on American troops came at a time when it was believed Filipino resistance to American rule had all but collapsed. The massacre at Balangiga was a wake-up call for Americans living in Manila. Men began wearing side arms. Tension and fear became the rule of the day. Helen Taft, wife of William Howard Taft, was so distraught that she had to be transported to Hong Kong.

Response to the unprovoked attack was swift and brutal. General Jacob H. Smith sent a communique to Major Littleton Waller, the commander of a battalion of U.S. Marines, which read: "I want no prisoners. I wish you to kill and burn; the more you kill and burn, the better it will please me... The interior of Samar [province] must be made a howling wilderness..." Major Waller countermanded General Smith's order, and it was never implemented by his Marines.

Because of the language General Smith used, he became known as "Howling Wilderness Smith." He later ordered Major Waller to kill all persons who were capable of bearing arms and engaging in hostilities against the U.S. forces. When Major Waller requested clarification regarding the age of those to be killed, General Smith responded that he was to kill all those ten years old and older.

In response to General Smith's orders and with no fear of recrimination, American troops marched across the island, destroying homes and shooting people and work animals. In a written report to General Smith, Major Waller stated that over an eleven-day period his men had burned 255 dwellings, shot thirteen *carabaos* (water buffalo), and killed thirty-nine people. The true "Balangiga massacre" was the retaliation against the peasants who lived in Samar province. The Americans became worse than the guerrillas when they became arsonists, burning entire towns and villages, and began killing with impunity.

The exact number of Filipinos who were killed by U.S. forces will never be known. The Spanish census of 1887 and the American census of 1903 indicated the population had decreased by 15,000. Considering the number killed was offset somewhat by births, there was no way to determine the number killed in the carnage.

****

The horrible events in Samar resulted in immediate investigations. On April 15, 1902, the Secretary of War sent orders to relieve officers of their posts and to court-martial General Smith. Major Littleton Waller also faced court martial for the execution of twelve Filipino bearers and guides. Waller was found not guilty. Senior military officers took umbrage with the verdict, and Waller was told it would be in his best interest to leave the military. General Smith was found guilty, given a slap on the hands, and forced to retire. A third officer, Captain Edwin Glenn, was also court-martialed for torturing Filipinos, was found guilty, and given a relatively light sentence. The court martials brought a measure of closure to the brutality of the treatment of the people of Samar province and seemed to mollify the American public, to some extent.

****

Nathan and his platoon were used to search for guerrillas in the outlying areas of Samar province. They normally encountered little resistance, and the guerrillas they found typically surrendered without firing a shot. The resistance fighters were starving, had little, if any, ammunition, and many were suffering from disease. Nathan could understand that a response to the attack in Balangiga was a military necessity. He couldn't understand the brutality and utter devastation inflicted on the Filipino people. He did his part without complaint but never killed any of the guerrillas unless they put up a fight. All those he captured were transported to Basey in Samar Province for confinement.

On June 13, 1902, Nathan and his Buffalo Soldiers were ordered to Manila, boarded a steamer for San Francisco, arrived at the Presidio, and were transported by train back to Fort Bliss, where he looked forward to resuming his normal duties. The Philippine experience was one he would never forget but also one that he wouldn't recall with fondness. He had performed his duty with dignity and honor. Many hadn't.

Chapter 18

Military historians call the years between the Spanish-American war and World War I "the New Army period." Inventions and innovations to bring the Army into the 20th century began to emerge. The Army underwent several organizational restructures, including major changes in 1901 and 1903. The service schools grew stronger, and additional emphasis was placed on creating a professional officer corps. Twentieth-century inventions and technology produced the machine gun, the airplane, improved artillery, and motorized modes of transportation. Amidst all the changes, Fort Bliss remained a small post on a distant frontier, and the early years of the New Army period went by basically unnoticed.

Colonel Frank West, representing the Inspector General office, visited Fort Bliss, Texas, in 1902. West, one of the old breed of career Army officers, wrote a long-winded scathing report regarding the disrepair of the facilities at Fort Bliss. Lieutenant Colonel H. H. Adams commanded the post in 1902 and didn't take exception to West's report. In fact, he added that only nine of the post's thirty-nine buildings were in "good" repair. He described the temporary pump house as "worthless." The hospital steward's quarters needed "extensive repairs," and the other twenty-seven buildings on the post were "in need of repairs."

Following Colonel West's report, most of the post's available funds were directed to upgrade and improve facilities on the post.

****

When Lieutenant Nathan Baxter returned to Fort Bliss on June 20, 1902, he reported to Lieutenant Colonel Adams and was told of his immediate duty assignment change. He was to aid Major James French with the construction and repair effort regarding the buildings on the post. Nathan wasn't overjoyed with the news. He was, after all, a cavalry officer and wanted to be with his horses and men. He informed Colonel Adams that the only thing he knew about building construction came from watching his father build a cabin when he was a child.

Lieutenant Colonel Adams looked at Nathan and said, "Life is a learning experience. I expect you will learn if you are interested. I suggest you get interested." Nathan accepted the new duty with grace and a smile. He had little choice because the circumstances weren't going to change.

Nathan got settled back into the routine at Fort Bliss. He was shuffling paperwork, standing officer of the day duties, monitoring work details, and attending to his personal equipment and firearms. The mundanity of life at Fort Bliss wasn't to change until the Mexican Revolution when the post would assume its role as a great border cavalry post.

When Nathan met Major James Madison French, he found him to be a most unpleasant, uncouth, and disagreeable man. French was a hold-over from the Civil War where he had been a brevet colonel. French was obese, in his mid-sixties, had no chance for advancement, was prone to passing gas without regard to who might be present, and spent considerable time with the bottle. He was tired, lazy, and resentful. Nat figured out early on that the workload and responsibilities were going to be his as well as the blame if things didn't go well.

After three weeks of planning and starting limited renovations, Lieutenant Colonel Adams called Nat to his office and asked him to sit down. He then asked him, "Lieutenant, how are things going? How are you and Major French getting on? You haven't come complaining to me, and I'm wondering why?

Nat look at the colonel momentarily and said, "My father was a military officer during the Civil War and taught me that complaints were for those who couldn't get it done. He didn't want to hear whining from me or my brothers. I figured you didn't either. It would change nothing anyway. I would still have my job to do."

Lieutenant Colonel Adams smiled at Nat and said, "You'll do, Lieutenant. You'll do."

****

Between July and the end of 1902, Nathan laid plans for the refurbishing of the post. He wanted to be ready when the War Department released the funds so that the real work could commence. After the Christmas holidays, work was begun in earnest. Nathan and his workforce worked ten to twelve hour days, six days per week, with Sunday off for attendance of chapel services. The day off also provided much needed physical rest for the men and mental rest for Nathan's harried mind. By mid-July of 1903, the improvements in the facilities were starting to become obvious. Nathan and his workers continued to toil all during 1903, into 1904, and then 1905. Lieutenant Nathan Baxter had put all his energy into the refurbishing and construction efforts and felt at times like he was in the engineering corps. For all practical purposes, he was.

In June 1904, Brigadier General Jesse M. Lee, the new department commander, toured the facilities at Fort Bliss and noted that improvement was evident. He also noted that a new Post Exchange and gymnasium had been completed. The general also commented that Fort Bliss remained one of the most unattractive posts in the department. Undaunted, Nat keep at the contractors and held their feet to the fire on completion dates and quality of workmanship. His own military workers were doing the best they could, and he had no complaints.

General Lee returned in 1905 and submitted a report that strongly contrasted with his earlier statements. "The material improvements as to repairs of buildings, construction of roads, fences, general improvements of grounds, etcetera, have not been equaled elsewhere in the department."

Major French had retired in early 1904 leaving a vacancy at Fort Bliss. In 1905, Captain Jonathan Wise was promoted to Major to fill the opening. Lieutenant Nathan Baxter, on the recommendation of Lieutenant Colonel Adams and endorsement of General Lee, was promoted to Captain effective July 1, 1905, filling the new vacancy left by Captain Wise. Nathan was two years behind BJ but was being promoted to captain ahead of his older brother. While it was more luck and being in the right place at the right time than anything else, he felt bad for his brother whom he idolized.

Unbeknownst to Nathan, Lieutenant Colonel Adams, or General Lee, Secretary of War William Howard Taft was in a meeting up the street from the White House with a bespectacled man who wanted to review the Army promotion roster before it was released. The man skimmed through the list for promotion to captain and saw the name Nathan Forrest Baxter. The gentleman asked Taft if this was the Baxter who was involved in the taking of Kettle and San Juan Hills. When he was told it was, the man rolled a large cigar around in his mouth and said, "Why isn't his brother, James Baxter on the list? I believe he has more seniority."

Secretary of War Taft was totally unprepared for the question, and at a loss for words. Normally, reviewing a promotion list of mid-grade officers was just a formality, if done at all. He responded, "I would assume there was no captain's billet available for Lieutenant J. B. Baxter, Sir."

The man looked at Secretary Taft and said, "If I'm not mistaken, Major General Corbin's aide de camp just resigned to accept a teaching position at some college. Why don't you see about getting Lieutenant Baxter that billet?"

Secretary Taft said he would see what he could do, and the man laughed and said, "Bully."

A week later, Captain James Budwell Baxter, Jr., was on his way to Washington, D.C., as the new aide de camp to Major General Henry C. Corbin. When he reported in to General Corbin's office, a staff officer greeted him, told him to have a seat, and that the general would be notified he was in the office. In a few minutes, BJ was told to report to General Corbin. He walked to the general's desk, gave a crisp salute, and told him he was reporting for duty. General Corbin looked at BJ and said, "Captain Baxter, stand at ease. Have you ever had any dealings with a general officer?"

BJ looked at the General without the hint of a smirk and replied, "Yes, Sir. I actually had a very personal and intriguing conversation with General of the Army Miles just a few years ago."

General Corbin looked surprised and said, "If it wouldn't compromise the content of your conversation with General Miles, would you provide me with the anecdote?"

BJ smiled and said, "General Miles looked me directly in the eye and said, 'Thank you,' right after I passed him the salt.'"

Corbin roared with laughter and said, "Captain, you will need that sense of humor around here. Good to have you on my staff." BJ went to his grave never knowing that President Roosevelt had interceded on his behalf.

****

El Paso, Texas, was moving into the twentieth century. The El Paso Electric Railway Company unveiled its new trolley car service which replaced mule drawn passenger cars on January 11, 1902. The little town had grown into a city with more than 25,000 residents.

When Nathan was given the task of refurbishing Fort Bliss, he didn't know beans about building repairs or construction, so he decided to ride into town, visit the El Paso Public Library, and see what he could pick up from the books concerning building construction. After tying his horse to the hitching rail in front of the library, Nathan walked into the building. When he walked up to the service counter, he encountered a young woman who would alter his life.

The woman was twentyish, slight of build, sported long blond hair which she wore in a bun and blue eyes that twinkled when she looked at Nathan. She was also affable and slightly flirtatious. Nat was impressed and nervous. He had called on a few girls while in school in Dallas and then the mixers while at the Academy but none of the girls struck his fancy. This one did. Nat asked the young lady where he could find books on building construction. Rather than telling him, the lady walked him to the section of the library where the construction books were located. Before leaving, she said, "My name is Lily Jane Thompson."

Nathan was taken aback and finally got out that his name was Nathan Forrest Baxter, but his friends called him Nat. Lily said she was glad to meet him. When Nathan found a couple books he thought would be helpful, he went to the service counter to check them out to take back to the post. Lily filled out the necessary paperwork, smiled, and handed him the books. Nathan was feeling brave, so he asked, "Would it be possible for me to call on you sometime soon?"

Lily smiled and said, "I'll tell you what, Lieutenant. There is a play at the municipal theater on Friday night. Why don't you come by the library at 6 PM, pick me up, and you can escort me to the play." Nathan said he would be at the library promptly at 6 PM. On Friday, Nathan had the sergeant in charge of the stables at the fort provide him with a horse and buggy and picked Lily up at 6

PM as promised. They went to a Shakespeare play called Hamlet. Lily thought it was wonderful. Nat didn't see the big deal in guys running around in tights and talking funny. However, he wisely didn't share his opinion of the play with Lily.

After the play was over, they went to the El Paso Café, had a late dinner, and talked until the café closed. Nat then took Lily to her parents' home in the buggy. After that evening, Nat would come into town at least once a week and take Lily to dinner, and after the first few dinner dates, he had dinner with her and her parents at their home. On September 20, 1902, Nathan went to the First National Bank of El Paso and asked to speak to Mr. Thompson, the vice-president of the bank. Mr. Thompson knew what Nathan wanted but made him squirm before finally asking for his permission to marry his daughter Lily.

Mr. Thompson was frank and told Nathan that he thought he was a fine young man but he had reservations about Lily marrying a career military man. An Army officer could be called to war at any time and possibly killed, leaving her with no means of support. But he conceded that was his concern and he wouldn't try to stand in the way of Nathan and Lily marrying. They were married at the base chapel in Fort Bliss, Texas, on Saturday, April 18, 1903, at 2 PM. Bud and Sara Baxter made the 640 mile train trip from Dallas to El Paso and attended the ceremony. They were both impressed with Lily and liked her parents. Nat and Lily moved into quarters on the post, which the groom had prepared, and Lily then turned into a home.

Chapter 19

On January 20, 1904, Lily gave birth to Kelli Ann Baxter, a beautiful blond haired baby girl. Then on July 7, 1905, James Nelson Baxter came into the world. He was named James after Nathan's older brother and Nelson after Lily's father. On May 15, 1906, Lily gave birth to William Nathan Baxter, a fine looking little boy. William was named after Nathan's younger brother.

****

In January 1904, the sergeant major retired. A replacement sergeant major reported to Captain Nathan Baxter. The man's name was Peter Seth Cheyhill. When Sergeant Cheyhill reported to Captain Baxter, he was obviously agitated and said, "Captain, I mean no disrespect to you, but I'm a cavalry sergeant. I didn't sign on in this man's Army to be no damn carpenter."

Nat looked at Cheyhill and replied, "Sergeant, I'm a cavalry officer, and I didn't envision being a construction engineer. We go where we are ordered and do what we are told. Do I make myself clear?"

Sergeant Cheyhill didn't smile and responded, "I will do my job, Captain."

To which Nat replied, "That's all I require of you, Sergeant Cheyhill. If we had to be happy with every posting and task, most of us would be in trouble." Sergeant Cheyhill proved to be a good NCO and worked well with the men, gave them reasonable breaks, and helped them when he could. He proved to be an asset to Nat and took some of the load off his shoulders. During the construction work at Fort Bliss, Cheyhill and Nat never became anything more than officer and subordinate. They shared a mutual respect, one for the other. Peter Cheyhill just wasn't the type of outgoing individual with which one tends to make friends, but he was strong of character and dependable.

****

The Mexican Revolution was one of the important events of its history. In 1910, Mexico had been independent from Spain for nearly a century, and the country was plagued by problems. Rich landowners, the Catholic Church, and the military ruled the country. Pastoral land was in short supply and controlled by a small number of affluent families.

The revolution was basically in opposition to the Porfirio Diaz government. After gaining the presidency in 1876, Diaz ruled Mexico with sham re-elections for decades. In 1910, the worm turned, and his opponents called for "effective suffrage, no re-election." Diaz was overthrown in 1911. Several revolutionary leaders struggled for power. Among them were Francisco I. Madero, Victoriano Huerta,

Emiliano Zapata, Alvaro Obregon, and Francisco "Pancho" Villa.

During the fighting between the different factions vying for power, hundreds of towns were destroyed, and an estimated 250,000 Mexican people lost their lives.

Predictably, the fighting in northern Mexico spilled across the Rio Grande into the United States. These incursions led to Fort Bliss becoming a major horse cavalry post. Border violations, violence, and arms smuggling demanded an increased American presence along the border. Because of its strategic border location, Fort Bliss became the focal point in the international confrontations which occurred during the revolution. The Punitive (Pershing) Expedition received most of the publicity. The Zimmerman Telegram, a secret communication from the German Foreign Office that proposed a military alliance between Germany and Mexico should the United States enter World War I, gained the attention of the American government. Even though they didn't get the lion's share of the press, the troops from Fort Bliss made the difference in controlling the border and preventing Mexican incursions into the United States.

****

On March 6, 1911, Secretary of War Henry L. Stimson ordered the formation of the Maneuver Division to be headquartered at Fort Sam Houston,

Texas "for the purpose of maneuvers and to render the civil authorities any aid that might be required…"

Fort Bliss had four companies of the 23rd Infantry Regiment, a band, and a few machine guns. Infantry had no way of chasing men riding on horses, so they were basically useless in providing anything other than presence. Major General William H. Carter was in charge of the Maneuver Division and immediately recognized that cavalry was required to chase down men riding horses. Both Emiliano Zapata and Francisco "Pancho" Villa were Mexican horsemen who were leading bandits across the United States border, doing mischief, getting arms from smugglers, and then returning to Mexico. Someone whispered in the General's ear that there was a fine cavalry officer at Fort Bliss who was working basically as an engineer. General Carter ordered three platoons to Fort Bliss to be under the command of Captain Nathan Baxter. Within two weeks, three lieutenants, three sergeants, troopers, and horses arrived at Fort Bliss. The unit was comprised of forty-five men total.

General Carter's chief of staff called Fort Bliss and set up a time for Captain Baxter to be in the command office to receive a telephone call. Nathan arrived ten minutes before the scheduled 2 PM call. The phone rang at 2:01 PM. The chief of staff instructed Captain Baxter that he was to report his activities directly to him, and he would convey what he thought pertinent to the General. Nathan was expected to keep his troopers in the field, and his highest priority was to take punitive action against Zapata or Pancho Villa should they bring forces into Texas. The chief of staff closed the call by telling Nathan that General Carter was depending on him to get the job done and to let him know, through the chief of staff, if he needed anything. Nathan responded, "Yes, there is something, or rather someone, I need."

The first thing Captain Baxter did when he left the command office was find Sergeant Major Cheyhill. Sergeant Cheyhill walked up to Captain Baxter, saluted, and said, "Yes, Sir, what can I do for the Captain this fine day?"

Nathan looked at Sergeant Cheyhill for a couple seconds and said, "Sergeant, I have been tasked with putting together a three platoon cavalry unit to patrol the border. No doubt, you have seen the officers, horses, and men reporting to the fort. I don't want to take you away from your love of construction, but would you consider being the Sergeant Major of the unit?

Sergeant Cheyhill looked at Nat, smiled, and said, "Is it against Army regulations for a sergeant to kiss an officer!" Nat smiled and said he would take that as a yes.

****

The border between Texas and Mexico is 1,954 miles in length, starting at the Gulf of Mexico and following the Rio Grande to Ciudad Juarez, Chihuahua, Mexico and El Paso, Texas. Of course Captain Baxter wasn't expected to patrol the entire length of the Rio Grande, but, on the other hand, the scope of his area of responsibility wasn't clearly defined. On May 15, 1911, Captain Baxter sent Lieutenant Jackson Frederickson and his platoon south along the border, and he accompanied Lieutenant Frank Smith and his platoon to a ranch west of present day Cornudas, Texas, that had reported Mexican bandits stealing their cattle.

Some thirty miles southeast of Fort Bliss, Nathan and the platoon encountered a group of ten to twelve Mexicans driving twenty head of cattle southwest. Nathan halted the platoon and sent Sergeant Forbes and two troopers to examine the brands on the cattle and ask for a bill of sale. Before the troopers arrived at the herd, the Mexicans fired on them. The three troopers retreated back to the column. Nathan brought the platoon to bear on the Mexicans at the gallop. The platoon was armed with the shortened barrel version of the 1903 Springfield bolt action, clip fed rifle in .30-06. The Springfield was an extremely accurate and hard hitting weapon.

When the platoon got to within fifty yards, Nathan gave the order to fire. In the first volley three Mexicans and one horse were shot. The Mexicans broke off the engagement and hightailed it south. Nathan slowed his horse, and the troopers checked the downed Mexicans. Two were dead and the other severely wounded. The horse that had been shot was thrashing around, and Nathan ordered it put out of its misery. Nathan sent two troopers to notify the ranch owner the location of his cattle. He and the rest of the platoon followed the escaping Mexicans. After five miles, the Mexicans turned and headed northwest towards the Mexican border. After following them for five miles, Nathan broke off the chase and returned to the fort. When he arrived he had the platoon stable their horses and went into the headquarters building and filed his report to Fort Sam Houston. In about an hour, while he was attending to his mount and discussing the foray with Lieutenant Smith, an orderly brought him a message from the chief of staff which consisted of a simple "well done." Nathan's participation in the Mexican Revolution had begun.

Between patrols, Nathan spent as much time as he could with Lily and the children who were growing like weeds. The patrols were sometimes a few hours, and at other times, were three to five days as they patrolled the border south of El Paso. In addition to the standard issue Springfield rifle, the troopers carried the Colt Model 1873 single action .45 revolvers. They were well armed and well supplied while on their patrols. The only complaint was that they never knew what they were riding into. One time, it would be harmless Mexican peasants who had crossed the border to get away from the violence. The next time, it might be Mexican bandits trying to steal cattle to drive back to Mexico to feed the revolutionaries. The next time, it might be arms smugglers and, less likely, but certainly always a possibility, revolutionaries trying to ambush the American soldiers. Constant vigilance was the order of the day.

On July 2, 1911, Captain Baxter and a platoon led by Lieutenant Mark Walker were in Butterfield, Texas, looking for Mexicans who had stolen cart loads of fruits and vegetables from the packing sheds. Fifteen miles southeast of El Paso, the platoon intercepted three horse drawn carts laden with fresh food stores to be delivered to the revolutionaries across the border. When the platoon pulled up, the Mexicans dropped their weapons. Nathan commandeered the wagons, had the troopers load the bandits' weapons in them, and assigned Sergeant Cheyhill and two troopers to escort the Mexicans to the border. He then had three troopers drive the wagons back to the packing sheds while he and Lieutenant Walker and the other soldiers accompanied them.

****

Butterfield was located on the old Jim Hogg Highway south of Alto and north of Forest in southern Cherokee County. In 1906, a group of investors purchased a large tract of land to develop a fruit orchard. The operation was known as Butterfield Farm or Butterfield, after Fremont Butterfield who served as manager. Several packing sheds were erected to process the fruits and vegetables. In 1910, a railroad spur for the Texas and Southwestern Railroad, also known as Butterfield, was constructed around three miles from the packing sheds. The orchard operated for several years but never turned a profit. The land was finally sold to a dairy farming operation.

****

After returning the carts, Nathan and Lieutenant Walker went to the commissary to get a bite to eat while the troopers watered their horses and then found a place in the shade to sit and eat their field rations. After they sat down at a table, a man dressed in civilian clothes, wearing a large slouch hat, sporting a big bushy mustache, and wearing a pair of Colt .45 revolvers strapped to his hip, walked over to the table and said, "You're the ugliest damn captain I ever did see. Is the Army promoting according to ugliness now!"

Nathan came out of his chair, grabbed the man in a bear hug, and said, "Well, I'll be damned. Fred Brubaker, it's great to see you." Nathan let the man go and shook his hand, turned to Lieutenant Walker, and asked, "Have you ever seen a lawman with a badge from Sears and Roebuck before?" Both Nathan and Fred laughed, and the Lieutenant just looked puzzled. Nat asked Fred to sit down with them and introduced him to Lieutenant Walker as his boyhood friend from Texas and Montana.

Fred explained that he was going to the prison farm to pick up a prisoner for transport back to Dallas to face murder charges. The prison farm was used to provide charcoal for the Texas State Penitentiary foundry at Rusk. Prison authorities had no knowledge of the murder charges against Jefferson Davis Freeman when they placed him with the trustees. Luckily, Freeman hadn't escaped while on work details under limited guarding as a supposed petty thief.

Nathan wanted Fred to come to El Paso and meet his wife and children, but Ranger Brubaker begged off because he was under a time constraint to get the prisoner on the train and back to Dallas. He had just been reassigned to the Troop at Dallas and wanted to make a good showing in his new location. The short visit was wonderful for both men, and they exchanged childhood memories for almost an hour. They then shook hands and said their goodbyes.

Fred picked up his prisoner, and Nathan and the patrol returned to Fort Bliss.

Chapter 20

Fred got Jefferson Davis Freeman's wrists bound with manacles, attached a chain to a belt around his midsection, and loaded him on the train without incident. Fred felt that he had the convict under control and would have no difficulty transporting the man from El Paso to Dallas. Sometimes what you think and reality are two entirely different situations!

When the train neared Midland, Texas, Freeman said he needed to use the Hopper toilet. Passengers weren't allowed to use the Hopper while the train was stopped at a depot because fecal material would accumulate on the tracks. Fred thought the demand was reasonable and decided to allow Freeman's request. Fred sat for a few minutes waiting for a young Catholic Nun who had entered the toilet to come out. When the nun exited the facility, he took Freeman to the Hopper. Fred was always meticulous in checking everything before taking any action. This time he wasn't!

When Freeman came out of the toilet, Fred was leaning against the wall across from the door. The outlaw shot Fred twice. The first bullet struck him in the upper left arm, and the second hit him in the chest. Had it not been for the train jerking and swaying as it slowed, Fred would have been killed outright. Freeman relieved Fred of the keys to the manacles, waited for the train to almost stop, jumped off, and caught a waiting horse. One of the three other men on the coach came and checked on Fred after Freeman had jumped from the train. Only one of the three was armed, but he had shown no interest in getting involved. A man removed the bandana from around Fred's neck and used it to put pressure on the chest wound. On July 6, 1911, Texas Ranger Fred Brubaker was unconscious, and the situation looked grave.

When the train stopped in Midland, a physician and nurse met the train within minutes of its arrival. Fred was taken to the doctor's office on a horse drawn stretcher and placed in a small, four-bed room. Doctor Martin VanHall was young, as was his nurse, but he was competent. The bullet wound to the arm didn't require anything other than cleaning, applying some salve, and binding the entry and exit sites. The chest wound was another matter. Doc VanHall had noticed Fred's Texas Ranger badge and sent for the town marshal. The marshal notified the ranger office in Dallas, who sent a ranger to notify Bill and Betty Brubaker.

Bill and Betty were having supper when the ranger arrived with the news. They immediately started packing a valise. Bill checked on the train schedule going from Dallas to Midland and discovered the next train was scheduled to leave Dallas at 9 AM the following day. They were standing at the depot loading area well before the train started loading passengers. They boarded the train and took seats in the passenger car for the eight hour, including depot stops, trip to Midland. Bill went to the dining car, drank enough coffee to float a ship, tried to play a few hands of poker but couldn't concentrate, and went back to sit with Betty. They arrived in Midland shortly after 5 PM. Bill asked directions to Doctor VanHall's office, left the valises at the depot for safe-keeping, and he and Betty walked the short distance to the doctor's office.

When they arrived, the scene was more like the site of a wake than a doctor's office. A Texas Ranger who was in Midland to serve a warrant was there wringing his hands and pacing. The doctor was grim faced. Bill got right to the point, "What are his chances, doctor?"

Doc VanHall looked at Bill and then at Betty and began, "The bullet went through his left lung and, as far as I can tell, lodged in soft tissue in his back. I have inserted a drain tube in his lung, and blood and mucus are draining well. My concern is that he is still unconscious which isn't normal. I'm afraid it is a waiting game now. I've done all I can for the moment."

Betty said, "I want to be with my son." The doctor said that was certainly fine and led her to the small ward where a young woman was sitting by Fred's bed holding his hand and talking to him. Betty looked at the young woman and blurted out, "Who are you?" Betty immediately realized how her question sounded and said, "I'm sorry for my tone. I'm understandably upset, but that doesn't excuse bad manners. Please forgive me."

The young woman smiled at Betty and replied, "That's perfectly alright. I'm Shelia Jean VanHall, the doctor's sister. I act as Doctor VanHall's nurse from time to time when needed."

Betty looked slightly confused and asked, "Do you know my son?" Shelia responded that she had never laid eyes on Betty's son before he was brought to the doctor's office, but, even though it might seem silly, felt a strange attachment to the man. Betty smiled a knowing smile, nodded, and took Fred's other hand. Bill walked to the Midland Hotel and rented a room for a week. He asked for the valises to be picked up from the train depot and brought to the hotel. The waiting game began.

Betty and Shelia Jean never left Fred's bedside other than for bodily functions, all that evening and night. Shelia looked at Betty on the morning of the 8th of July and said, "Mrs. Brubaker, why don't you go to the hotel, eat breakfast, freshen up a bit, and take a nap. I'll be with your son until you get back."

Betty had to agree that she was completely exhausted. She hadn't slept since she had received the news and could barely function. Doctor VanHall walked Betty over to the hotel and to her room, where Bill was dressing to go to the doctor's office. Bill suggested to Betty - he had long since acknowledged that he could tell her nothing - that she take a short nap. He assured her that he would come and wake her so they could get something to eat, and she could go back to the ward. When Bill arrived at the ward, Fred was speaking in barely understandable tones to the girl at his bedside. Bill took that as a doubly good sign. Fred was awake and interested in the girl. Both indicated that he was probably going to make it.

Fred started to recover from his chest wound and began taking nourishment, broth at first, and then some type soup laden with vegetables. Then, on the 10th of July, Fred asked Shelia to get him a beefsteak from the hotel dining room. After seeing that Fred was up to eating a steak, Bill made arrangements to leave the next morning. He and Betty were comfortable that they were leaving him in capable and caring hands.

Fred stayed in bed for two more days and then began getting up and attending to his toilet functions and taking his meals. Shelia was around all the time, attending to his needs, helping him get out of bed, and visiting with him. On the 17th of July, Fred said he was well enough to take a room in the hotel until he felt up to traveling back to Dallas.

Texas Rangers Nate Fuller and A.J. Beard were sent to find Freeman and bring him to justice. They arrived in Midland on the same train with the Brubakers. They started poking around at the saloons and other places in town until they found someone who knew Freeman and was willing to talk. Early on the morning of July 9, they cornered

Freeman and his girlfriend, Susan Brand, the woman who had pretended to be a nun. She and Freeman were in a cabin on the side of Beals Creek. Freeman refused to surrender, saying that he wasn't going to prison or hang, and came out shooting.

When Fuller and Beard brought Freeman and Ms. Brand into Midland to the sheriff's office, the undertaker and a newspaper man were both counting the bullet holes in Freeman. The reporter turned to the Rangers and asked why they shot Freeman twelve times. Ranger Fuller responded in a very even tone, "Since Colt revolvers only hold six cartridges, we couldn't shoot him more than twelve times without reloading, and we didn't see any reason for that." With that, he and Beard went to get something to eat at the Midland Hotel café after returning Fred's pistol. The shooting of Ranger Fred Brubaker had been avenged!

Fred left on the 20th of July on the train to Dallas. Shelia went with him to the depot and cried when he boarded the train. Fred looked back, smiled, and waved. When he got back to Dallas, he reported in to the ranger office and was told to take another week off to recuperate.

That evening, he went to his Dad and Mom's home and had dinner with them. During his second piece of apple pie, his mother looked at him and said, "In case you are like your father and are too thick-headed to notice, that girl is in love with you. You are thirty-eight years old, cranky, and set in your ways. You might think about going back to

Midland and marrying that woman before you become a grumpy ole man living alone and talking to your horse for companionship." Fred's dad just looked at the ceiling and said nothing. He was no help at all.

Fred procrastinated for two days and then got the courage to call Doc VanHall's office in Midland. Shelia answered the phone, and he said, "This is Fred. I've been thinking that I would like to be with you."

Shelia laughed and replied, "Fred who?"

Fred said, "Fred Brubaker. You know that."

Shelia said, "What exactly does that mean? You plan on getting shot again?"

Fred said, "No, I'm not. Now don't make this harder than it is. I was thinking that you might consider becoming my wife."

On Saturday, September 23, 1911, Frederick William Brubaker and Shelia Jean VanHall were married at the Methodist Church in Midland, Texas. Bill and Betty Brubaker and Bud and Sara Baxter made the trip from Dallas to Midland for the ceremony.

Fred took a couple days off for a honeymoon and bought a small house on the outskirts of Dallas where he and Shelia set up housekeeping.

****

Shortly after getting settled into married life, Fred was tabbed to go to arrest one Roy Daugherty, aka Arkansas Tom Jones or, sometimes Skunk Breath Jones, who had robbed the Brady mercantile store in Stephenville, Texas. The man had killed the stock clerk when he refused to turn over the cash box. Mrs. Maude Mayfield was entering the mercantile store just as Daugherty shot Jonathan Brock, the stock clerk, and then ran past her on his way out of the store. She had made a sworn statement that she had no doubt it was Daugherty.

Fred was to proceed to Stephenville, meet a ranger coming from Abilene, and then track down and capture the murderer. When Fred got to Stephenville, he met Texas Ranger Joshua Enoch Cheyhill at the sheriff's office. After introductions, they walked to the Erath Café, ate a meal, got to know each other a little, and discussed their plan of action. Daugherty had worked at a small ranch in Erath County for a couple years shortly after the turn of the century and was well known by locals.

Daugherty had no known associates in Erath County. But Fred and Josh had to start somewhere, so they headed to the small ranch that the killer had worked on previously. They rode to the ranch and pulled up in front of the ranch house. They talked with Teamore Cardwell, the owner, who denied having seen Daugherty since he left the ranch in 1903. As Cardwell was talking to the Rangers, he kept repeatedly shifting his eyes towards the barn. Fred and Josh noticed Cardwell's obvious signaling.

They thanked Cardwell and rode off from the ranch. When they had ridden a mile or so, they veered left into a copse of trees that provided them cover. They walked their horses until they got within 100 yards of the back of the barn and dismounted. Josh pulled his rifle out of its scabbard, and Fred took out his shotgun.

They decided that they would approach the barn from the rear, and Josh would attempt to move along the left side of the barn and cover the front entrance. Once they were in position, they would call out to Daugherty come out of the barn and surrender. All plans are wonderful when they work. This one didn't.

Daugherty saw movement through one of the cracks in the sidewall of the barn as Ranger Cheyhill walked by and knew something was up. No doubt Cardwell had tipped off the lawmen that he was in the barn. He aimed his rifle, and the next time he saw movement, he fired. Fred heard the rifle shot and called out to Josh but received no answer. Daugherty had no idea how many lawmen were outside. He had seen one and heard another, but there could be others.

Fred went to the corner of the building and peeked around. He saw Josh lying on the ground next to the barn wall with a pool of blood accumulating next to him. Fred knew that if he went along the wall, he would probably be the next one shot. He decided to go in the back door of the barn and trust his luck to surprise Daugherty. Fred went to the double doors. Since there was no bar securing it, he tried the one on his left. He slowly opened the door just enough to slide though the opening and dropped to the floor just as a bullet hit the door. Fred saw the flash of the gun and fired a load of 00 buckshot where he had seen the flash. Fred pumped the shotgun ejecting the spent shell and loading another. Daugherty came crawling out of a horse stall holding his stomach. The shotgun blast had missed Daugherty, but when a board that the pellets had hit splintered, a large shard flew off and entered the outlaw's abdomen. When Daugherty cleared the horse stall he raised his rifle and Fred shot him with a load of 00 buckshot from thirty feet. To say Daugherty was a mess was an understatement. Fred walked up to the man to make sure he was dead. He was, very!

Fred ran out of the barn to Josh and discovered he was still alive, but barely. The bullet had entered his side at an angle, and exited leaving a fair sized hole. Josh was losing a lot of blood, so a vein or artery had obviously been hit. All Fred could do was use a length of cloth he had the foresight to pick up in the barn to make a compress. He put firm pressure on the entry and exit sites and hoped that Josh's blood would coagulate before he bled out. After a few minutes, the bleeding seemed to subside somewhat. Cardwell had come to the barn once the shooting was over. Together, he and Fred carried Josh very carefully to the porch of the ranch house and laid him down.

Fred told Mr. Cardwell to ride to town, get the doctor, and bring him to the ranch. About an hour later Cardwell and a man driving a buggy raced into the ranch yard. Doc Blanchard examined Josh and said he had lost a lot of blood and shouldn't be moved. A wagon trip to Stephenville would, no doubt, start the bleeding again and kill him. Cardwell said he had a spare bedroom that the ranger could stay in. They carefully moved him to the bed, took his boots off, and got him settled.

Fred got Daugherty's horse, saddled it, loaded the man's carcass on the mount, tied the dead man's hands to his feet under the horse, led the horse to the front of the ranch house, and hitched it to the rail. He then walked to the trees and retrieved his and Josh's horses. He took Josh's horse to the barn, removed the saddle, and stabled it. He then led his horse to the ranch house, told Cardwell and Cheyhill he would be back in a few hours, and headed out to Stephenville.

When Fred got to the town, he took the body to the undertaker, wired the Texas Ranger office in Dallas, made an abbreviated report, and asked them to notify the Abilene office of Josh Cheyhill's condition. Fred rode back to the ranch, stayed three days with Cheyhill, and helped take care of his needs. On the third day, Doc Blanchard visited Josh and said he thought it would be safe to move him to town if they were careful and didn't jostle him too much. Fred and Cardwell got Josh loaded on a farm wagon. The rancher drove, and Fred followed, leading Josh's horse.

Once they got Cheyhill settled in the doctor's sick room, Fred shook hands with the ranger and said he was headed back to Dallas. He told Cheyhill his horse would be in the livery when he was ready for it.

Cheyhill thanked Fred repeatedly for saving his life. Fred said, "I don't consider myself a necessarily brave or foolhardy man. You were bleeding to death, so I had to go into the barn and try to take care of Daugherty or let you die. Hopefully, you would have done the same if our roles were reversed." With that, they shook hands, promised to stay in touch, and Fred left.

Chapter 21

Captain James (BJ) Baxter served as aide de camp to Major General Henry Clark Corbin until the general retired in September 1906. Shortly after being promoted to Lieutenant General, Corbin was placed in charge of the Northern Division, The Department of the Missouri. The general was a congenial man whose demands were always realistic. BJ enjoyed working for him but didn't enjoy the assignment because it kept him away from the cavalry which he dearly loved, and the constant travel demands kept him from the family he loved more than his horses.

After the retirement of General Corbin, Captain Baxter was reassigned to the staff of General Leonard Wood, was promoted to Major, and became assistant adjutant. He accompanied the general's staff to the Philippines when Wood was assigned as Commander of the Philippine Division of the Army. The staff officer job entailed making sure the Army troops in the Philippines were combat ready. In addition to lots of inspections and coordination with regimental commanders, the job seemed to mainly consist of moving tons of seemingly innocuous paperwork from one basket to another. The promotion was nice, but BJ hated being tied to a desk and out of the flow of front line action.

****

Leonard Wood was an unusual Army officer. He started his military career as an Army physician on the frontier. He received the Medal of Honor while a member of the 4th U.S. Cavalry, which was searching for Geronimo during the summer of 1886. Assistant Surgeon Wood volunteered to carry dispatches through an area infested with hostiles, rode seventy miles in one night, and then walked thirty more miles the next day.

Wood served as Chief of Staff of the U.S. Army, Military Governor of Cuba, and Governor General of the Philippines. During the Spanish-American War, Wood commanded the Rough Riders, with Theodore Roosevelt as his second-in-command. Wood was passed over for consideration of a major command during WWI. After Wood was passed over, he elected to retire from the Army and went into politics.

****

The assistant adjutant position gave James a broader understanding of the inner workings of the Army and prepared him for possible upper echelon assignments. He stayed in the Philippines without his family and missed Marie and the kids terribly. One of the elements of his job while in the Philippines was assisting in the formation of the

First Philippine Assembly, which ultimately led to Filipino independence. Major Baxter's role was relatively minor but did allow General Wood to keep his finger in the pie, so to speak. The formation of the Philippine Assembly was the brain-child of William Howard Taft, and most everything Major Baxter was involved in had to be done with great diplomacy. General Wood didn't want the future president to think he was interfering in the process. Walking a political tightrope wasn't BJ's forte, and he was extremely relieved when that part of his duties was concluded.

In 1908, General Wood was reassigned back to the United States to take command of the Army's Eastern Department and served in that capacity for almost two years. Major Baxter rotated back to the United States with General Wood and was on his staff at the Eastern Department Headquarters located at Fort Jay on Governors Island in New York Harbor. BJ was assigned quarters, and Marie Elizabeth and the kids moved to Fort Jay. It was a wonderful period for the Baxter family. BJ had been gone for almost two years, a long time when children need the influence of their father. Most of all, Marie enjoyed having a husband at home and the kids loved having a father at home to spoil them.

When General Wood became Army Chief of Staff in 1910, Major Baxter stayed on his staff, was promoted to Lieutenant Colonel, and was assigned to the planning staff. BJ held that position until 1914 when General Wood retired. After being assigned to the planning staff, BJ moved his family from Fort Jay to Fort Myer, Virginia, and was assigned military housing for him and his family. Fort Myer is adjacent to Arlington National Cemetery, the burial place of many military members who were killed in action.

General Wood was impressed with BJ, and they built an association which was to last until the general's death on August 27, 1927. While James was a major, and then a lieutenant colonel, General Wood could always count of him to be candid, vigilant, extremely loyal, and always truthful. Wood respected these attributes in a man and officer and rewarded BJ for his abilities and diligence by recommending him for advancement.

After General Wood retired on April 21, 1914, there was a succession of generals who served as Army Chief of Staff. William Wallace Wotherspoon served from April 21 to November 16, 1914, when he was forced to retire at age sixty-four. Hugh L. Scott served from November 17, 1914, to September 22, 1917, when he, too, was forced to retire because of age. Tasker H. Bliss served from September 23, 1917, to May 19, 1918, when he also was forced to retire because of age.

****

On July 28, 1914, World War I, the war to end all wars, began. On April 6, 1917, two days after the U.S. Senate voted eighty-two to six to declare war against Germany, the U.S. House of Representatives endorsed the decision by a vote of 373 to 50 and the United States formally entered the First World War. The horrible war lasted until November 11, 1918.

During the course of the war, 9,911,000 uniformed soldiers were killed, and 7,700,000 civilians lost their lives. Unfortunately, the war to end all wars didn't serve that function!

****

Lieutenant Colonel James Baxter continued to serve in his position on the planning staff, first under the command of Major General Wotherspoon and then Major General Scott, until February 1915. General Scott called BJ to his office and offered him the job of helping to establish a training facility to prepare army soldiers for deployment and engagement in the ongoing war in Europe. The general went on to say that he thought the assignment would be good for BJ's career and might well lead to a promotion to full colonel. BJ thanked the general for his confidence in him and the consideration.

The facility was concealed from the public because the Chief of Staff of the Army felt that the American civilian population would become outraged if they knew soldiers were being prepared for deployment to Europe to participate in the war.

Lieutenant Colonel Baxter was appointed as Executive Officer of the clandestine training facility. Marie and the kids stayed in their quarters at Fort Myer. BJ would return to the fort on the weekends when he had no fires to put out at the training facility.

The facility was in the hills of Virginia and was equipped with trenches, barbed wire, and other realistic obstacles designed to replicate the situation which would be found in the war in Europe. The logic for the facility was to introduce as much realism as possible into the training regimen. The flares, smoke bombs, rockets, and general confusion which the soldiers who attended the facility were exposed to were designed to prepare the Army regulars for the real thing should they be deployed.

On September 1, 1917, Lieutenant Colonel BJ Baxter was promoted to Colonel and was appointed vice-commander of the training facility. General Scott had been correct. Advancement in the Army was contingent upon having a "sponsor," a general who would guide a junior officer into assignments which would prepare him for more responsibility and advancement in grade.

Colonel Baxter was to learn that the training at the clandestine facility, though designed to be realistic, was grossly inadequate for the reality on the ground once they were engaged by the Germans. There was nothing that could prepare men for the nightmare of actual battle in terrifying and deplorable conditions! Nothing!

Chapter 22

When the United States entered World War I on November 20, 1917, things weren't going well for the Allies on the European fronts. A French offensive, supported by the British, began in April 1917 and was an absolute failure. The fiasco led to widespread mutinies in the French armies. To their credit, the British maintained strong pressure against the Germans all along the front during 1917. The British attacked the Germans at Messines Ridge on June 7, Passchendaele on July 31, and at Cambral on November 20, but each initiative failed to reach their objective. Closing the German submarine bases at those locations was the goal. After the attacks, they remained in operation. The British lost a great many lives while achieving little beyond establishing themselves as a tough fighting force.

Three American engineering regiments: the 11th, 12th, and 14th, were engaged in construction activities behind the British lines at Cambral in November 1917. Nathan Baxter's work during the renovations and construction projects at Fort Bliss didn't go unnoticed. Because of the experience Nathan gathered at Fort Bliss, he was assigned to the Engineering corps and rose to the rank of Lieutenant Colonel. In early 1917, Nathan was assigned to the 11th Engineers. The unit consisted of 1,400 volunteers from New York State. Many of the volunteers had previously been railroad workers. He met the unit in Jersey City, New Jersey, as the **Battalion Commander for the 11th**. After completion of training, the 11th boarded troop ships for the crossing of the Atlantic Ocean and landed in France in August of 1917. Upon landing, they were almost immediately deployed to Gouzeaucourt, just south of Cambrai, to improve the rail facilities in the area. The 11th Engineers were tasked with preparing the lines for railway transportation of supplies and equipment and repairing abandoned railway lines. They were also tasked with unloading and positioning tank fleets in case of a German attack. The 11th was the first American unit to enter the European theater. Shortly after arrival in France, Colonel Waters, the regimental commander, became ill, and Lieutenant Colonel Nathan Baxter was named as the new Regimental Commander.

Nathan had been briefed that the American Expeditionary Forces were going to be involved in a support mission and that their objective wasn't to engage the enemy in combat. When the 11th was called to the front lines after the Germans overwhelmed the British and French soldiers, they became the first American Expeditionary Force unit to meet the enemy.

****

On September 5, 1917, the 11th Engineers came under German artillery fire. German spotters had pinpointed the American location and let go with a barrage of cannon fire that was withering and kept the unit pinned down. During the shelling, Sergeant Matthew Calderwood and Private William Branigan were injured by flying shrapnel. They were the first two American casualties of the war in Europe, but they certainly wouldn't be the last. The shelling of the American engineers earned them the moniker of "first to fight." Nathan's engineers helped with the deployment of tanks and other heavy equipment, built berms and staging areas, and completed anything else they were asked to accomplish.

On November 9, 1917, after the Allies had advanced sufficiently to provide them with a reasonable level of protection, the 11th Engineers began re-laying the railroad track on the main line running north into Cambrai. While the engineers were working on the tracks, the Germans attacked in force. Lieutenant Colonel Nathan Baxter was ordered to pull his workers back and keep them off the line until the German troops had been repelled. Instead of falling back, the German Sturmtruppen (storm troops) overran the British lines and ambushed the 11th Engineers where they were working in a presumed safe zone.

The engineers were totally unprepared for the attack and were only armed with discarded rifles. The only other weapons they had were spades and other hand tools. The workers managed to hold their position and hang on for dear life until British forces could mount a counterattack. During the melee, Lieutenant Colonel Baxter took cover, fired at the advancing German troops with his M1911 .45 pistol, and managed to wound two or three. He hollered to Lieutenant Malcolm McLoud to get the engineers into the trenches where they would be somewhat safe. McLoud and Sergeant Donald MacIsaac were successful in getting the men to safety. For their acts of heroism, both McLoud and MacIsaac received the Distinguished Service Cross. A few minutes into the attack, Nathan found himself pinned down and unable to escape the advancing Germans. He kept firing, and the British arrived just as he was inserting his last clip of ammunition.

After the Germans were driven back, Nathan started checking on the wounded engineers and helped get them to the field hospital. Being a commander carried a heavy burden. It was impossible to keep 1,400 men safe when the Germans were hell bent on killing them. Nathan did what he could for the wounded and made sure the dead were handled with dignity. He then went off by himself and shed tears of sorrow. He was covered with blood, some of it his own from small flying shrapnel shards. His entire body was camouflaged by filth, sweat, scrapes, and lacerations. Losing men that he had talked with just an hour or so before was almost unbearable. It was to get much worse.

The spring offensive began on March 21, 1918, with three German armies involved in the assault on the assembled British defense lines. The British weren't able to hold the line, and their lines of defenses were pierced in several places in rapid succession. By March 26, Amiens was seriously threatened. On the 27th, a gap was created between the French and British armies. Fortunately, the Germans lacked reserves to exploit their initial successes. By April 6, the Allies had moved in enough reserves to bring the offensive to a halt. The Germans had occupied forty miles (1,500 square miles of ground), taken 70,000 prisoners, and inflicted 200,000 casualties. However, they had failed to reach their objective. The destruction of the British forces and the capture of Amiens hadn't been accomplished.

Nathan and his engineers were again caught in the middle of the action. The British trench system in Cambrai was incomplete, which left a weakness for the Germans to exploit. On March 21, 1918, the Germans attacked and fired an estimated one million artillery shells at the British 5th Army, which was commanded by General Hubert Gough. Nathan and his engineers were pinned down and at the mercy of the protection provided by the British. When it became obvious that the British were being routed, Nathan ordered a retreat to avoid capture. Nathan's decision proved prudent as 21,000 British soldiers were taken prisoner by the Germans. The German breakthrough at Cambrai was the biggest advance in three years of warfare on the Western Front, and General Gough ordered the entire 5th Army to withdraw.

The Germans continued to advance under an artillery bombardment that was horrendous. The 11th just couldn't outrun the big guns. There were body parts strung out all along the line. Men were screaming, crying, and moaning in pain. A shell fragment hit Nathan in the lower leg causing a large laceration. The gash produced a lot of bleeding before a corpsman could get a compression bandage on the wound. The frustrating thing was there was no one to shoot at. All he and his men could do was hunker down and hope that they weren't among the unlucky that a shell found. Nathan's engineers retreated along with the remaining British troops who had avoided capture. As they withdrew, Lieutenant Mark Wilson took a direct hit from an artillery shell and was obliterated. There was nothing left but blood and small pieces of tissue.

On March 25, 1918, at the height of the German push, General Pershing offered his four American divisions to help stop the German drive and placed them at the disposal of the French. Unexplainably, only a few American units were allowed to engage the Germans. Nathan and his men became riflemen and fought for their lives in the face of an aggressive and committed enemy. All around Nathan, men were dying. The bullets didn't care if it was engineers or regular infantry. Both were equally easy targets for the advancing Germans.

The Germans became overconfident and overplayed their hand. German General Ludendorff ordered the 18th Army to advance on the important railroad city of Amiens. He was confident that if they took the town, the British and allies would be cut off from supplies. Nathan and his engineers were holed up in any structures they could find still standing in Amiens. The anticipated German attack on the city never materialized. The 18th Army ran out of supplies, and their cargo horses were killed for food. As they neared Amiens, the Germans began looting the shops in the small town of Albert. German soldiers began fighting among themselves for the meager food stores. All discipline was lost, and the German advance to Amiens stalled.

Nathan and his engineers were exhausted and short on rations, but most were alive. The 1918 German Spring Offensive had cost 230,000 casualties. By the end of March 1918, 250,000 fresh American soldiers poured into the Western Front to join the British. Nathan and his engineers stood and cheered like little boys at a parade as the American soldiers entered Amiens.

Once the Americans took control of Amiens, the 11th Engineers came off the front and got some much needed rest and decent, well almost decent, food. Nathan went to the field hospital and looked in on his wounded troops and then sorrowfully looked at the lines of dead soldiers awaiting burial. Nathan's leg had festered, and a corpsman lanced the wound and let the pus drain. Eventually, the wound healed.

Nathan and his engineers were now neck deep in the fighting. The Germans mounted more offensives on the western front, with mixed results. The first offensive was the Battle of the Lys which was fought from 7 to 29 April, 1918, in Flanders. After an initial objective proved unproductive, the operation was changed to the German's goal of capturing Ypres.

The German bombardment began on the evening of April 7 and was concentrated on the southern part of the allied line between Armentieres and Festubert. The artillery barrage continued until dawn on April 9 and was followed by the German 6th Army attacking with eight divisions. Nathan and his engineers were in Armentieres working on the railroad tracks and had to suspend work and find cover in order to escape the barrage. Armentieres was under the protection of the Portuguese Second Division which was quickly overrun and withdrew towards Estaires leaving the 11th Engineers to fend for themselves—again.

Nathan and his beleaguered engineers fought against overwhelming odds. Lieutenant Colonel Baxter had procured more and better weapons for his men along with sufficient ammunition to form a viable resistance and protect themselves. The 11th Engineers found secured positions that gave them some protection and fought on. Nathan's engineers were, by definition, soldiers. But they were trained for engineering work, and their military training with weapons had been sorely neglected. Nathan found himself instructing men on military maneuvers, weaponry, and tactics as well as building or repairing lines of transportation.

Luckily, the British 55th Division to the south and 40th Division to the north mounted minor counterattacks which caused the Germans to abandon their positions where they had the 11th Engineers pinned down. Once the Germans withdrew, Nathan and his men started attending to the wounded and placing the dead in a central location. Dozens of men were wounded, and more than two dozen killed, during the onslaught. The British 55th Division managed to hold their position despite the Germans calling up two additional reserve divisions. The British 40th Division collapsed under the German attack and fell back to the north. Nathan was able to get his men back to a reasonably secure position where they could get some hot food and receive medical treatment for their wounded.

Based on Lieutenant Colonel Nathan Baxter's obvious leadership skills and management of the defense of his 11th Regiment, he was promoted to Colonel on the recommendation of General John Pershing, commander of the American Expeditionary Forces on the Western Front during World War I.

****

The 11th Engineering Regiment, along with other engineering groups, were responsible for constructing more than twenty million square feet of storage space and built 800 miles of standard-gauge railroad lines plus an equal distance of yards and storage tracks. Other engineering groups enlarged French port facilities, tank yards, and cut and processed millions of feet of lumber.

****

Colonel Nathan Baxter survived the Great War with only an ugly scar on his leg and a few minor cuts and bruises. Hundreds of his engineers were wounded, and more than 100 killed, during their various engagements in France. For a group whose only function was to support the war effort, they contributed mightily with rifles as well as shovels. It was a horrible experience, a tremendous loss of life and limb, and would emotionally scar Nathan for the rest of his life.

Colonel Nathan Baxter boarded a troop ship and returned to the United States along with a boat load of soldiers. His new assignment was at Fort Riley, Kansas, as the Commandant of the Army Cavalry School. Nathan had a wonderful homecoming and then moved Lily and the children with him to Kansas. No one knew for sure how Colonel Baxter landed the coveted assignment to the Cavalry School. Most thought it was a reward for his service as an engineer.

Nat was in his own little world as Commandant of the Cavalry School. He was amongst men who loved and worked with horses. What could be better? Colonel Nathan Baxter served as Commandant until his retirement in June 1924, having served thirty years as an Army cavalry officer. For the most part, it had been a fulfilling and interesting experience.

Chapter 23

Army Chaplain William Huzzah Baxter spent five years at Fort Riley, Kansas, and was promoted to Captain in the Army Chaplain Corps. In the spring of 1907, Captain Baxter was given a plum assignment to the newly constructed Fort Shafter which is located in Honolulu, Hawaii, between Kalihi and Moanalua valleys. The transfer came as a complete surprise to Bill who hadn't requested the assignment. He thought it might be Divine intervention. Actually, there was a fellow in Washington, D.C. who had a very high opinion of the Baxter brothers and had suggested the assignment.

****

Fort Shafter is the senior Army headquarters in Hawaii and command center for the United States Army Pacific. Construction of the fort began in 1905 on the *ahupua'a* (a subdivision of land) of Kahauiki. Kalihi is the name of the *ahupua'a* between Kahauiki and Kapālama in the Kona district of O'ahu. They were formerly Hawaiian crown lands that were ceded to the United States government after annexation. When the new facility opened in 1907, it was named for Major General William Rufus Shafter, who led the United States expedition to Cuba in 1898.

****

After getting settled in, visiting the post chapel, and checking out his office, Captain (Chaplain) Baxter started his official duties by paying a courtesy call to Lieutenant Colonel (Father) Adolphus McGuire, the command chaplain and, technically his boss. After chatting for an hour or more with McGuire, Bill visited the 2nd Battalion, 20th Infantry Regiment Commander, Major Maxwell Jones. After meeting and chatting with Major Jones, Bill visited with some of the troops, invited them to chapel, and told them he was always available should they need him for any spiritual matter.

Bill and Father McGuire formed a close friendship while he was billeted at Fort Shafter, which was to continue for several years. Bill stayed on the island of Hawaii for almost eleven years and enjoyed the laid-back environment and easy life. On May 1, 1918, shortly after his promotion to Major, Bill Baxter volunteered for duty in France. Lieutenant Colonel Adolph McGuire talked with Bill and tried his best to talk his friend out of his decision, but Major Baxter wouldn't budge.

Bill told Adolph, "Brave soldiers are being wounded and killed in France and I don't feel right about sitting here in the sunshine. I have been more than lucky to have stayed here in paradise for years. Now I feel the least I can do is go to the war area and minister to the soldiers that need my spiritual encouragement more than I need to lie on the beach."

Colonel McGuire wasn't happy about Bill's decision but said that he understood and would approve his request for the billet in France. Within three weeks, Bill was on a troop ship headed for France and landed at Saint Nazaire on June 1, 1918. After processing in, Major Baxter was assigned to the 9th Infantry Regiment as the regimental chaplain. Colonel James Blunt was the regiment commander. When Bill reported in to the officer, he was warmly greeted and asked to sit and visit. After chatting and having a cup of coffee, Colonel Blunt said, "Major, I have read your file. You are quite a story. Colonel William Bisbee made an entry in your file that indicates that you are brave to the point of being foolhardy and that he had to order you off the line in the Philippines."

Bill looked at Colonel Blunt and replied, "Sir, with respect, I don't think of myself as brave. Those young man who are firing their weapons and being fired upon are the brave ones. Colonel Bisbee and I had a disagreement concerning my function with the war effort. I thought I should be with the men to comfort them. He thought I should be in a headquarters tent or visiting the field hospital. I did spend a great deal of time visiting with wounded soldiers, but I also went into the field to perform religious services and counsel the men."

Colonel Blunt looked at Bill and said, "Major, just so you know, I'm not a spiritual man, but I won't interfere with your religious work. If Colonel Bisbee didn't want to lose a lieutenant chaplain, I certainly don't want to lose a Chaplain Corps major. I don't want you on the line, period."

Will looked at the Colonel and said, "Yes, Sir, I understand."

****

The 9th Infantry Regiment was assigned to the 3rd Infantry Brigade of the 2nd Division. The 2nd Division was organized on October 26, 1917, at Bourmont, Haute Marne, France. The 1st Provisional Brigade was redesignated as the 3rd Infantry Brigade on September 22, 1917. The 9th and the 23rd Infantry Regiments, along with the 5th and 6th Marine Regiments, 6th Machine Gun Battalion, 2nd Brigade of field artillery, and various support units, came under the 2nd Division. On two occasions, the division was commanded by Marine Corps generals: Brigadier General Charles A. Doyen and Major General John A. Lejeune (after whom the Marine Corps Camp in North Carolina is named). This was the only time in U.S. military history when Marine Corps officers commanded an Army division.

The 2nd Division spent the winter of 1917 – 1918 training with French and Scottish veterans of the war. Though the French tacticians felt the American Expeditionary Force was unprepared for combat, it was tasked with the mission of halting the German advance toward Paris in 1918. Before being deployed to reinforce the French along the Paris to Metz road, the 2nd Division fought at the Battle of Belleau Wood.

****

Bill went back to the field chapel to think over what Colonel Blunt had told him when a corporal walked up, saluted, and said that he was wanted at brigade headquarters. Bill's first thought was, *"What could I have done wrong, I just got here."* When he arrived, he was escorted to an office where a voice said, "Come in, Major Baxter."

Behind a desk sat Lieutenant Colonel Adolph McGuire who smiled and said, "I thought about what you said about enjoying the sunshine while men were dying in France, so I volunteered to come over. I am the brigade chaplain, so you are working for me again."

Bill looked at his longtime friend and asked, "Does this mean that I can do my job, visiting with the men on the front, or do you want me behind a desk and safe?"

McGuire looked at Bill and said, "Major, why don't you just get right to the point? I thought we might enjoy a meal together and chew the fat some before getting down to brass tacks. To answer your question: I don't want you dead, but I won't stop you from doing your job as you see fit as long as you don't try to play soldier."

Bill smiled and replied, "Now, we've got that settled. Would you like to go to the officer's mess with me and find a slightly cooked piece of beef to chew on?"

****

On the evening of June 1, 1918, German forces managed to punch a hole in the French lines to the left of the American Marines' position. The U.S. reserve consisting of the 23rd Infantry Regiment, 1st Battalion, 5th Marines, and part of the 6th Machine Gun Battalion marched six miles to plug the gap. Major Baxter walked every foot of the march with the men. He spent his time talking to this soldier and that, encouraging them, telling stories to break the tension, and listening to them talk about their families back home. By dawn, they had closed the gap. By nightfall on June 2, the U.S. forces held a twelve mile front line north of the Paris-Metz Highway, which ran through grain fields and scattered woods. The German line ran from Vaux to Bouresches to Bellea, setting the stage for a bloody clash between the two forces.

At 3:45 AM on the morning of June 6, the Allies launched an attack on the German forces. Unbeknownst to the allied forces, the Krauts were preparing their own strike. The French 167th Division attacked to the left of the American line while two companies of the 1st Battalion, 5th Marines, attacked across an open field and came under withering German machine gun and artillery fire. The 49th Company lost all five junior officers. The 67th had one lone officer who survived the attack. Captain Hamilton of the 49th combined what was left of the two companies. His troops established strong points to fire on the Germans and established a defensive line.

The 2nd Division, 23rd Infantry Regiment, captured the ridge overlooking Torcy and Belleau Wood and then occupied and held Belleau Wood. Unfortunately, the Marines had failed to scout the woods and discovered too late that a regiment of German infantry was hiding with a network of machine gun nests and artillery. They cut the soldiers down in waves as they climbed the hill towards the ridge. All around Major Baxter, men were screaming and wriggling in pain. He stopped and helped make men as comfortable as possible, bound wounds, gave those not shot in the stomach water, and stopped and held the hand of those who were dying. While he was bent over a soldier, trying to hold a compress on his chest, he felt a sharp punch in his back and saw blood starting to cover his tunic.

Bill continued to bandage the wounds of soldiers and looked up to see two German soldiers advancing with bayonets attached to their rifles. Bill had a decision to make. He was a non-combatant, and wasn't supposed to get involved in combat. On the other hand, he wasn't inclined to allow the wounded men to be killed. Perhaps the Germans wouldn't kill him because he had a cross on his headgear, and perhaps they would.

Bill removed the M1911 pistol from the nearest man's holster, cocked the hammer, shot the German nearest him, and then shot the other. Both men hit the ground and didn't move. A .45 slug is highly lethal. Bill returned to placing bandages on the men when it occurred to him that he was no longer a noncombatant. Once he picked up a weapon and killed the enemy, he was part of the military force. Bill had several shrapnel wounds, along with the bullet wound, and was seeping blood in several places.

Chaplain Baxter continued talking to the severely wounded soldier, while he held a compress to his own chest and attempted to keep both of them conscious. The soldier was named Michael Frederick Cheyhill, Jr., and during their chat, Bill learned the man was from the Yellowstone area in Montana. When the medics arrived, they found Major Baxter lying on Corporal Cheyhill with the compress in one hand, pressed against his chest, and a M1911 in the other hand.

Bill was attended to by the medics and loaded into a horse drawn ambulance along with Cheyhill and other wounded soldiers and taken back down the hill to a field hospital. Bill passed out during the trip and woke up that night with horrible pain in his chest where the bullet had exited. When Colonel McGuire was informed that one of his chaplains was wounded and in bad shape, he immediately knew it had to be Major Baxter. When he got to the field hospital an hour later, his initial presumption was confirmed. Major William Baxter was lying in a bed, his chest and shoulder bound with a large dressing, and a young Voluntary Aid Detachment (VAD) nurse was placing a cool towel on his forehead.

McGuire walked up shaking his head and said, "Major Baxter, you will never survive this war. This makes three times you have been wounded, and you aren't even supposed to be in combat. The medical corpsmen who treated you in the field said you were holding a M1911 pistol, and there were two dead Germans just a few feet away from you. I won't ask you if their report is accurate."

The nurse looked at Colonel McGuire and said, "Sir, the Major needs to rest. Could you come back and visit with him later please."

McGuire looked at Bill, smiled, and said, "Looks like you are in good hands. I will come back and see you tomorrow."

Bill replied, "Would you check on the men I was trying to help while you are here. I did the best I could at bandaging them."

Bill spent five days in the field hospital. Upon his release, Colonel McGuire told him he was making arrangements to transfer him back to the United States. Bill protested and said, "My place is with the men until the war is over. I believe we all have a time to die. When it is my time, I will die whether here or riding a horse in Texas." Colonel McGuire just shook his head and walked out of the hospital tent.

On June 21, 1918, the Army surgeon who was treating Bill released him to return to limited duty.

Chapter 24

When Major William Baxter returned to duty, it was limited duty. He was to do nothing stressful or strenuous. Having been given his orders, Bill stayed off the line and visited soldiers in the hospital every day. He just happened to look in on a young nurse on each visit. Amy Margaret Binder had been widowed in 1917 when her husband, an American officer, was killed in a training exercise. After Captain John Binder was killed, Amy lived with her parents at the United States consulate in Kehl, Germany, where her father was the vice-consul. Once war was imminent, Amy left Germany and went to France, and joined the VAD to help with nursing wounded soldiers. Bill would schedule his visit at the hospital to arrive just before lunch and eat with Amy each day. Being an army chaplain had its benefits.

While the soldiers who Bill had helped were in the field hospital, an Army investigator came and interviewed them asking if they saw an Army chaplain shoot two German soldiers. All the men interviewed said they had seen a chaplain helping with the wounded and trying to comfort dying soldiers. They didn't remember seeing a chaplain shoot anyone. When questioned, Michael Cheyhill said he had head trauma and had trouble remembering certain things.

****

On July 6, 1906, thirty-five nations met in Geneva, Switzerland, and adopted the "Convention for the Amelioration of the Condition of the Wounded and Sick in Armies in the Field." This meeting improved and supplemented the 1864 convention, but nowhere in its code did it preclude an officer from protecting soldiers under his care. The investigation of Major Baxter went nowhere, and nothing more was ever mentioned regarding the alleged shootings.

****

Amy's father wasn't available to contact, so there was no way for Bill to ask his permission to court his daughter. He did, however have Lieutenant Colonel Adolphus McGuire formally introduce Major William Huzzah Baxter to Mrs. Amy Margaret Smith Binder before even asking her to lunch.

****

Courtship prior to the 1920s could begin when a young lady was seventeen to eighteen years old. This was typically the age when they began attending adult social functions. Courtship could only begin with the couple first having a conversation preceded by a proper introduction. A woman couldn't introduce herself to a man, nor could she speak to a man without proper introduction. The courting couple was not allowed to touch until after they were engaged, and even then, it was limited. A man always asked a woman's father for permission for her hand in marriage. The couple was allowed some time alone once engaged but only for things like going for a walk. They were also permitted to hold hands and might even sneak a kiss from time to time.

****

Bill and Amy were in Europe and, within reason, felt they should comply with the Edwardian rules of conduct between men and women. Even though Bill was in his forties and Amy thirty-something, he was very cautious about propriety. He didn't want to allow her to be the subject of gossip. Because they were separated from their parents, Bill couldn't introduce Amy to his parents. Bill and Amy discussed the situation and decided that even though the courtship rules were silly and old fashioned, it would be better if they just went ahead and got married. By skipping all the nonsense, they wouldn't be giving tongues a reason to wag.

Bill went and talked with Colonel McGuire, and a wedding was scheduled for September 1, 1918, at the headquarters chapel. Actually, it was a large field tent. Bill and Amy found quarters in the headquarters compound, and their honeymoon was limited to an evening together having a candlelight dinner and then enjoying each other in a biblical way.

Bill didn't return to the front and confined his duties to visiting the sick and wounded in the hospital and conducting religious services. The war ended on November 11, 1918, and Bill knew he would be sent back to a duty station in the United States within a few weeks. Bill and Amy didn't think it wise for her to travel to Germany. They were faced with a logistical nightmare in trying to get her to the United States. Colonel McGuire had met General Pershing on several occasions and contacted him with regard to the Baxters' problem. General Pershing knew Major Baxter's brothers, interceded, and made arrangements for Amy to travel to the Unites States on the S.S. George Washington. She would be part of the entourage accompanying President Woodrow Wilson on his voyage back to the United States after his trip to Europe. Bill arranged Amy transportation to Brest, France, and she boarded the ship back to the United States on July 1, 1919. When she boarded the ship, Amy thought she was seven months pregnant. As it turned out, she had miscalculated by almost two months and delivered William Huzzah Baxter, Jr., while crossing the ocean.

President Wilson's personal physician delivered the baby, and the President visited Amy shortly after she gave birth. The ship docked at Hoboken, New York, on July 8, 1919. Amy and William, Jr., boarded a train to Dallas, Texas, to stay with the Baxters until Bill returned on a troop ship. Bill had sent his parents a wire and told them that Amy would be arriving on a train out of New York. When she got to New York, Amy sent the Baxters a wire and told them her train schedule. She was scared to death, alone in America with an infant, and going to stay with people she had never met.

When Amy and William Jr. "Billy" arrived in Dallas, she was met at the train depot by Bud and Sara Baxter. Sara embraced Amy, saw Billy, and immediately fell in love with her newest grandchild. Amy immediately felt at ease with the Baxters. Bill's father talked a lot, and Mrs. Baxter, Sara, went out of her way to make her comfortable and part of the family.

Bill was required to stay in France until most all of the soldiers were placed on troop ships and the wounded moved to ships equipped to somewhat attend to their needs. There were thousands of men with missing limbs from bullet shattered bones and shrapnel from artillery blasts. Finally, when most of the vast numbers of men were moved out, Major William Huzzah Baxter boarded the American ship El Sol on August 5, 1919. He arrived at New York on August 18. Bill sent a wire to his parents' home in Dallas letting them and Amy know he would be in Dallas in a few days. Bill arrived in Dallas and was met at the train by Amy and his parents.

Bud and Sara had been convinced that Bill would be a bachelor his entire life, and they wondered silently how a marriage between a forty-five year old man and a thirty-some year old woman would work in the long term. On the other hand, there was quite a bit of age difference between Bill and Betty Brubaker, and they got on well. Bill and Amy spent three weeks in Dallas and then caught a train to El Paso where Major William Baxter reported in to the post commander to discover that he had been promoted to Lieutenant Colonel and was the new Brigade Chaplain.

****

In 1919, the 2nd Cavalry Brigade, which consisted of the 5th and legendary 7th Cavalries, had been deactivated at Fort Bliss. The post was now home to the 82nd Field Artillery (Horse) and the 8th Engineering Regiment. The Army was changing and moving away from horse mounted troops. The 401st Truck Company operated the M1917 Liberty and the 1916 Jeffrey Quad trucks. During the transition period between the horse and mechanized transportation, the truck's function was to support the horse. Specifically, trucks were used primarily to carry supplies and fodder for cavalry horses. In addition to the main units stationed at the fort, the 19th Infantry Regiment and the 9th Engineers were scattered along the border.

****

After getting Amy and Billy settled into their quarters on the post, Bill went to the brigade headquarters and found his office. He met Sergeant Gregory Masters, his chaplain's aide, chatted with him for a few minutes, and established what he expected from the NCO. He then went to the post chapel and met the two chaplains assigned to the post.

Life at Fort Bliss developed into a routine. Bill would go to his office at the brigade headquarters, review paperwork, visit with soldiers on the post, stop at the base chapel, check on the two chaplains, go to his quarters, have lunch with Amy, and help feed Billy. Some days, he would have a horse saddled for his use and visit the outlying troops guarding the border. Other days he would conduct visits to the base hospital. Every few weeks, he would prepare a sermon and preach at the base chapel.

November 9, 1919, was unseasonably cold, twenty-seven degrees when he awoke and then moderating to a chilly thirty-three degrees by mid-morning. When Bill rode his horse to the 9th Engineering Regiment stationed along the Rio Grande River, he arrived chilled to the bone. Bill visited with the regiment commander and spent some time visiting with individual soldiers at their duty locations. During the mid-afternoon, Bill rode back to Fort Bliss, turned his horse over to the stable personnel, and walked to his quarters.

When Bill entered his quarters, he found both Amy and the baby sick, very sick. Both were running high fevers and coughing. Bill bundled Amy and Billy up in blankets and called for an ambulance, which arrived shortly. They were taken to the base hospital where the surgeon on duty diagnosed them as having ordinary LaGrippe or influenza. As the evening progressed, Amy became sicker and exhibited cyanosis, a condition in which the skin and mucous membranes take on a bluish color. The discoloration is caused by the body not producing enough oxygenated blood.

Once Amy started exhibiting cyanosis, she and Billy were isolated in a room, and Bill was ordered to stay out. By 9 PM, Amy had developed pneumonia and was getting worse by the minute. At 9:15 PM, the doctor feared it was just a waiting game until William Huzzah Baxter, Jr., died. At 4:30 AM, William Jr. was pronounced dead. At 10:30 AM on November 10, 1919, wracked with horrible coughing seizures and an uncontrollable fever, Amy Margaret Baxter succumbed to the horrible sickness. The hospital surgeons were mystified. The influenza outbreak of 1918 was supposed to have been over. They couldn't explain how Amy and the baby contracted the disease. There was no viable treatment at the time. No one else on the post had developed flu symptoms. It was as if Bill's family alone was cursed by the horrible disease.

****

The influenza pandemic of 1918 – 1919 killed more people in absolute numbers than any other disease outbreak in history. The estimate of deaths worldwide was put at twenty-one million at the time of the pandemic. Epidemiologists and scientists have revised that figure upward several times since the early twentieth century. Modern estimates place the death toll at somewhere between fifty and one-hundred million. The world population in 1918 was only twenty-eight percent of today's population. Extrapolating the figures to today's population would indicate a comparable death total of 175 to 350 million people worldwide.

****

Bill called his parents in Dallas, gave them the sad news, shared some tears, and sent a wire notifying Amy's parents of her and the Billy's death. Bud and Sara Baxter arrived by train on the late afternoon of November 11, 1919. The funeral was held on November 12, 1919. Amy and William Jr. were buried in the post cemetery.

Bill didn't want to return to his quarters and asked Sergeant Masters to get his personal effects and take them to the bachelor officer quarters. He just couldn't face being in the place where his wife and child were stricken.

Bill's parents stayed on for two days and returned to Dallas. There was no way they could console him. Bill was simply overcome with grief. The death of his wife and child had been so immediate, so unexpected, that he was overwhelmed. Bill was a mere shell of his normal self for several weeks and went through times of deep depression, denial, anger, and resentment. Over time, Bill was able to deal with the loss of his wife and only child, but it wasn't easy. Only his spiritual strength allowed him to survive the ordeal. He never married again.

Chapter 25

On January 31, 1918, Colonel James Baxter was assigned to the 369th Infantry Regiment "Harlem Hellfighters" as their commander. He was tasked with the assignment, in large measure, because of his experience with the Buffalo Soldiers while serving in the cavalry. The endorsement of General Pershing didn't hurt. The 369th was in place just in time to participate in the Champagne-Marne offensive of July 15 thru 18, 1918.

****

Leading up to the Champagne-Marne offensive, the Germans had gained considerable ground between March 21 and June 13, 1918. Even though they controlled more real estate, they were unable to achieve a decisive advantage at any point on the front. Moreover, the meager success was purchased at a high price in manpower and material, which the Germans could ill afford.

The war was becoming one of attrition. The allies had lost around 800,000 killed and wounded during the German offensives. Fortunately, they were being replaced by new American units arriving at the front in ever-increasing numbers. By comparison, the Germans had suffered more than 600,000 causalities. The problem was that Germany had few replacements for their killed and wounded.

By July 1918, Allied troops outnumbered German soldiers on the Western Front, but the Krauts weren't ready to quit!

On July 15, 1918, the Germans mounted a two-pronged assault on both sides of Rheims. Plans for the attack had somehow leaked out of Berlin. Allied airplanes had detected unusual activity behind the German front, and the Allied forces were prepared for the attack. The German attack west of Rheims succeeded in pushing across the Marne near Chateau-Thierry but stalled at that point when met by French and American units.

****

Colonel Baxter's 369th was dug in east of Rheims and confronted the advancing Germans head on. The Germans attacked Colonel Baxter's troops at 8 AM on July 16 and came at them, wave after wave, supported by light artillery and machine gun fire. BJ had deployed his machine guns at strong points toward the opposite ends of his lines and had the Germans caught in a pincher maneuver. When the Germans advanced, they were harassed by machine gun fire from two sides and withering rifle fire towards their advancing front.

Even though Germans were being killed and wounded by the thousands, the Americans were catching hell as well. While BJ was outside his headquarters bunker checking the troops on the line, a courier came running up to Colonel Baxter with a note.

BJ asked the corporal, "Why are you on foot, Son? Where is your mount?"

Corporal James Wadfer replied, "Sir, I have had three horses shot from under me this morning. The Germans target couriers because they want the commanders to be denied access to current information."

BJ said, "Well, go behind the lines, get a bite to eat and water, get another mount, and come back here, and I will give you a reply." With that, the corporal departed. James read the note which was inquiring about how he was holding his position.

BJ penned a response, "General, we are holding the line at great cost in human lives but costing the Germans even more dearly. We will hold. And by the way, Sir, Corporal Wadfer is deserving of a medal. He has outlived three mounts." Colonel James Baxter, Commander, 369th. After scribbling his name on the note and folding it, he waited for the courier to return.

While he was waiting for the courier, Second Lieutenant Mark Johnson ran up to tell him that the Germans were concentrating their men about 300 yards up the line. While he was giving the information to Colonel Baxter, he was hit in the neck by a rifle bullet which severed his carotid artery. Lieutenant Johnson bled to death within a couple minutes. All BJ could do was watch the young man bleed out. This was a horrible war. How many times had he lectured his officers about keeping their heads below the trench line! Lieutenant Johnson paid a fatal penalty for being tall and forgetful!

BJ hollered to Sergeant Fredric Micklos to tell two of the lieutenants to get their platoons on the move to fill the gap the Germans were exploiting. Micklos was Colonel Baxter's personal messenger and every man, officer or otherwise, knew the message he delivered was from the lips of Colonel Baxter. Micklos was the only son of dairy farmers near Falmouth, Michigan. Micklos delivered the message to Lieutenants Spicer and Cranker. They immediately got their platoons on the move. When Sergeant Micklos was on his way back, ten yards from BJ, a German artillery shell hit just a few feet away from the Sergeant and tore his right leg off just above the knee. Another shell fragment tore into Micklos' stomach and spilled out his intestines. BJ rushed to Micklos, tore the Sergeant's belt loose, using it for a tourniquet on the man's leg, and nestled the man's head in his lap while he took his last breaths. This was a horrible war.

The attacks, counter attacks, and repulsions continued all through the evening and night. At times, the fighting was hand-to-hand with fixed bayonets. BJ personally killed two German soldiers with his M1911 service pistol and wounded at least one more. During one of the early morning attacks,

BJ was hit immediately above his left shoulder blade by a German bullet, which left a nasty looking gouge and hurt like fire. As he looked at the dead and dying men in the trenches, he felt very lucky to just have a divot taken out of his shoulder.

The 369th held, and early on the morning of July 17, the Germans finally tucked tail and withdrew, dragging or carrying their wounded as they pulled out. BJ knew he had lost a lot of soldiers. He wouldn't know exactly how bad the losses were until the field reports got to him. Two hours later, the reports were in. The dead totaled 131 men, and 403 were wounded. About one-fourth of his original command was either dead or wounded. The 369th Infantry Regiment was nicknamed the Black Rattlers. They preferred Harlem Hellfighters. The 369th spent 191 days in front line trenches, more than any other American unit. They also suffered the most losses of any American regiment with 1,500 casualties.

****

On July 18 thru August 6, 1918, the French mounted the Aisne-Marne offensive. Five French armies: the 10th, 6th, 9th, 5th, and 4th had surrounded the Marne salient by the 18th of July. Spearheading the attack were the soldiers of the American 1st and 2nd Divisions, consisting of some 30,000 men. The two American divisions met little initial opposition. Then the Kraut resistance stiffened as the Germans reorganized. The American doughboys penetrated seven miles before they were relieved. They secured the town of Soissons and captured 6,500 German prisoners. The gains were made at the expense of 10,000 Americans killed or wounded. Colonel James Baxter had been given no instructions to mount a counter-offensive, so when the Germans started withdrawing, the 369th allowed them to retreat without needlessly killing more humans.

The contribution made by American troops in the Aisne-Marne Offensive gave General Pershing an opening to press for the formation of an independent American Army. Preliminary steps to organize the American First Army had been taken in early July 1918. Orders issued on July 24, 1918, announced formal organization of the First Army, effective August 10, 1918, and designated General Pershing as its commander. Its headquarters was located at La Ferte-sous-Jouarre, west of Chateau-Thierry. Fifteen months after the Unites States declared war; it had autonomy to lead its soldiers on the ground. By August 6, the Aisne-Marne Offensive was over.

****

After the conclusion of the Aisne-Marne Offensive, Colonel James Baxter was assigned to General Pershing's headquarters staff as Chief of Operations and Strategy. BJ served in this capacity at headquarters until late September 1918 when it became obvious that the war to end all wars was winding down. BJ went to General Pershing and asked for a short meeting.

Colonel Baxter started by saying, "Sir, it has been an honor to serve under your command. This war is on its last legs, and I would like to get back to the United States and to a cavalry assignment. I kinda have my eye on Fort Bliss and the Mexican uprising that is impacting the border areas."

General Pershing looked at James for a couple moments, smiled, and said, "BJ, you need to be careful of what you wish for. I led an expedition to capture Pancho Villa in 1916 – 1917 and didn't get it done. Stay with me, and you will be a Brigadier General within a year. If you go to Bliss you are going to be on a dead end street with no chance of catching anyone's eye, probably bound for failure, and will retire a colonel."

James looked at the general and replied, "General, I'm nothing but an old horse soldier. No offense, but I'm just not cut out for a desk, paperwork, and the politics required to be a general. I need to be in the field, leading men from the back of a horse. You have other officers who aspire to be generals." Pershing knew that BJ and Georgie Patton had butted heads a couple times, and there was no love lost between them. He suspected Baxter was referring to Patton without invoking his name.

General Pershing smiled, sighed, and replied, "BJ, you're a good officer and I won't stand in your way, if that is what you want. I feel compelled to reemphasize that this is a dead end assignment."

James looked at General Pershing and said, "General, I appreciate your candor and concern. I have been in this man's Army since 1892. I'm forty-eight years old. It was never my ambition to have a star on my shoulder and sit in an office. No offense, Sir."

The General said that he would have the transfer orders put into effect and notify the War Department of Colonel James Baxter's new duty assignment. James stood, saluted, and as he was exiting the general's office, General Pershing said, "If you happen to meet that bastard Villa, kick him in the butt for me." They both had a good chuckle, and James said, "Yes, Sir, if I have that opportunity, I will."

On October 1, 1918, Colonel James Baxter was assigned a berth on the Italian ship Duca D'Aosta which was carrying a full complement of wounded soldiers, nurses, and physicians to New York. When he arrived in New York harbor and got his feet back on dry land, he sent a telegram to Marie at the old ranch in Montana and another to his parents in Dallas. After letting them know he was back in the United States, he boarded a train bound for Montana.

After changing trains a couple of times, followed by a horseback ride, he arrived at the Emory ranch. Marie greeted him with open arms, tears, and relief. Being an Army wife wasn't much fun. James Budwell Baxter III was away in his second year at West Point, and Madison was in Helena attending school. Being a military man and missing a lot of your children's lives wasn't much fun either.

After spending a few days at the ranch, BJ and Marie boarded a train for Dallas to visit with Bud's parents. After visiting a few days, they went on to Muncie, Indiana, for temporary duty before Colonel James Budwell Baxter was to take command of the 2nd Cavalry Brigade. While in Dallas, BJ sat on the porch with his dad and talked about his military experiences. He shared what General Pershing had said about Fort Bliss being a career ending assignment.

Bud Sr. smiled and said, "Son, I was a lieutenant in the army that lost the Civil War. You and your brothers have accomplished far more rank and status than I ever achieved. If you are happy leading a cavalry brigade, then I think that is what you should do. Happiness is more important than prestige or rank."

BJ replied, "Thanks, Dad. I appreciate your advice and support. Do you get any feed-back on how III is doing at the Point?"

Bud Sr. said, "The last I heard, he was doing fine, a sophomore now and playing on the football team like his uncle Nathan. I expect he will do fine. He is my grandson you know." BJ looked at his Dad and said, "Some years ago, I sent you a letter asking whether you and Captain Brubaker hung cattle thieves on the drive from Texas to Montana. I don't recall ever getting a reply.

Bud Sr. looked out across the field in front of the house for a few moments and replied, "Yes, we did. I will tell you the entire story. Do you remember shooting the man at the chuck wagon? That was part of it." His Dad went on to tell him the entire story. After which, they finished their drinks and went into the house.

Chapter 26

While the Baxters were fighting "over there," Texas Ranger Fred Brubaker was trying to keep the peace in Texas. On a windy and cold Friday morning on January 25, 1918, Ranger Captain J. M. Fox called Fred into his office and asked him to sit down. After taking a sip of his morning coffee, Fox looked at Fred and said, "Brubaker, I'm sending you on a mission to find and arrest Abraham Rosenberg, aka the Jewish Jesse James. The best time to arrest Rosenberg is between an hour before sunset on a Friday and sunset on a Saturday. That is the Jewish Shabbat. Orthodox Jews aren't allowed to work or carry anything on their religious holiday. Brubaker, in case you are wondering, I went to the library and read up on Judaism so I could give you a few tips. That's why I'm a captain. I stay prepared." Abe Rosenberg was wanted for a string of robberies of stores, cafes, hotels, and anything else that had money. So far, he had never shot anyone, but that would be the next logical progression in his career as a bandit.

Fred wasn't really all that impressed with the assignment, but he humored Captain Fox and asked, "Why do you want me to get on the road over the weekend?"

Fox looked at Fred and said, "I don't know what that has to do with my orders or your mission, but since you seem to want to know troop business, the rest of the unit is going to Porvenir to check and see how many of the Mex living there were involved in the Brite Ranch raid."

****

On December 25, 1917, a group of Mexican guerillas crossed the border into Presidio County, Texas, and attacked the Brite Ranch. They murdered three people, robbed a general store, and rode back to Chihuahua, Mexico, with a motorized posse in hot pursuit. The Americans engaged in a running battle with the Mexicans all day on the 26th, resulting in the deaths of several of the Mexican raiders. The posse recovered some of the stolen money and goods, but some of the raiders managed to avoid arrest and disappeared into the countryside.

****

Fred read the report on the man he had been assigned to find and arrest. He discovered that Rosenberg's last robbery was the Hill General Store in Gainesville, Texas, on January 23, 1918. The bandit had made off with around $200.00 in cash and some food stores. Rosenberg had been positively identified as the bandit. He had worked on a local ranch, and virtually everyone in Gainesville knew him because of his peculiar attire and his refusal to do anything even resembling work between Friday evening and Saturday evening.

Fred got his rifle, shotgun, mount, and pack horse, loaded the panniers with provisions for a few days, and headed north towards Gainesville.

****

Gainesville, Texas, is a town with a past. A hideous crime against humanity was a part of its legacy. On a rainy morning on October 1, 1862, somewhere around seventy men were jerked from their beds, rounded up, ushered inside a vacant store, and charged on suspicion of treason. Two weeks later, the good citizens of Gainesville had rounded up an additional eighty men. A court consisting of prominent members of the town of Gainesville were appointed as a citizen's jury which found seven men guilty of treason. They took the convicted men out to a large tree and promptly hanged them.

Tensions mounted, and the town became concerned that the remaining prisoners were made up of bandits, John Brown loyalists, or had given aid to the Indians who raided nearby ranches. Within a week, forty more men were hanged and another two shot trying to escape. The Great Hanging in Gainesville is recorded as the greatest act of mob violence in United States history.

****

Fred wasn't in any great rush to get to Gainesville and spent the first night of his journey with a family on a small farm a few miles north of Plano. Jonas and Mary Snyder were delighted to have company. They made Fred feel welcome, fed him a nice meal, and fixed him a pallet near the fireplace. The floor was cold, and the night air came through the floorboards. But his ground cover blocked the draft and made it much more comfortable than trying to get some sleep under the sky.

Fred up was up early, had coffee, headed out again, and arrived in Gainesville during the afternoon. His first stop was at the office of the town marshal to see what, if anything, he had done in an effort to apprehend Rosenberg. Marshal Stan Witherson was short, rotund, balding, and lethargic. He had interviewed the owner of the Hill store but, beyond that hadn't really done anything of consequence to try to find or capture Rosenberg. No, Witherson didn't know where Rosenberg might be hiding. He wasn't aware of any known associates and had no idea if he was still in the local area. Fred thanked Witherson for all the help, walked across the street, got a room at the Barbwire hotel, stowed his gear in his room, went downstairs to the café, and had supper. After eating, he returned to his room and got some shuteye. Wherever Rosenberg was, he would keep til the next day.

****

On January 26, 1918, while Fred was enroute to Gainesville, Texas Rangers of Company B, led by Captain J. M. Fox, entered and searched the homes of villagers in Porvenir. The raid was prompted by the suspicion that the villagers had been involved in the Brite Ranch raid during December of 1917. Only two weapons were found. They consisted of a pistol, which belonged to an Anglo who was being entertained by a Mexican woman, and an old Winchester rifle which belonged to a Tejano villager. The weapons cache was confiscated, and three Tejanos were arrested and detained in the Ranger camp. The men were released the next day.

During the early morning hours of January 28, all the villagers were taken out of their hovels by the ten rangers, eight members of U.S. Cavalry, and four local ranchers. Fifteen men and boys, all ethnic Mexicans, were separated from the women, children, and the few Anglos in the village. The Texas Rangers and ranchers led the men and boys out of the village to a nearby hill and executed them all.

The bodies were left where they fell. The next day, the bodies were discovered by the villagers. The survivors of the village of Porvenir crossed the border to Pilares, Chihuahua. They later returned and buried their friends and family members. The cavalry soldiers burned the village to the ground in the days following the massacre.

The incident wasn't reported to the Texas Ranger hierarchy for almost a month. Captain Fox stated that the fifteen Mexicans ambushed the rangers and that stolen property from the Brite Ranch was found on the bodies of those killed.

None of the rangers were convicted, but the killings blighted the institution. Due to the event the Texas Rangers organization was downsized and the troop office in Dallas eventually closed.

****

Fred was just pulling his new boots on when someone began knocking on his door with urgency and said, "Ranger, ranger, the marshal wants you." Fred opened the door, and a boy of around twelve years of age was standing there. Fred told the boy to tell the marshal that he was on his way.

When Fred arrived, Marshal Witherson was talking to a man who appeared to be a farmer, judging by the way he was dressed. Witherson looked at the man and said, "Jed, tell the ranger what you just told me."

Jedidiah Maloney shook hands with Fred, introduced himself, and said, "This morning about 4 AM, when I went to the barn to milk Gennie and Elsie, a man led his horse out the back of the barn, mounted, and started north into the foothills. It was Abe Rosenberg. I'd know him anywhere. It's Sunday, so he can ride today. If you want to catch him, I would suggest you get on your way.

Rosenberg knows these hills like the back of his hand and has about a three hour head start on you now."

Fred thanked Mr. Maloney, got directions to his farm, retrieved his horses from the livery, and took off. Thirty minutes later, Fred was at the farm and picked up Rosenberg's trail with little difficulty. Fred followed the tracks and, within a few miles, entered an area of rolling hills, arroyos, and small copses of trees. There were lots of hiding places. So far, this was way too easy. The numerous places that provided potential to hide and drygulch someone gave Fred a degree of concern.

Fred had followed the tracks for more than two hours when his horse stumbled, and he immediately heard the report of a rifle shot. The horse went to its front knees, and rolled to its side. He released the lead on the pack horse, got his left boot out of the stirrup, and rolled off the horse as it fell. He pulled his rifle out of its scabbard, took cover behind the dying animal, and watched the pack horse disappear over a ridge. One hundred fifty yards away, a man came out from behind a large boulder riding a gray horse. Fred quickly aimed and snapped off a shot. The man's horse fell, and the rider ran for cover. Now both men were afoot and were a long walk from any town.

Fred crawled out from behind the now dead horse, ran to some boulders large enough to use for cover, and started inching his way towards the large boulder Rosenberg was hiding behind. When Fred got to with fifty yards, he hollered, "Rosenberg, you would do well to give it up before one of us gets killed. I won't quit until I have manacles on you, or see you dead. It's your choice."

A voice hollered back, "Lawman, you will have to come and get me. I have no plans to give up." Fred and Rosenberg were at a stand-off. Rosenberg couldn't get away without exposing himself, and Fred couldn't close the open space between them without exposing himself. To make matters worse, for both men, there was to be a full moon and no cloud cover. Both men's canteens were still on their horses. Fred saw Rosenberg's canteen exposed on the near side of the dead horse, took careful aim, squeezed the trigger, and saw the water container explode. Score a point for the ranger!

Rosenberg screamed, "You, son of a bitch. You must be a Christian. Now you have forced me to kill you. I can't outwait you without water. Don't go to sleep!"

Fred knew he was in a precarious position. There was no doubt that without water to sustain him Rosenberg would now be infuriated and desperate. The outlaw would be fine tonight, but tomorrow, the lack of water would start to take a toll. Even though it was cold, dehydration would make a man weak and unable to think properly or defend himself.

Fred decided to be proactive. When darkness set in, he crawled on his belly to his dead horse, removed the saddle bags, canteen, and bedroll, and crawled back to the rock. Now with water, some jerked beef, and a warm blanket, he would be able to wait out the outlaw. He decided to wait a couple hours and retreat back a hundred yards or so under the cover of darkness, find a hiding place, and plot a strategy for the following day. After crawling a few dozen yards, Fred walked at a quick pace until he came to a slight rise with some heavy brush. He crawled into the brush on all fours, wrapped himself in the blanket, and settled in for the night.

All during the night, Fred would doze off and awake with a start. He would look around, listen for a few minutes, hear nothing, and doze off again. When he awoke the last time right after daybreak, he looked toward the area that Rosenberg had been hiding and saw the man walking north. He was only a speck, but he could see him nonetheless. Fred took a sip of water, bit off a piece of jerked beef, and started after his quarry.

Fred stayed well behind Rosenberg, always out of rifle range, and just kept pace with the man as they both headed north. Fred's only concern was that they would come upon a ranch or homestead and then other people would be endangered. Fortunately, they didn't. During mid-afternoon, Rosenberg began to slow his pace somewhat. Fred closed the gap slightly but kept a safe distance between them. At nightfall, both men hunkered down and slept fitfully.

Both men began walking again at daybreak. Around noon, Rosenberg got to Hickory Creek, drank his fill, and headed towards the Arbuckle Mountains. Fred drank til he was full of water, filled his canteen, soaked his boots and aching feet, and continued after Rosenberg. Neither man realized it, but they were only about three miles from Ardmore, Oklahoma Territory, when they stopped at the creek. Rosenberg just kept walking, and Fred just kept following. They had walked nearly forty miles and Fred's feet were killing him. New riding boots just weren't intended for long walks. He decided that this adventure had to end!

Both Rosenberg and Fred stopped at dark to wrap themselves in their mackinaws and blankets to try to stay warm. Shortly after dark, Fred saw the glow from Rosenberg's camp fire and decided to skirt the outlaw's camp to the right and come out ahead in the direction Rosenberg had been walking. His plan was contingent upon the element of surprise. The fact that he would be ahead of Rosenberg had to be unsuspected in order to take the bandit by surprise. Everything went like clockwork until Fred got to within sight of the campfire. Rosenberg wasn't there! Fred's first thought when he realized he had been outfoxed was, *"Oh shite, what do I do now?"*

Chapter 27

Fred lay down and stayed perfectly still. He had no idea where Rosenberg was hiding. He didn't know if Rosenberg had walked on towards the mountains or was lying in ambush, waiting for Fred to show himself. As the sun was just starting to peek over the tree line to the west, Fred saw subtle movement from behind a cluster of Barberry bushes perhaps thirty yards from his location. Fred was miserable, cold, had blisters on his feet, and was bone tired. When Rosenberg exposed himself, Fred shot him. Fortunately for Rosenberg, and unfortunately for Fred, the bullet went through the man's shoulder, exited, and produced a lot of bleeding but not a fatal injury. Fred got up, walked towards Rosenberg, and said, "Don't even think about trying me. I will kill you if you even twitch." Rosenberg lay on the ground holding his wounded shoulder. When Fred got to Rosenberg, he took the man's pistol out of its holster and threw it and his rifle well out of reach. He then examined the wound and said, "You'll live." With that bit of encouragement, he placed manacles on the bandit. Fred then held pressure on the exit side of the wound until the bleeding subsided. He bound the outlaw's shoulder with cloth that he'd cut off the man's blanket. What to do now seemed to be the reoccurring question.

Fred had no idea where he might find a farm, town, or help. He did know that there was no help to be found on the route they had taken to get to their present location. It seemed impossible that they could have walked so far and never encountered another human. Fred was in the horns of a dilemma. He had no idea where he was or how far a town might be located if they kept on their current direction. On the other hand, he knew that there were no towns the way they had come. Fred looked at Rosenberg. He was sickly-looking. Fred was wondering if Rosenberg could walk much farther considering the blood he had lost. One thing was for certain, they had to do something. Staying where they were and waiting for help to ride by didn't seem a sensible option. Fred looked at Rosenberg and said, "You able to travel or do I need to find a tree, cuff you to it, and come back and get you when the weather gets better, maybe next May?"

Rosenberg smiled at Fred and replied, "You're about as compassionate as Rabbi Swartz. Are you a Jewish Christian by any chance?" Fred assured Rosenberg that he wasn't Jewish, and some would say he wasn't Christian. As near as he could figure, he was a Methodist, although he rarely attended church. With the religious discussion concluded, Fred repeated the question. Rosenberg assured him that he would be able to keep up. Fred figured with his blistered and bleeding feet, that probably wouldn't be very difficult.

Fred set out south by southwest in the hopes of coming upon someone who would help them. He had Rosenberg walk slightly ahead of him in order to keep watch and discourage any attempt to escape. They were a couple of motley looking specimens as they limped along. Fred shared a sip of water with Rosenberg from time to time. After what seemed to be days but was in fact, just a few hours, they crested a slight rise and saw a small homestead in a valley below them. The place was bare-bones at best. It consisted of a small cabin, tack shed, and corral. There were a couple horses in the corral, but they didn't appear to be saddle stock. The place looked well kept.

When the two men walked, actually stumbled, down the hill, they were met by a large bearded man who introduced himself as Jacob Tuttle. Fred introduced himself to Tuttle and advised the farmer that he was a Texas Ranger. He went on to inform Tuttle that Abraham Rosenberg, the man in manacles, was his prisoner. Tuttle studied both men a few moments and said, "Come into the house. It looks like both of you are about done in."

Fred said that they would sit on the porch for a while and try to catch their breath. A dipper of water would be nice though. Rosenberg lay back on the porch. Fred just sat on the edge and let his feet dangle over the side. After resting for a few minutes, drinking a few dippers of cool water, Fred stood up next to the porch, shook Rosenberg, and said, "Let's go inside."

Once inside the rustic cabin, Fred was introduced to Mary Tuttle who invited him and Rosenberg to sit down. Mrs. Tuttle looked at the wound on Rosenberg's shoulder and asked if she could examine the wound and change the dressing. Fred had no objections. Rosenberg certainly made no protest. Mrs. Tuttle looked at Fred and said, "I can't help but notice that you are walking mighty gingerly. Why not take off your boots and I'll take a look at your feet when I get finished with Mr. Rosenberg." Mrs. Tuttle cleaned Rosenberg's wound, put some horse salve on the entry and exit sites, and bound his shoulder with a clean cloth.

Fred allowed Mr. Tuttle to pull on his boots to help get them off and said, "I'm afraid I picked a poor time to break in a new pair of boots. I didn't figure on having to walk half-way across Texas to capture Mr. Rosenberg." Even Rosenberg laughed at his comment. After Mrs. Tuttle finished with Rosenberg's wounds, she turned her attention to Fred's feet. When she saw the condition of his blistered feet, she gasped. She couldn't begin to comprehend how the lawman could even be walking. His feet were a mass of blisters and several were bleeding.

She walked over to a small cabinet, took out a jar of Turpentine, and walked back to Fred. She looked at the lawman for a couple moments and said, "I'm afraid this is going to hurt, but it's necessary to get you some relief." With that, Mrs. Tuttle poured a generous amount of the liquid on a rag and began dabbing Fred's blisters. The woman was certainly right. It hurt like fire. After allowing Fred's feet to air off for a few minutes, Mrs. Tuttle applied some horse salve on the blisters but didn't bind his feet. Mrs. Tuttle said that it would be best to allow air to get to the blisters. It would speed the healing process. Mrs. Tuttle took Fred's boots and placed them by the fireplace.

Fred and Rosenberg stayed with the Tuttles for three days. On the second day, Mrs. Tuttle took a sharp knife and removed the dead skin from all Fred's blisters. She then put some pickle brine on the blisters. She set a jar of pickle brine on the table and told Fred to pat some on his feet every few minutes. It hurt, but seemed to toughen the skin somewhat. On the morning of the third day Fred was preparing to leave to go to Ardmore, Oklahoma, to secure mounts. Mrs. Tuttle came over with the can of horse salve and told Fred to put a dab on the blistered areas before pulling on his boots. Fred borrowed one of Mr. Tuttle's horses to make the trip to Ardmore. The horse was a nag plow horse but better than the alternative - walking. After securing Rosenberg to a horse ring in the barn, he rode off to Ardmore, Oklahoma. After arriving in Ardmore, Fred went to the marshal's office. Fred told him that he had a prisoner on a farm outside of town and needed to contact his ranger office in Dallas. Marshall Jeff Jones made arrangements with the livery for two horses. As Fred was preparing to leave, the marshal told him that the train to Dallas would leave the following morning at 9AM. Neither man mentioned jurisdiction issues.

Fred got back to the farm, unsaddled all three horses, and put them in the corral. He then went into the barn, undid Rosenberg's right hand manacle, freed it from the ring, and reapplied it to the man's wrist. He then led the prisoner to the cabin and relaxed with a cup of hot coffee. The swelling and pain of his feet had subsided. He took off his boots and stood them by the fireplace and relaxed in his sock feet. He wasn't up to another cross-country hike, but his feet had stopped hurting.

The following morning, Fred was up at daylight, got the two livery horses saddled, helped Rosenberg onto one, mounted the other, thanked the Tuttles, and headed to Ardmore. Once at the town, Fred rode to the livery and turned in both horses. He walked with Rosenberg to the marshal's office, thanked Marshal Jones, and took his prisoner to the train depot. Fred got Rosenberg situated in the train Pullman car and attached one ring of the manacles to the outlaw's arm rest. Nothing eventful happened during the train ride.

The tracking and apprehension of Rosenberg had been an expensive ordeal. Fred had lost two horses, his panniers, provisions and utensils, and most importantly, the Winchester Model 97 shotgun his mother had given him as a present.

Once in Dallas, Fred deposited Rosenberg in the Dallas County jail. When he went to the Ranger office, only then did he learn of the event at Porvenir. Even though he wasn't present, Fred was linked by association to the massacre. Later in 1918, the Dallas ranger office was closed. The Texas Rangers organization had been decimated by the fall-out from the killing of the unarmed Mexicans. The hierarchy of the rangers was aware that Fred wasn't a participant in the massacre. Fred was reassigned to the Laredo, Texas, office and moved his family there. If Fred knew what the Baxter brothers were going through, he would have rejoiced in his circumstances.

Chapter 28

When BJ returned from France, he was placed on temporary duty with the Student Army Training Corps at Ball State University in Muncie, Indiana. General Pershing had told BJ that the 2nd Cavalry Brigade would soon be reactivated at Fort Bliss, Texas. Ball State was to be just a temporary duty assignment, pending the unit being restructured and activated. The Student Training Corps needed a full bird colonel about as bad as a nun needed a riding habit. BJ felt like a fancy saddle on a plow horse. There was nothing for him to do but stay out of the way and wait. True to his word, General Pershing's promise materialized. The 2nd Cavalry Brigade was reactived on August 31, 1920, at Fort Bliss.

Colonel James Budwell Baxter, Jr., arrived at Fort Bliss on August 27, 1920, to command the 2nd Cavalry Brigade which comprised the 5th and legendary 7th Cavalries. After getting his family settled into their quarters, he took care of his next priority. BJ stopped a trooper and got directions to the brigade chaplain's office. He walked over to the chaplain's office and made contact with Lieutenant Colonel William Huzzah Baxter. BJ offered his condolences concerning the loss of Bill's wife and child, and visited for a couple hours. After their visit, BJ started making the rounds. He found that good order and discipline within the newly activated unit were in short supply. When he entered the recently opened brigade headquarters administrative office, there were three men working. One was sitting at a desk writing. One was posting something on a bulletin board, and one was sweeping the floor. None of the soldiers stopped what they were doing and came to attention when Colonel Baxter entered the office.

Colonel Baxter walked over to the desk where a corporal was sitting writing on a pad. The man remained sitting, looked up, and said, "What can I do for you, Colonel?"

BJ replied, "Private, you can start by telling me where the Sergeant Major might be found."

The soldier smirked and said, "It's Corporal, Colonel."

BJ responded, "No, it was corporal two minutes ago. Now it's private. Would you like to try for a stay in the stockade?" With that, the soldier jumped out of his chair, came to attention, and hollered, "Room, attention."

BJ went on to remind the soldier he needed to know where to find the Sergeant Major. The soldier told him that Sergeant Blevins was at the horse training facility. BJ said, "Thank you, Private, as you were."

After BJ had walked out the door, the soldier sweeping the floor said, "I don't think that colonel was very impressed with us. I'm glad he didn't ask me anything."

When BJ arrived at the equestrian training facility, he saw a man, whose blouse was hanging on the fence, whipping a Morgan horse. BJ hollered to the man. "What are you doing, Soldier?"

Without turning around, the man replied, "What the hell do you think I'm doing? I'm trying to teach this dumb Morgan some manners. What's it to you?" He then turned around, blanched white, and came to attention.

BJ said, "Put away that whip. Put on your blouse, and follow me." With that, BJ turned and started back towards the headquarters building with the sergeant at his heels, trying to get himself properly militarily attired.

When they got to the headquarters building, the men in the office snapped to attention, and BJ walked into his office without saying a word. Sergeant Blevins was hot on his heels. BJ walked around his desk and sat down. Sergeant Blevins started to pull up a chair to sit down when Colonel Baxter said, "You won't need that chair, Sergeant. Stand at attention. This is going to be a listening session, not a chat about the weather."

BJ told Sergeant Blevins that cavalrymen at his post would not mistreat a horse. The next thing on the agenda was telling the sergeant there was a new sheriff in town, and his name was Colonel James Budwell Baxter, Jr. Pausing for a moment, BJ called out, "Private, come in here, please."

The young soldier who still had corporal chevrons on his sleeve came at the run, slid to a stop, and said, "Yes, Sir." BJ told him to find the officers who had been assigned to the 2nd Cavalry Brigade, round them up, and have them assembled in the headquarters building in exactly one-half hour.

While waiting for his staff officers, BJ continued chewing on the sergeant. When he finished, the Sergeant Major had very sore buttocks, but a very clear picture of how military life would be at Fort Bliss from that day forward. BJ finished by saying, "Sergeant, it appears you know little about horses. I think we need to find you another job. You're dismissed." The sergeant saluted, did an about face, and walked out of the office.

BJ had another few minutes to wait for his staff officers, so he had the clerk connect him with the Commandant of the Cavalry School at Fort Riley, Kansas. In a few minutes, the private knocked on BJ's office door and said that there was a Colonel Baxter on the phone. BJ picked up the handset and said, "Nathan, are you there, little brother?"

The reply was, "Yep, what can I do for you today, big brother?" After chewing the fat for a few minutes, BJ got down to business.

"Nat, I need two favors from you. If you have one, I need a fine specimen of horseflesh in the form of a Black Brandenburger for my personal mount here at the 2nd. The second thing I need is for you to find that Sergeant Major named Cheyhill you told me about. I need a mean-mouthed NCO here to help me get, and then keep, this brigade in order." Nat said he had five Brandenburgers and would have the best of the lot sent to Fort Bliss by railcar. As to Sergeant Major Cheyhill, he would see what he could do to find him, relay BJ's request to the powers that be, and get back to him.

At 11AM, two first lieutenants, one captain, and Lieutenant Colonel William Baxter were standing in the administrative office that had been assigned to the brigade. BJ went to his office door, opened it, and said, "Come in, gentlemen. Please introduce yourselves. You don't have to do that, Colonel Baxter. I seem to remember you from someplace."

The captain was named Max Dennard, and the lieutenants were Kenneth C. Brekker and Mark Battles. The introductions completed, BJ asked the men to sit down and began to explain his requirements for success in providing leadership in his brigade. The rules were very simple. He expected his officers to dress appropriately, act appropriately, and lead by example. He went on to say that the 2nd would be receiving a large number of mounts and soldiers within the next few weeks. It was to be their job to coordinate the off-loading of troopers and mounts from the train, keep things moving smoothly, and make sure confusion was held to a minimum. He expected to see his officers and troopers in full uniform, blouses buttoned, hats on, and boots shined at all times. There were to be no exceptions. He turned to the captain and said,

"Captain Dennard, you are my acting executive officer. The first thing I need for you to do is generate the paperwork to reduce Corporal Fields in grade from corporal to private. Next, I want the troopers and their mounts assembled on the parade ground at 6 AM tomorrow morning and ready for inspection."

BJ turned to Lieutenant Colonel Baxter smiled, and said, "It will be your function to pray for me, my officers, and men, and to provide them with spiritual guidance." BJ finished by asking if there were any questions, and of course, there weren't any.

At 4 PM, the phone rang. Colonel Nathan Baxter was on the phone desiring to speak to Colonel James Baxter. When BJ got on the phone, Nat told him that Sergeant Major Cheyhill was with the U.S. Army Artillery School at Fort Sill, Oklahoma, and would probably eat a basket of horse apples to get back in a cavalry outfit. BJ made a couple phone calls, and one week later, Sergeant Major Seth Cheyhill reported for duty at the 2nd Cavalry Brigade headquarters. Sergeant Blevins was immediately assigned to the newly formed motor pool. BJ met with Cheyhill for thirty minutes and went over his expectations, and the sergeant major said, "Sounds reasonable to me, Colonel. Let's get a cavalry outfit assembled and ready for action."

At 6 PM on the same day, a young private named Jonas Breckridge hitched two

Brandenburgers, a stallion and a gelding, to the hitching post in front of brigade headquarters. After securing the horses, he walked inside and asked to see Colonel James Baxter. Privates don't normally seek an audience with a colonel. BJ overhead the private and got up to see what was up. When BJ came out of his office, Breckridge popped to attention and said, "A gift for the colonel at the hitching post outside, Sir, with Colonel Nathan Baxter's compliments, Sir." BJ walked outside and saw the two most beautiful horses he had ever seen in his life. BJ turned to Private Maynard Fields and said, "Private, take Private Breckridge and these mounts to the equestrian center, please. Have the stallion saddled and bring him back. I think I'll take a ride."

In a few minutes, Private Fields returned to his desk. Thirty minutes later, Private Breckridge was standing at attention in front of BJ's office door. BJ told the private to stand at ease. Private Breckridge said, "Begging the colonel's pardon, but Colonel Baxter suggested I ask you if I could stay on here at Fort Bliss. I would be honored to personally attend to the Brandenburgers and any other duties the colonel might desire."

BJ looked at the young private and said, "The horses look fine, and the fact that you got them here without a scratch was no small feat. I will call and make the arrangements." Private Breckridge wanted to hug the colonel but restrained himself and merely said, "Thank you, Colonel. I will give your personal mounts the best of care and do whatever else I am told to do."

BJ got to know the black stallion for a few minutes, mounted the animal, walked the horse around for a couple minutes, and then cantered the mount out the main gate. BJ rode for almost an hour, trotting the horse, galloping, holding him to a canter, stopping, and seeing if he would stand still. He was impressed. His little brother had sent him a wonderful animal. BJ decided to call the horse Sergeant Sonny. A private wasn't a suitable rank for the brigade commander's personal mount. The next morning, when he walked into the headquarters building, Private Fields handed him a steaming cup of black coffee and said, "Good morning, Colonel. Shall I have the gelding brought over so you can evaluate him, Sir?"

BJ was surprised at the transformation in the private and said, "Yes, please have him saddled and brought around." BJ was equally impressed with the gelding and called him Sergeant Jack in honor of General Pershing.

By September 20, 1920, about ninety percent of the mounts and troopers were in place at Fort Bliss. When fully staffed, Colonel Baxter would have 2,000 cavalry troopers, with around 3,000 mounts, a staff consisting of ten captains, one major who served as executive officer, and forty 2nd and 1st lieutenants under his command. When the full complement of newly assigned officers had reported in, BJ ordered an officer's call at the training center. After a few opening comments, BJ introduced Sergeant Major Seth Cheyhill and said, "Sergeant Major Cheyhill is my voice. He answers to me, and only to me. Is that understood?" There was a booming "Yes, Sir," from the assembled officers. BJ then told Private Fields to step forward and said, "This trooper is Corporal Fields, my chief clerk. Coordinate through him if you need to see me." Fields was grinning like a Cheshire cat. BJ contained his urge to grin. He told the assembled officers they had two days to get all the troopers assigned to platoons, billeted, outfitted, and ready for their first inspection with their mounts. Colonel Baxter told the officers that 6 AM Thursday would be a fine time for the inspection. They would then have five more days to get their troops ready for deployment into the field for duty, securing the Mexican border.

By the time the 2nd Brigade was put into service, Pancho Villa and the other Mexican revolutionaries were, for the most part, living peacefully on haciendas or were dead. Pancho Villa lived on a government supplied hacienda at Hidalgo del Parral, Chihuahua, surrounded by his staff of bodyguards. However, Mexican bandits and rustlers were crossing the Rio Grande and raiding Texas ranches most every night. BJ ordered night patrols, with two platoons of cavalry to patrol the area between El Paso and the Mexican border and the areas immediately north and south of the town. The other platoons were to monitor activities up and down the border. Their job was to intercept bandits and rustlers, turn them back to Mexico, or engage them with prejudice.

BJ's troopers did their job so well that Mexican incursions into the area around El Paso were reduced by around twenty-five percent within the first ninety days that the 2nd was in operation. BJ was pleased with the effectiveness of his unit, but he wanted the cattle rustling, robberies, and killings to stop. He stepped up the pressure!

Chapter 29

The next officers' call was a twofold meeting. BJ began by commending his staff for their hard work and success in reducing the Mexican problem along the border. Then BJ said, "Sergeant Cheyhill and I agree that we are capable of much more than what we are accomplishing. You are a fine group of officers, but we are tasked with stopping the Mexican incursions into Texas. We are going to step up our patrols and range further from the fort. I want those patrols that go south along the border to be provisioned and stay in the field for five days."

On October 3, 1920, Sergeant Major Cheyhill walked into the stables. A six man patrol led by Second Lieutenant Marcus DuPont had recently returned from patrolling an area west of El Paso. Six troopers and Private Breckridge were wiping down mounts and getting ready to curry them. Sergeant Cheyhill walked up to Private Breckridge and asked, "Is this your horse, Trooper?"

Breckridge replied, "No, Sergeant Major, it's not my mount."

Sergeant Cheyhill looked at Breckridge for a few moments and said, "Well, Private, don't keep me in suspense. Who rode this mount in from the patrol?"

Breckridge swallowed hard and replied, "That would be Lieutenant DuPont, sergeant major."

Sergeant Cheyhill already knew who had ridden the mount on the patrol. He just wanted confirmation. He asked, "Did Lieutenant DuPont order you to attend to his mount?" Breckridge told Sergeant Cheyhill that the lieutenant hadn't ordered him exactly, just told him to take care of his mount.

Sergeant Cheyhill headed for the mess hall and found Lieutenant DuPont sitting with two other young officers drinking coffee. Sergeant Cheyhill walked up to the table and said, "A word, if you please, Lieutenant DuPont." Reluctantly, DuPont got out of his chair and walked with Sergeant Cheyhill out of earshot of the other officers and said, "What is it, Sergeant Major?"

Sergeant Cheyhill looked at the lieutenant and said, "Your mount needs your attention, Lieutenant."

Lieutenant DuPont replied, "One of the stable boys is taking care of him, Sergeant Major." With that, he turned to walk back into the mess facility.

Sergeant Major Cheyhill was now pissed and said loud enough to wake the dead, "Lieutenant, I'm not finished."

DuPont turned to Sergeant Cheyhill and said, "Do you know who you're talking to?"

Sergeant Cheyhill glared at Lieutenant DuPont, took two steps forward to where their noses almost touched, and said, "Yes, I know who you are. You are a shave tail lieutenant who just got out of the Point. You're also a spoiled brat from a rich family back east who wants to play soldier. Now hear this! I'm gonna tell you this only once, so give me your undivided attention. You're a member of the 2nd. I'm responsible to Colonel Baxter, and I will make sure that every man in the 2nd can and does pull his own weight."

Lieutenant DuPont smirked and said, "Are we finished, Sergeant Major?"

Sergeant Cheyhill was so angry he could chew nails and responded "I'll let you know when I'm finished, Lieutenant. You need to get your butt to the stables and attend to your mount. You will never, as long as you are in this unit, leave your mount to the care of another trooper. It's your mount, your responsibility. I'm hoping this will act as a wake-up call for you. If Colonel Baxter gets wind of your negligence, you, your captain, and his major will all need salve for your arses, and you will be on your way back to the DuPont mansion to explain to your highfalutin family why you couldn't cut it. Do I make myself clear, Lieutenant?" Lieutenant DuPont finally understood the gravity of Sergeant Cheyhill's remarks and said, "Yes, Sir." He then did an about face and scurried off towards the stables.

The next day, Sergeant Major Cheyhill was in the brigade headquarters building when Colonel Baxter walked by him and said, "Honing up your baby sitting skills on my lieutenants, Sergeant Major!" BJ laughed and kept on walking.

On January 17, 1921, a platoon of cavalry was on patrol ten miles south of El Paso when they were attacked by a Mexican raiding party of twenty or more bandits. Lieutenant James Fremont was taken prisoner, one trooper was killed, and two were wounded. BJ was notified by Corporal Fields at his quarters at 2:30 AM. He got dressed, went straight to brigade headquarters where Sergeant Cheyhill and Major Ragsdale were awaiting his arrival. BJ said, "Give me the details, Major." Major Ragsdale proceeded to fill BJ in on the details of the attack. He stated that he was about to call the war department and report the detention of Lieutenant Fremont so diplomatic efforts could get started to secure his release.

BJ said, "No, Major, delay any such call. Sergeant Major, get attired in civilian clothes, eat some breakfast, and meet me here with Sergeant Sonny, a pack horse with provisions for a week in the field, and your mount at 6 AM. We want nothing which would identify us as American military. We're going for a ride."

Major Ragsdale spoke up and said, "Begging the colonel's pardon, but can I speak to the colonel in private?" They proceeded into BJ's office, closed the door, and Major Ragsdale said, "With respect, Sir, I think this foray would be ill-advised. It's bad enough that Lieutenant Fremont is held prisoner. It would cause an international incident if a brigade commander was captured. If you enter Mexico without permission, it could get you in trouble, Sir."

BJ thanked Major Ragsdale for his counsel and concern, smiled, and said, "I fail to see where Sergeant Cheyhill and I taking a couple days' vacation in Mexico would cause an international incident." He winked at Ragsdale and walked out of the headquarters building. Two days later, BJ and Cheyhill arrived at the Villa hacienda at Hidalgo del Parral at mid-morning. BJ and Cheyhill dismounted and were escorted into the hacienda where BJ asked to see Pancho Villa. In a few minutes, a large Mexican man appeared and took BJ and Cheyhill's weapons, led them to a large room, and asked them to wait. In just a couple minutes, Pancho Villa walked into the room followed by two body guards. Villa looked at BJ and said, "You're American Army, no?"

BJ said, "Yes, I am American Army from Fort Bliss. One of my officers was taken by a Mexican raiding party. I doubt you were involved. But I know you know, or can find out, who took my officer and where he's detained."

Villa looked at BJ and replied, "And if I don't help you, Senor Gringo soldier?"

BJ looked at Villa for a couple moments and said, "General Jack Pershing asked me to kick you in the butt for him if I had the opportunity. Georgie Patton killed your lieutenant back in 1916. It can get much worse than that. If I don't get my man back post haste, you are going to find your peaceful retirement interrupted by being in the middle of a shite storm."

Pancho Villa looked at BJ, burst out laughing, and said, "I doubt you could bother me, but I like a man with balls. Start back to the border. Your man will join you along the route." BJ thanked Pancho Villa and bid him good day. He and Cheyhill were given their weapons, walked out of the building, mounted their horses, and rode off toward the border. As BJ and Cheyhill were riding through the village of Ejido El Vergel, Lieutenant Fremont came riding out from between some adobe buildings, saluted, and said, "Good afternoon, Colonel. Hi, Sergeant Major. Good of you both to come to Mexico and check on me." BJ and Cheyhill just looked at each other, shook their heads, and chuckled. This was one tough kid.

BJ commanded the 2nd Cavalry Brigade until his retirement on July 31, 1922, when he had completed thirty years of military service. General Pershing was correct. The assignment to the 2nd was a career ending move, but BJ had the best of all worlds. He got what he wanted and wanted what he got.

There were minor border skirmishes and several Mexican bandits captured or killed. Thanks to Colonel Baxter's leadership, the 2nd was credited with establishing good order on the border. When BJ retired, border incursions were largely stopped and robberies and murders rare. BJ sent a memo to

General Pershing and thanked him again for allowing him to live his dream of commanding a large cavalry unit. He never received a reply!

Chapter 30

Following his retirement on July 31, 1922, Colonel James Budwell Baxter, Jr., took up residence at the Baxter Ranch outside of Dallas, Texas. Colonel Nathan Forrest Baxter retired on June 30, 1924, and also moved into the sprawling ranch house on the Baxter Ranch. Nat and BJ had been talking back and forth on the phone for more than a year regarding breeding Brandenburger horses for sale to the cavalry, pleasure riders, or for pulling carriages, and for people like Nat and BJ who just loved the breed. James Baxter, Sr., had left the Baxter siblings well provided for. Mattie Lea and William received two-thirds of the cash assets, and James Jr. and Nathan the other one-third and the small ranch. The polled Hereford cattle had long since been disposed of in a sale. The three Baxter children had used the four bedroom ranch house with two separate living quarters as a vacation home since their parents had died. BJ Sr. died in 1913 and their mother in 1917. BJ found the house and outbuildings in fine condition when he returned to the ranch.

Lieutenant Colonel William Huzzah Baxter also retired from the U.S. Army on June 30, 1924, after twenty-five years of service to his country. Bill was one of the very few military chaplains who were wounded in two different wars. Bill also returned to Dallas and was asked to serve as the interim pastor of Cochran Chapel United Methodist Church. He accepted the position and filled it for a little more than three years. Bill stayed in a small guest house on the ranch.

Fred Brubaker had been with the Texas Rangers for thirty years and was fifty-one years old. Fred was slowing down some but wasn't ready to retire. He had been promoted to lieutenant but had never progressed further in rank with the Texas Rangers. He had let it be known that he had little interest in riding a desk and preferred to be in the field. He was transferred from the Laredo office back to the ranger office in Dallas when it reopened. He had lived on the Brubaker ranch since his parents' death.

BJ had made arrangements to purchase Sergeant Sonny from the Department of the Army. He transported the beautiful Brandenburger stallion via railcar to Dallas and then saddled and rode him to the ranch. He had purchased Sergeant Sonny to use at stud on the ranch to start a breeding program. He had found a Brandenburger mare on a horse farm outside Austin, went and inspected the animal, purchased her, and led her back to the ranch in Dallas County. The mare was named Black Rose. BJ bred Sergeant Sonny to Black Rose on May 1, 1923. She delivered a beautiful male foal on the 2nd of April 1924. The Baxter ranch breeding program had started.

When Nathan showed up at the ranch in July, he brought two Brandenburger mares he had purchased from the Army. Prissy and Missy were the names of the two mares. Sergeant Sonny did his job in early August, and both mares were with foal during the winter. Building a horse farm from the ground up was a slow process. Ideally, mares shouldn't be bred until they are three years of age to foal when they are four. By July 1925, the Baxter brothers had three colts on the ground and needed to purchase more mares if they were going to have anything more than a hobby operation. With their military retirements, the money their father had left, and the fees for providing Sonny to stud, they were able to live comfortably and avoid using their savings. It wasn't so much the quest for money but their love for the horse that motivated their desire to breed the animals.

In early 1926, BJ and Nathan decided to go to the source of the best Brandenburger horses in the world. The Brandenburg State Stud at Neustadt (Dosse), Germany. The Neustadt Brandenburger studs were known the world over as the premier bloodline of the breed for more than 125 years. After conversing back and forth by cablegram, the Baxters were able to strike a deal for a Brandenburger stud and dam. A date was set for the purchase. Cargo space was reserved on the Ramsden steamship from Germany to the United States for both horses and their human companion. BJ and Nathan flipped a coin to see who would go and pick up the horses. Nathan won. The ocean crossing to Germany took four days. Nathan picked up the horses, got them loaded on the ship, and spent most of his time eating, exercising the two horses, and looking for a latrine. On the second day of the return voyage, he ate something in the ship's dining room that disagreed with him. He often had to find a latrine facility in a hurry.

As miserable as the Atlantic crossing was for Nathan, the horses weathered the crossing in fine shape. Next on the agenda was getting the two prize horses on a livestock car from New York City to Dallas, Texas. Nathan spent the bulk of his time on the train with the two horses. He kept them calm, watered, and as stable as possible considering the pitching and rocking of the train. On May 15, 1926, the Baxter brothers had two of the finest Brandenburger specimens in the world to bolster their stock. The two horses cost $1,500.00, plus the cost of steamship and railroad transportation. It was a very high price for two horses in 1926.

****

On October 24 through 29, 1929, the New York stock exchange collapsed. Stocks that had made men wealthy were suddenly just worthless paper. Men who were rich in September 1929 were financially ruined the following month and were jumping out of New York windows to their death. The Baxter brothers were fortunate. All three had their military retirements. Their money was in the form of greenbacks for the most part since they had liquidated their bank accounts immediately after the stock market crash. In all, 744 banks failed during the first ten months of 1930.

BJ and Nathan had heard their father talk about times when they couldn't sell their cattle for any price. They had been forced to just wait it out until conditions changed. Nat and BJ found themselves in the same circumstance. They kept at the breeding program and continued to train horses. They were lucky. They had enough money to weather the storm. Many Americans didn't.

****

BJ's daughter, Madison Kay, had married Jay McElroy, an attorney, and the son of a prominent Dallas banker. They had two children, Bud and Marie. Marie was a pretty little girl, and BJ loved her, but Bud was the apple of grandpa's eye. Nathan's daughter, Kelli Ann, had married a Dallas physician named Cliff Hagan and had two daughters, Mary and Francis. On June 20, 1930, Madison and Kelli Ann had taken the children to White Rock Creek, a tributary of Elm Fork Trinity River, for a picnic and to allow the children to play in the water. The children had a great time. Madison and Kelli were putting the blankets, towels, and food baskets back in the surrey, when two men with bandanas over their faces rode up on chestnut colored horses. One man had grabbed Bud from the river bank and slung the little boy up in front of him. The other man handed Madison an envelope. Both men rode away at a gallop.

It had happened so quickly that Madison and Kelli Ann were in complete disarray. Kelli Ann got the other three children, who were screaming and crying, into the surrey. The men followed White Rock Creek upstream and were out of sight within a couple minutes. Madison opened the envelope and was horrified. The handwritten note said, "*We know that the boy's father and grandfather have money. If you want to see the boy again, follow our instructions and we'll return the boy. If you don't, we'll kill him.*" Madison was made of pretty solid stuff, but the note shook her to her core. She and Kelli Ann headed for the ranch as fast as the horses could run.

****

In July 1874, Charley Ross, the four year old son of a Philadelphia dry-goods merchant was abducted. It was the first known kidnapping for ransom in American history. Two days after the abduction, the kidnappers sent Christian Ross, the boy's father, the first of twenty-three ransom demands. Mr. Ross wanted to pay the ransom, but the Philadelphia Police Department convinced him that a payment would only encourage more kidnappings.

Five months after the boy disappeared, Joseph Douglas and William Mosher, two small-time burglars, were shot while robbing a house on Long Island, New York. Douglas was mortally wounded and, as he was dying, told a witness "It's no use lying now. Mosher and I took Charley Ross." A policeman asked Douglas where they could find the boy. His response was, "Mosher knows. Ask him." He was told that Mosher was dead. Douglas' final words were, "Then God help his poor wife and family."

Over the next sixty years, some 5,000 men turned up claiming to be Charley Ross. None could prove their identity. The fate of the boy remains unknown.

Charley's father, Christian Ross, wrote a book recounting his experiences which detailed his "varied expressions of horror" during the ordeal.

****

Madison got to the ranch where she, Kelli Ann, the children's fathers, and the grandparents were assembled for a family dinner. The surrey was followed by two Dallas Police vehicles. When the group stopped, the entire family came out of the house. Madison grabbed Marie, ran to Jay, and fell into his arms crying, "Bud is gone. Someone took Bud."

A police sergeant walked up to Colonel James Baxter and said, "Colonel, we don't know exactly what is going on. Mrs. McElroy screamed at us as she dashed by in the surrey that her son was taken at White Rock Creek. I sent a car to the picnic area, but we have received no word."

BJ said, "Thank you, Sergeant." He then turned, walked into the ranch house, picked up the phone, and called Fred Brubaker. After telling Fred what little he knew, Fred said he would be right there. In less than five minutes, Texas Ranger Fred Brubaker was pulling up in the drive in his official vehicle.

Without preamble, Fred walked up to Jay and Madison and said, "Madison, I need to ask you some questions. Can you calm yourself enough to help me get an idea of what is going on?" His tone was filled with compassion but firmness. Time was of the essence if they were to have any chance of finding the child.

Through sobs Madison said, "Yes, Uncle Fred. I will tell you what I know." And with that, she handed the ransom note to Ranger Brubaker.

Fred opened the envelope, looked at the note for a couple moments, turned to Madison, asked Kelli Ann to come over please, and said, "I need you both to think of every detail about the two men that you can remember. How tall, what color hair, fat or skinny, what kind of horses were they riding? Anything you can remember may help." BJ was standing nearby, so he could hear every word. This was his grandson, and he intended for him to be found, and found alive.

About all Madison or Kelli Ann could remember was that the men were average size, medium brown hair, dressed like outdoorsmen, and riding chestnut colored horses. They had worn bandanas on their faces, so there wasn't much to help identify them. It was getting close to dusk, but Fred thought it would be best to go and see if he could see anything peculiar or distinguishing about the horses' hoof prints. He turned to BJ and asked if he wanted to ride along, and of course, he did.

Chapter 31

Fred jumped into the Ford Model A with the Texas Rangers emblem on the door, and BJ got in on the passenger side. Fred took off as fast as he could and still keep the vehicle under control. When he got out of the ranch lane and onto the road, he turned on the Sireno siren and went about as fast as the vehicle could safely travel. The rest of the family went into the ranch house. Madison lay down on a sofa and tried to regain her composure. Everyone was understandably upset.

When Fred and BJ got to the picnic area on the creek, Fred stopped the vehicle, stepped out, and asked BJ to stay behind him. The hoof prints of the horse that the man who delivered the note was riding were easy enough to see. After looking at the imprints for a few moments, Fred saw nothing remarkable about them. The two men walked to the creek and found the prints of the second horse. Again, Fred saw nothing unusual about the hoof prints. Fred turned to BJ and said, "You have probably forgotten more about tracking than I know. Do you see anything distinguishing about either horse's prints?

After looking at both hoof prints, BJ was thoughtful for a couple moments and replied, "No, Fred. And you're just being kind. You do this for a living. I saw nothing that is really helpful. The man who took my grandson was a much larger man than the man who delivered the note, but I wouldn't call that very helpful."

Fred smiled and said, "You never know. We know that there were two men. We know one was much bigger than the other. We know both had brown hair. We know both were riding chestnut colored horses. I doubt there are many men carrying a five year old boy who fit that description. I will report what is going on to the Texas Ranger headquarters. Let's plan on getting our horses and being here at first light tomorrow morning. We will see if we can track these fellows or at least get some idea of where they might have been going. With a plan in hand, they got in the car. Fred dropped BJ off and went to his ranch.

When they arrived, BJ went directly to his office, called Brian McElroy, Jay's father and Bud's grandfather, to tell him what little they knew at the time. Brian said that Jay had called and told him that Bud had been taken. BJ filled the elder McElroy in on what little he knew. He also told him that there would undoubtedly be a demand for money. The demand would probably come sooner than later. They agreed to stay in touch.

After talking with the elder McElroy, BJ went into the parlor and tried to assure Madison, Jay, and Marie that he and Fred would do everything possible to find and return Bud home. Jay was trying to keep a stiff upper lip but wasn't doing well. Madison and Marie were basket cases.

Fred showed up at the Baxter ranch house at 4AM and hitched his horse beside Sergeant Sonny at the porch rail. He went inside and had coffee with BJ, Madison, Jay, and Nathan. BJ had on a light jacket under which he had a shoulder holster with a Smith & Wesson M1917 revolver which used a half-moon clip to fire .45 ACP cartridges. He probably wouldn't need it, but it was always best to be prepared. Fred said, "Let's get going. By the time we ride to the creek, it will be daylight." They mounted their horses and took off, held their mounts to a canter, and arrived just as the sun was peeking over the tree line. Fred said he would follow the tracks at the creek, and BJ could follow the tracks of the note carrier. The two trails converged about 300 yards up the creek. The tracks were easy enough to follow until they came out on a well-used road. Then the tracks just blended in with all the other hoof prints. Fred and BJ agreed that the horses were headed north, but even of that, they couldn't be completely certain. If headed north, they would be traveling towards present day Berkner Park.

Fred and BJ rode along at a slow trot, stopping when they saw a house whose occupants may have seen the riders with the little boy. They made a few stops. None had seen anything of value. The farther north they rode, the fewer houses and people they encountered. Fred looked at BJ and said, "I think we are wasting our time. This is like looking for a needle in a haystack. They could have veered off on any of the roads or trails off this road. Unless we just happened to stumble into someone who saw the riders, there's no chance of finding them." With that bit of encouragement out of the way, they headed their horses back to the ranches.

The following day, around noon, a young Mexican boy riding a burro came up to the Baxter ranch house. When BJ answered the door, the boy handed him an envelope. BJ told the boy to sit down on the porch swing and not move. The gist of the note was simple enough. The men holding Bud wanted $50,000.00 in $20.00 bills. The Mexican boy said he was supposed to wait for an answer, take it to a certain spot, and leave it. The other thing the note stated was that if the Mexican boy was followed, they would kill the McElroy boy. Saying "I'm sorry" or anything else wouldn't help. They would kill the boy. BJ called Brian McElroy and told him the contents of the note. McElroy said that coming up with his half of the $50,000.00 didn't present a problem, but how could they be sure of what they were getting for their money? How would they know that Bud was still alive? BJ acknowledged the problem and merely said, "I agree. I'll think on it."

****

Jay and Madison were still at the ranch, and Uncle Bill, Reverend Baxter, was there to comfort the family. BJ called the three into his office. Once they were seated, he began, "I know you both are scared to death, as am I. But we need to think this thing out together and decide what we want to do. You are Bud's parents, so it will be your decision as to what we do."

Jay and Madison held hands and Madison was fighting back tears. BJ began by saying, "I have prepared a response to the demands of the people who took Bud. I will read it, and then I want your input." Reverend Bill Baxter moved to the sofa, sat next to Madison, took her other hand in his, and gave her a strained smile. As BJ started to talk again, there was a knock on his office door, and Texas Ranger Fred Brubaker entered, took a chair, smiled at Jay and Madison, and nodded to Bill and BJ.

BJ proceeded to read the response, "*To the cowards who took our son and grandson, we will be willing to pay the ransom as you request, but with certain provisions. First of all, we want to see Bud alive, and we must see him alive and unharmed before we give you the money. Without proof that the child is alive, there will be no payment. How you want to supply proof that Bud is alive and unharmed is up to you. You took him. Next, there are people who saw you with the child. If we don't get Bud back and unhurt, I will place an ad in the Dallas Express and Daily Times-Herald, offering the $50,000.00 to anyone who can identify you or bring you to my ranch dead or alive. Now that we understand each other, I will await your response.*"

Madison teared up again and said, "Dad, do we need to be this firm? Aren't you afraid that you will make them mad, and they will take out their anger on Bud?"

BJ thought for a moment and responded, "Madison, as I said initially, you and Jay are Bud's parents, and you have to make the decision. Some years ago, I negotiated the release of one of my officers who was taken prisoner and held in Mexico. I learned from that experience that people who would do something as despicable as taking a child would only understand strength and fear. They are counting on our fear to get the money they want. In my opinion, we need to transfer some of that fear to them."

Jay had been quiet throughout the ordeal but now spoke up, "Colonel Baxter, Sir, I'm a lawyer. My Dad is a banker. You and Uncle Fred are experienced with dealing with hard men. We will just have to allow you to do what you think is best. I know you love Bud as much as we do and will do nothing to endanger him more than he already is."

BJ looked at his family and said, "It's settled then. We send this response, but make no attempt to follow the Mexican boy. We don't want to chance being seen."

****

After the reply was given to the Mexican boy, Fred called the ranger office, talked to the dispatcher, and said, "Have our people get 'eyes' on a Mexican boy wearing white pants, a red plaid shirt, and riding into Dallas on a burro. Don't be obvious. Don't follow the boy. Just note where he is seen, and the direction he is traveling, and get the Dallas police to do the same thing. But I can't overemphasize: don't follow the Mexican boy."

****

The next morning, the same Mexican boy showed up with another note. BJ answered the door and told the boy to sit on the porch. He went to his office, called Fred, and told him to please get the Texas Rangers and Dallas police deployed along the route at the last point they had seen the boy on the day prior. He then opened the envelope and read the note, *"We don't have to show you anything. Pay the money, or we will kill the boy."*

BJ picked up his pen and a piece of stationary and wrote the following *"My phone number is Emerson 5-7137. When I get to talk to my grandson, we can discuss this further."* BJ took the note to the boy and thanked him for coming.

****

Fred had every available ranger and the Dallas City police deployed along the route that he had devised based on where they had seen the Mexican boy travel the day before. None of the rangers or Dallas police appeared to notice the Mexican boy as he rode by them on the burro, but they were fine tuning the location he was headed. After the second trip, they had narrowed it down to the boy delivering the message at a remote spot. The only buildings in the vicinity were a group of abandoned warehouses near what is today the Baylor Scott and White Medical Center in Irving, Texas. They were getting close to finding Bud and the men who were holding him!

Fred called BJ and asked how he wanted to proceed. Fred's fear was that if they went into the area in force with uniformed police, the men might get spooked, kill the boy, and simply attempt to get away. BJ replied, "We have to presume that the men who took Bud have been watching us for some period of time. This wasn't just some random grabbing of a child. They knew that I, and Bud's other grandfather, have money. That is why they targeted the boy. I think I will borrow a horse from one of the ranch hands, use a well-worn saddle, put on some old work clothes, go into the area, and sniff around a little. I don't think they will recognize me without my normal clothes and riding one of the Brandenburgers. As an added precaution, I will make sure I roll around in the ground and get real dirty. Perhaps I will try that tomorrow morning."

Contrary to what he had led Fred to believe, BJ left the ranch during the mid-afternoon on the borrowed horse and arrived at the warehouse area around 4 PM. BJ knew that Fred wouldn't be happy about being deceived, but if anything happened to his grandson, he knew he would always think he could have made the difference. As trustworthy as Fred was, it would only take one ill-advised act by a ranger or Dallas policeman to get the boy killed. When he arrived at the warehouse complex, he realized that this wasn't going to be easy. There were carts, delivery wagons, and half-dozen run-down buildings. Trying to find two men and a little boy in this maze would be like looking for a needle in a haystack.

BJ slowly rode around each building as if he was trying to find a door though which he could get into a building. On the off chance he was being watched, BJ stopped at each large door, shook it to confirm it was locked, and then rode on. There was evidence of looting so BJ thought he would look like someone looking for something to steal. As he rode down the front of a large building and neared a large warehouse door, he heard a horse whinny from inside the building. BJ continued on as if he hadn't heard the horse, turned the corner of the building, and rode off down the road. He stopped in a copse of trees once he was out of sight of the building. He tied the horse's reins to a small tree and waited for more than four hours until it was completely dark and started walking towards the warehouse.

Chapter 32

BJ had absolutely no idea what he was getting himself into. He had heard a horse whinny. That meant nothing in the grand scheme of things. It could be the men who had abducted Bud, or it could be someone stealing things from the warehouse, or it could be a night watchman who had put his horse in the warehouse.

BJ had exchanged the Model 17 pistol for his old Model 73 Colt revolver that he had carried since graduating from The Point. One thing was for sure, if he was going to wager his life and the life of his grandson on a weapon, he wanted it to be one in which he had the utmost confidence. BJ was an excellent shot with a pistol and had practiced for hours while in the military. In fact, BJ was good enough with a pistol to have competed with the Army pistol team, but his duties keep him out of the competition. He had found that going to the range and shooting a few dozen rounds was therapeutic and relieved the stress that accompanied the responsibility of command. Besides, the ammunition was furnished by the government as were the practice pistols.

As BJ slowly and deliberately walked along the building, he came to a window that was covered with dust and grime. He stopped and peeked through the glass and saw nothing but a few assorted boxes and the faint glow from a fire somewhere out of his field of view. He ducked down and went past the window and peeked in from the other side. From that viewpoint he could see there were two men, two horses, and one little boy across the warehouse perhaps fifty feet away from where he currently was located. Both men were on one side of the small fire, and the boy was on the other side with his hands tied together. The men were talking, but BJ couldn't hear a word they were saying.

BJ tiptoed up close to the warehouse door, sat on his haunches, and waited. There was no reason to get in a hurry. The safety of his grandson was the main consideration. BJ looked at his pocket watch and noted the time, 8 PM. He had only been in the warehouse area for about four hours. It seemed much longer. His knees were beginning to ache, so he stood and flexed his legs and stretched a few times. He didn't dwell on his aches and pains, but at fifty-three years of age, the years of riding, combat, and the various small wounds were beginning to take their toll. There was a time he could have sat on his haunches for hours. Those days were long past.

He sat with his back against the building and waited, and waited. Every few minutes, he would get up, stretch his legs, slowly walk to the window and peer in. Nothing had changed. Around midnight, one of the men saddled his horse and led it to the door. BJ had heard the animal, but not the man. The door creaked slightly as it opened, and the smaller of the two men came out leading the horse and closed the door. When the man got one foot in the stirrup, BJ hit him on the head with his pistol. It wasn't BJ's intention to kill the man, but the stress and pent up anger had caused his adrenaline level to rise. The result was the man's skull was bashed in. The man was dead shortly after he hit the ground.

BJ placed the man on his horse and led it away from the building and to the copse of trees where he had left his horse. He tied the man's hands to his feet under the horse's belly, got a drink of water from his canteen, and tried to calm down. BJ had been in many stressful circumstances and had managed to stay calm until the ordeal was over. This was different. This was his grandson and one miscalculation could get the boy killed. This wasn't business as usual!

When BJ got back to the warehouse, he looked through the window and saw the large man was basically where he had been sitting since he first looked in the window. Didn't the man ever need to use the privy? BJ looked at his watch again, and it was 1:30 AM. He had no idea where the man he had thumped on the head had been going or how long he would have been gone. Perhaps, it was to be a couple hours, and perhaps the remainder of the night. The one thing he didn't want was for the man inside the warehouse to become suspicious because the man didn't return as anticipated.

BJ looked in the window and saw that Bud was now lying on his side and fast asleep. The man was sitting with his back against the wall and nodding off then awakening with a start each time he dozed off. BJ decided it was time to get this over with. He walked to the door, eased it open, and entered. Fortunately, the door didn't make a sound. He closed the door as quietly as he could and eased himself partially behind a large crate which was against the wall. Given the glow from the small fire and the relative darkness of the building, BJ was fairly sure the man wouldn't be able to see him unless and until he moved.

BJ watched the man, and the next time he nodded off, he stood erect, moved away from the side of the crate, and walked directly towards the man. When BJ got to within about thirty feet, the man awoke with a start, saw him, and went for his rifle which was lying across his knees. The warehouse was basically open, and the sound of the .45 barking reverberated around the walls in a deafening roar. He shot the man four times. Once was all that was necessary. The last three bullets were to relieve some of the stress and anger that had built up in BJ since the child had been taken. The man was a mess. A .45 bullet makes a fair sized hole. Four bullets make four fair sized holes! BJ rushed over to Bud, took out his Imperial Schrade pocket knife, and cut the cords that were binding the child's wrists.

Bud put his arms around BJ's neck, cried for a minute or so, composed himself, and said, "I knew you would come and get me, Grandpa. I knew it.

That man is named Elmer. I told him that my grandpa would kill him if he didn't let me go. He just laughed and told me to shut up. He should have listened to what I said!"

BJ smiled at Bud and asked, "Are you ready to go home?" That question didn't really deserve an answer. BJ took the boy's hand, walked together out of the warehouse, and to the copse of trees. He mounted the horse, leaned over, took Bud's wrist, and pulled him up and behind him. BJ untied the dead man's horse and led the animal to the warehouse, opened the door, and allowed the animal to go in. He then closed the door.

It was dark until they got to Dallas, and then the street lamps provided enough light to make it easier to travel. They got to the ranch around 4 AM. BJ and Bud walked through the front door and BJ hollered, "Anybody in this house want to see a little boy?"

People started boiling out of bedrooms, and the joyous celebration at the return of Bud began. BJ sat in the kitchen and drank coffee until 6 AM and then called Fred and told him that Bud was home and that there were two dead men who had abducted his grandson at the warehouse complex. One was tied to his horse in the warehouse, and the other man was lying on the floor inside the same building. Fred wasn't happy that BJ had deceived him but understood. He probably would have done the same if the shoe were on the other foot.

Two weeks after BJ recovered Bud and killed the two men, there was a coroner's inquest. After listening to BJ detail the circumstances of his rescue of Bud, the coroner ruled both killings were justifiable homicides. Dallas prosecutor Matthew Dilbeck was in attendance at the hearing and approached BJ once the hearing had concluded. Dilbeck shook BJ's hand and said, "Colonel Baxter, because of your standing in the community, I am going to suggest that I empanel a grand jury. I don't want any hint of murder hanging over your head. I don't need your permission to seat a grand jury, but I would like your concurrence in this matter." BJ had been in meetings with Dilbeck and trusted the man to do the right thing. He granted Dilbeck his permission and said he would help in any way he could.

The next week, there was a grand jury presentation. Prosecutor Matthew Dilbeck might as well have been BJ's lawyer. Dilbeck led the jury through the events of the abduction and framed the killing of the two men in such a manner that the jury went away thinking BJ deserved a medal, and was lucky to have escaped with his life. No charges were made, and Colonel James Baxter walked out of the Dallas courthouse with his good name intact.

BJ placed his Colt revolver and the holster in a chest in his closet and was never to fire the weapon again. Life got back to normal around the Baxter ranch, and BJ and Nathan continued the Brandenburger breeding program. He never felt any guilt over killing the two men. They had taken his grandson. That was an ill-conceived decision that had cost them their lives.

Chapter 33

The invitation said that the Russell House on the outskirts of Dallas, Texas, had been reserved for the gathering of the Baxter, Brubaker, and Cheyhill males of the two families. It was April 1, 1933. The war over there, to end all wars, had been over for fifteen years. James Budwell (BJ) Baxter, Jr., Nathan Forrest Baxter, and William Huzzah Baxter had survived the harrowing experiences of the awful war and were retired Army officers. Fred Brubaker had survived a severe gunshot wound and had made it to retirement with the Texas Rangers. Preachers never really retire, and Reverend Bill was serving as pastor of Friendship Methodist Church outside of Dallas, Texas.

As the four men were awaiting the arrival of the Cheyhills, they were filled with trepidation. They had no idea how the Cheyhill men would receive the news regarding their fathers. Life is filled with many twists and turns, not the least of which were the events that had tied the Baxters, Fred Brubaker, and the Cheyhill brothers and cousins in a web of intrigue for years. Sometimes, life just was so complicated, so filled with chance meetings and events, that it seemed overwhelming.

Through the years, the Baxters and Fred Brubaker had found one constant with regard to their associations with the Cheyhills. They wanted revenge for the killing of their fathers. Only fairly recently had the Cheyhills figured out that the Baxters and Fred Brubaker were the children of the men who took their fathers' lives. They had spent lots of money and time to arrive at the confirmation of the identity of the killers.

Fred looked out the front window of the house and saw the headlights of three automobiles coming up the driveway. He wasn't the only one of his group that was armed. If the Cheyhills chose retribution, they would be outgunned. The moment of truth was at hand!

When the Cheyhills got inside the house and everyone had sat down, BJ Baxter took the lead. He told the story of the Cheyhills' fathers' attempt to steal cattle from the Slant BB herd as it was being driven to Montana and his recollection of shooting one of the rustlers. BJ said he had no idea which of the men he had shot, but he didn't think he was one of the Cheyhills. In any event, he had only wounded the man, Dorothea had killed him. He finished by saying that, as self-serving as it might sound, he felt no ill-will towards the men who had attempted to steal the cattle. Life on the frontier could be harsh. If his children were going without, he might have done the same thing. By the same token, decisions had consequences. The law of the 1870s was different than the law of the 20th century. In fact, in most cases, there was no law on the frontier in the 19th century other than that which was administered by the cattlemen.

There was complete silence for a few moments. Then Seth Cheyhill spoke and asked, "What happened to our Uncles Martin and Enoch?"

BJ looked at Nathan, Bill, and Fred, and all he got was a blank looks and shrugs of their shoulders. BJ looked at each of the Cheyhills, in turn, and said, "This is the first I have even heard any mention of uncles. I didn't even know you had uncles. My Dad didn't mention anything about them at all."

Caleb Cheyhill spoke up and said, "I remember that Uncle Martin and Enoch rode off together to find the herd and kill the men that were responsible for killing our fathers. They never returned."

BJ, who was the spokesman for his brothers and Fred, said, "Again, my father didn't mention them at all. I remember we had more than one close shave with hostiles while on the cattle drive to Montana. I don't recall more than one run-in with white men trying to take the cattle. I feel confident, since my Dad was forthcoming about hanging the rustlers, he would have mentioned dealing with two other men. But all that was a long time ago and I was a young boy. Perhaps they were killed by Indians?"

Since everyone involved in the incident was dead, BJ, his brothers, and Fred hoped that this "clearing of the air" would serve to bring closure to the Cheyhills.

There was a long silence. Then Seth Cheyhill spoke up, "Every Cheyhill in this room has either been helped, had their life saved, or otherwise found themselves involved with the Baxters or Fred Brubaker in some positive manner. I, for one, have no interest in rehashing something that happened almost fifty years ago. Our fathers are dead and the Baxters' and Fred Brubaker's fathers are long dead. I personally think it is time we got on with our lives and put this behind us."

After Seth finished talking there was complete silence in the room. The Cheyhills were looking at the floor, as if in deep thought, and the Baxters and Fred tried their best not to look overly concerned. After what seemed like hours, but was only a minute or so, Josh Cheyhill spoke up and said, "Other than what Colonel Baxter told us today, there is no way to confirm any details of the incident that led to our fathers' deaths. I do know that had it not been for Ranger Brubaker, I would have died many years ago. He risked his life to save mine. I'm unable to hold any grudge against him."

Michael Cheyhill spoke softly but his words sounded like gunshots in the room, "Had it not been for Reverend Baxter, I would be buried somewhere in France. I'm certainly not going to do anything to harm him.

Caleb Cheyhill cleared his throat and said, "Colonel BJ Baxter and a man named Mel Spurgeon who was later shot and killed saved my life back in 1897. I certainly have no malice against him.

Seth Cheyhill spoke up and said, "I served under both Colonels Nathan and James Baxter while in the cavalry. I never knew either one of them to lie, ever, even over little issues. If the Colonels James or Nathan say that is the way it happened, then that is the way it happened. It's over as far as I am concerned." With that, the Cheyhills stood, and the eight men began exchanging handshakes. The long years of hatred and desire for retribution were over. The Cheyhills, Baxters, and Fred Brubaker could finally put the lingering hatred and concern behind them and live in peace.

Chapter 34

BJ and Nathan continued to breed and sell their beloved cavalry horses. They sold a few to the Army, but mostly to people who loved the breed. In July of 1939, BJ and Nathan sold all their horses except for a couple they kept for their personal use. It was just becoming more work than they wanted and required more time than they wanted to continue to expend on selling, transporting, and tending to the animals.

James Budwell Baxter, III followed in his father's footsteps and entered the United States Military Academy in June of 1916, class of 1920. He rose through the ranks and was a Colonel and assigned to Fort Meade, Maryland. He shared his father's love for horses but was preparing to lead men in yet another war.

William Nathan Baxter developed a heart condition as a youngster and was rejected for military service. In June of 1938, at thirty-seven years of age, he had a massive heart attack and died.

Nathan's son James Nelson Baxter loved mathematics, applied for and was accepted at the Massachusetts Institute of Technology, Cambridge, Massachusetts, and graduated in 1924. After graduation, James attended Oxford University in England, fell in love with the island, married an English girl, and made the British Isles his home. On August 24, 1940, on the very first German bombing raid over England, James' home was hit by a German bomb, and he and two children were killed in the blast. His wife was away from the house attending to her grandmother and was unscathed. She was killed during a nighttime German bombing raid in 1941, when an ambulance backed into her. She was crushed against a building and died within minutes.

James Budwell Baxter Jr. died peacefully in his sleep on July 7, 1953. He had just celebrated his eighty-third birthday. Marie died the following year of a stroke.

Nathan Forrest Baxter suffered a heart attack and died at the ranch outside Dallas on May 3, 1954. Lily Jane lived another ten years.

William Huzzah Baxter never remarried, or even considered marrying again after the loss of Amy and his young son. He died in a Methodist nursing home on November 3, 1963, at ninety-one years of age.

Frederick William Brubaker retired from the Texas Rangers in June of 1933 and served warrants for the Dallas County court system just to have something to do. On May 1, 1934, Fred walked up to a house in North Dallas with a summons for a man to appear for a competency hearing. The man opened the door and shot the retired Texas Ranger in the chest with a shotgun. Fred died within minutes. Shelia Jean lived on the ranch for several years and then went to a retirement home in Dallas.

She didn't want to live with her daughter and disrupt her life.

Both the Baxter and Brubaker ranches were sold by their children, the proceeds shared equally, and the land used for a planned airport to serve Dallas and Fort Worth, Texas.

Epilogue

Between 1914 and 1918, the United States sent almost one million horses to the European forces, particularly the British. When America entered the war, another 182,000 horses were taken overseas by the American Expeditionary Forces. Only 200 horses returned to the United States after the end of the war. Somewhere around 60,000 were killed outright in France.

At Fort Riley, Kansas, there is a monument commemorating the operation of the 26th Cavalry Regiment. The unit was totally annihilated by the Japanese in January 1942 during engagements at Luzon and Bataan in the early moments of WW II. This was the last occasion that mounted horse cavalry was used in actual combat by the United States against the enemy.

A bay horse named Chief was the last government owned cavalry mount. Chief was foaled in 1932 and arrived at Fort Riley, Kansas, in April 1941. He was assigned to the 10th, and later, to the 9th Cavalry. In 1942, Chief was assigned to the Cavalry School and remained there until his retirement.

Chief died on May 26, 1968, and was buried at the feet of the statue "Old Trooper" at Fort Riley, Kansas. Chief was the last of thousands of horses that served in the military. He was a reminder of the days of boots and saddles, Custer and the 7th Cavalry, and the days of the Old West.

****

Most people probably think the cavalry became lost to history before World War I. Actually, the cavalry survived until a blustery day, on a treeless prairie near Crawford, Nebraska, in April 1942.

Three days prior, troops of the 4th Cavalry had ridden down the streets of Omaha as a crowd of 60,000 wildly cheered the troopers and their horses in their final public appearance. Old cavalry men came from all over the country to see the final parade as the horse soldiers and their mounts passed in review at Crawford for the last time. The horses pranced and held their heads high as if they knew something special was happening. Five hundred men rode their mounts out onto a parade field, dismounted, unsaddled their mounts, and turned the animals in for the Army to sell at auction.

There were few dry eyes in the crowd of former cavalrymen, dignitaries, and onlookers who were assembled for the final review. A time when man and steed worked as one had passed and was replaced by engines that belched smoke and rumbled along with no heart, no capacity for companionship or friendship. Colonels James Budwell and Nathan Forrest Baxter, Retired, were in attendance. It was a sad day indeed!

****

The 3rd Infantry (Old Guard) has twenty-eight government owned horses. These aren't cavalry horses. They are for ceremonial use, primarily for caisson-drawing, mounts for caisson leaders, or caparisoned horses for military funerals.

The Baxter brothers, Fred Brubaker, the Cheyhills and all the other horsemen are long dead. Their legacy as war heroes, cavalrymen, and trailblazers lives on.

Maggie's Pleasure Palace

The murder of Thelma Goodrich

Chapter 1

Maggie's Pleasure Palace was a brothel on the outskirts of Dallas, Texas. The establishment was operated by Maggie Ellen Branceer. The facility was staffed by twelve to fifteen girls of varying ages and dimensions at any given time. Technically, prostitution was illegal, but the luminaries around Dallas would occasionally enter Maggie's Pleasure Palace for an evening's entertainment. Maggie didn't entertain the clientele. She just made sure the paying customers were well taken care of and left happy. The bawdy house wasn't elegant. In fact, it was weather-beaten on the outside. But on the inside, it was comfortable and masculine. The furnishings obviously had men in mind and were made of earth tone fabrics and rich leather. The bar had drawings of ladies in immodest attire and paintings of western landscapes. The dining room featured a stuffed longhorn head with seven foot tip to tip horns, a large fireplace, tables to accommodate thirty diners at the same time, and T-bone steaks as the specialty. A Chinese cook named Ling Ching was in charge of preparing food for the guests and was a world class chef.

The employees' rooms were clean and always well maintained. The girls' rooms were on the second floor. The kitchen, dining room, and bar were on the ground floor. The building was built in a T shape. The one-story part contained Maggie's office, her private living quarters, and a comfortable room for Ling Ching. There was also a well-appointed room for a guest who might drop in to see Maggie. The rest was relegated to storage. There was one room on the second floor which was nicer than the others and was kept locked most of the time. The bar was well stocked with bonded whiskey that was shipped in from the east. Rot-gut booze wasn't allowed in the building. A piano player was hired to play from 6 PM to midnight every night of the week. Occasionally, a cello player from Boston, Massachusetts, who had moved to Dallas would come in at night and play tunes with the throaty deep sounds only the large string instrument could provide. Once a month, Maggie would usually host a bare knuckles fight in a ring which would be erected for the event. It always drew a big crowd. Men came for the fights, the excellent steaks, the good whiskey, and at times, the girls. Sometimes, the men just wanted female companionship and, at other times, more. Maggie gave attention to detail. She even had several loads of small rock hauled in and placed in front of the building so that men wouldn't track mud onto the carpet in the foyer.

The girls who worked in Maggie's were happy. The clients were happy, and Maggie was certainly happy. The money rolled in. The men who frequented Maggie's were of means, and she tolerated no nonsense. Maggie's was, after all, a gentlemen's establishment.

Maggie knew a gonorrhea infected employee would hurt her business. Thus, she had the girls regularly checked, and if an infection was detected or even suspected, the doctor would treat the woman with one of the medications available. The girl would be out of business until the doctor gave her a clean bill of health.

****

Gonorrhea, colloquially referred to as the "clap," is a sexually transmitted infection caused by the bacterium Neisseria gonorrhoeae. Infection may involve the genitals, mouth, or rectum. Infected men may experience pain or burning during urination, discharge from the penis, or testicular pain. Infected women may experience burning during urination, vaginal discharge, vaginal bleeding, and/or pelvic pain. Unfortunately, many women who are infected display no symptoms at all.

During the middle 19th century, the treatments of choice were cubebs, an Indonesian variety of pepper of which the dried powdered unripe fruit was used, and balsam of copaiba, which was extracted from a South American tree. Silver nitrate was also used and proved to be more effective than the organic plant extracts.

****

It was June 1874. Business was good, and the customers were leaving well satisfied with the food, liquor, and female companionship. Not every male customer who entered Maggie's tasted of the girls' wares. Some just wanted a good steak and a few drinks. That was fine with Maggie. All the income went to the bottom line. Maggie was generous to a fault with her girls. She allowed them to keep 30% of their take and didn't charge them a dime for room and board. Most women in their profession fared far worse. Some were basically held in slavery. The women who worked at Maggie's were there because they wanted the income. Most stayed a couple years, saved a few hundred dollars, and then went west to San Francisco or east to New York City in search of a husband or to go into business for themselves. They didn't necessarily stay in the oldest profession in the world. With seed money, they entered whatever vocation interested them. Maggie heard from some of the girls that left her employment occasionally and was pleased they were doing well.

Every Sunday morning, Maggie and all the girls had breakfast together at 8 AM sharp. At the breakfast, Maggie heard complaints, if there were any, and then she sponsored a Bible study. Maggie felt the girls needed a spiritual element in their lives. Certainly, they were engaged in the world's oldest profession, but that didn't necessarily make them bad people. In the 19th century, love often wasn't a consideration in marriages. A woman wanted security, and a man wanted sex and someone to cook and clean. Maggie kinda figured she was supplying a service the same as a wife would provide. She got reimbursed for her services with money. Married women got reimbursed in kind: a home, security, and whatever finery the husband could afford.

Once the Bible study was concluded, the girls had the rest of the day to themselves to do whatever they desired. Most went for a walk, sewed, or just laid around and relaxed.

One June 21, 1874, thirteen girls showed up for breakfast at 8 AM. Thelma Goodrich wasn't at the table by 8:10 AM, and Maggie sent Beverley Scott to go to Thelma's room to make sure she was awake and get her down to the breakfast gathering. In a couple minutes, Beverley was back, looked at Maggie, and said, "Thelma's gone. Her clothes and personal effects are all gone. She must have left sometime during the night. I saw her around 10 PM, so she was still here then. Peaches was the only living, breathing thing in the room." Peaches was the pale orange-tan colored cat which was kinda community property amongst the girls at Maggie's. The visitors to the establishment thought it interesting that a cat wandered the halls and rooms of the sporting club.

Maggie asked the girls if they knew where Thelma had gone and why. No one knew for sure. Joyce Baker said that Thelma was sweet on someone, but she never would say who it was. Joyce supposed Thelma left early Sunday morning and met whoever she was planning to run away with. None of this made any sense to Maggie. Her girls could leave any time they wanted and, normally, on good terms. There was no reason to sneak off in the middle of the night. Nope. Sneaking off to meet a boyfriend didn't wash. Something else was going on here.

Maggie's opinion was to prove prophetic. There was a whole lot else going on!

Maggie's Pleasure Palace

The murder of Thelma Goodrich

Will be available winter 2019

Bill Shuey is the author of several books and the weekly ObverseView column. He travels extensively in his Recreational Vehicle with his wife Gloria and his fly rods.

He can be contacted at: billshueybooks@gmail.com or his website at: WWW.billshueybooks.com